RIVER OF BLOOD

The two men rode out from the smoking fort
alone. They rode into the mountains, hard on the
heels of Blanco's Muache Ute and the warriors from
other tribes who followed his warpath.

There was a chill in the air, a dullness to the sky, a
feeling that death was only a breath away, whispering
in their ears, killing the things that grew on the
earth. There was a sadness to the land, yet the river
ran and the mountains stood lofty and solid, immutable and mysterious, brute monuments that marked
the graves of men and seasons, impervious to all
change.

Along the river they rode, outnumbered, but bound
for battle. . . .

Rivers West

Ask your bookseller for the books you have missed

The Arkansas River

Jory Sherman

BANTAM BOOKS
NEW YORK · TORONTO · LONDON · SYDNEY · AUCKLAND

THE ARKANSAS RIVER

A Bantam Domain Book / September 1991

ISBN 0-553-29180-7

Published simultaneously in the United States and Canada

PRINTED IN THE UNITED STATES OF AMERICA

RAD   0 9 8 7 6 5 4 3 2 1

For Ken Richman
of Wolf Ridge,
with thanks.

We will give the names of our fearless race
To each bright river whose course we trace.

Song of Emigration
FELICIA D. HEMANS (1793-1835)

≈ **PREFACE** ≈

The upper Arkansas River represented a gateway to fortune for many of the trappers and traders who ventured westward across the Great Plains to the Rocky Mountains. The white men drifted here from the Platte, South Park, Bents' Fort, Taos, and Santa Fe, from virtually every direction. Indians, explorers, and hunters traveled this *el camino real*, this royal road, and forged it into a link between the vast prairie and the formidable mountains. Some headed into the Rockies; some went farther southward to the great trading centers of Taos and Santa Fe.

During the quarter century between 1832 and 1858, a number of settlements and trading posts began to dot a hundred-mile stretch of the Arkansas and its tributaries in what is now south-central Colorado. The men who built these intrepid little settlements were ordinary men of uncommon determination. They (unwittingly perhaps) became the first white men to open up the Rocky Mountain West to others of their ilk: farmers, stockmen, merchants, hunters, tradesmen, trappers.

These men, and their women, exerted a strong influence on the pattern of development that would attract thousands of other Easterners to this wild region. Because they built their trading posts here, the settlers caused a disruption of tribal life among the nomadic tribes of Indians who used those same trails in and out of the mountains. The Indians never lived in that region, but when the trading posts opened, they moved to the Arkansas to trade with the whites. This migration caused a displacement of many tribes, a realignment of alliances and loyalties, and incremented startling changes, both obvious and subtle, in the Native American cultures.

At the time our story opens, there were no white men on the upper Arkansas. There were no settlements. There was only the broad empty plain and the mountains. And the river: the ancient, silent river.

Francisco Serrano, one of the fictional characters in this novel, was the first Mexican to live north of New Mexico in the Arkansas Valley. Many of his descendants live there today. According to historians, three hundred Mormons spent a winter near the settlements and carried to Salt Lake City skills and attitudes learned from their neighbors on the Arkansas. U.S. Army expeditions passed through the small villages and procured guides, provisions, and animals essential to their military operations. When gold seekers arrived in the territory, they found the Indians tamed by contact with the early settlers and friendly for just long enough to allow new towns to become well established. At first the gold seekers lived on produce from the Arkansas Valley; later, they became farmers themselves, using techniques of agriculture and husbandry already tested by the Arkansas Valley pioneers.

This is the story of these first American citizens to settle in the Rocky Mountains, of the men and women who struggled to make not only a living but a good life out of the stubborn soil, the thin grass, the hard winters of this dangerous and difficult valley.

This is a story of pathfinders and trailblazers, pioneers and scalawags, soldiers and poets, knaves and schoolmarms, farmers and hunters, gold seekers and merchants. These are the people who lived in places called Pueblo, Hardscrabble, and Greenhorn, along the

Fountain, Huerfano, and St. Charles rivers and dozens of creeks in between. These are the ones who triumphed, eventually, over every adversity, physical and moral, who tamed a stingy and hostile land, a land alien to any they had ever known before.

This is the story of three men and their families—the Serranos, the Stoneciphers, and the Burkes. Some believe that these pioneers were noblemen of the frontier, these men who forged new trails and paths on the plains and through the mountains. They came to the mountains and looked into the geological past, back to the beginning of the earth itself. After they saw the Rockies, they were never the same, could never get the mountains out of their minds.

It all started when a Mexican found a wild blue flower in a high mountain meadow.

The
Arkansas
River

≈ 1 ≈

A cloud of blackbirds flushed from the bulrushes upriver, wheeled in the sky like magnetized specks on a sheet of blue paper. Three of the birds broke loose from the flock to chase a red-tailed hawk sailing the shore on silent pinions, dragging its rumpled shadow like some vagrant inkblot across the water and over the rocks and cattails, into the high gamma grass. Seconds later, both shadow and hawk, with its three dark pursuers, disappeared over a low knoll that rose up like a sudden bump on the flat prairie.

Jacob Stonecipher rammed the prow of his dugout canoe into the bank of the river. He dropped the paddle, grabbed both gunwale to brace himself, but the shock of the impact jarred him, sent ripples of energy through his hands and arms. He was a tall, graceful man, lean as a hunter's whippet, shoulders wide as an ox yoke, with a shock of brown hair that hung spike-straight to the top of his spine. His eyes were as blue as the basking flame in a blacksmith's forge, his cheek-bones sharp and chiseled as sculptured cherrywood. His face was tanned to a deep burgundy by the sun. He wore soft thin buckskins, carried a possibles pouch, a big Green River knife, whetted to a hair-splitting edge, and a slender conical powder horn made from the graceful tip of a Texas longhorn's lance. His boot moccasins were sturdy, with hard cowhide glued to the deerskin soles. Stonecipher, for all his manly appearance, was but nineteen years old.

Jake looked up once again at the vast range of blue mountains beyond the foothills as the boat rocked in the shallow waters, settled to a state of inertia. He had been looking at the hazy silhouettes of those mountains for days, dumbstruck with wonder. Now he could see their jagged edges etched against the blue sky, the majestic snowcaps crowning their highest peaks, the stubble of trees on their massive chins. He had fought the river, stroked his way around its islands in the shallow stretches, plowed through muscular eddies and vagrant whirlpools in its deep spots, dragged the dugout over sandbars when the waters disappeared underground, only to reach this place.

They called this river the Arkansas down at Fort William where Bill Bent was building his fort, and this was as far as he could go alone. Ahead were turbulent rapids, boiling white water that would hurl him backward like a chunk of driftwood.

Jake scrambled ashore on nervous, quivering legs. He pulled the boat up into the stand of willow saplings, his corded arms flashing sinewy ridges as he wrestled with the heavy dugout. He had hacked the boat out of a cottonwood tree at the fort. It was bulky and unwieldy, loaded down with trade goods. In its crude bowels, the boat held kegs of glass beads in a variety of colors, looking glasses, finger rings, bells, wristbands, earbobs, axes, powder horns, scalping knives, brass kettles, vermillion, bright-colored cloth in short bolts, tools and light lumber for making adobe brick forms, lead and powder.

"Ah," he sighed, and sat on the gunwale to catch his breath. The tingle went out of his arms, and his legs firmed up as they became used to solid ground. He wiggled his toes to bring the circulation back to them, rocked back on his heels to test the flex of feet numbed from disuse in the boat. He picked up his Hawken .50 caliber caplock rifle and stood up.

He leaned the rifle in the forks of a willow sapling, stretched to remove the last of the kinks in his shoulder muscles, bone-hard from wielding the heavy oak paddle. He drew his knife and cut willow branches to cover the boat. When he was finished, he picked up his rifle, slid through the thicket, stepped out into the open. The nipple was capped, the cap snug, the hammer at half cock. Somewhat dangerous, he thought, to carry a loaded rifle in a skittery boat, but this was dangerous country.

Jake strode to the little knoll, wading through the tall gamma grass, leaving a swath in his wake. He climbed to its bare rounded pinnacle, looked to the east, knowing he might have to wait some. He had not seen his partner, Joe Perkins, for two days. Joe, a tow-headed kid of sixteen, homely as a darning egg, was bringing up Jake's horse and two mules, two of their panniers full of more trade goods. Jake figured they could fill up two more panniers and pile some of the goods on top of the pack frames without killing the mules.

It was Jake's idea to barter for pelts this spring, sell the furs in Taos or Santa Fe. He was not a trapper, but he had known many of them, listened to their lively talk around the evening stove or at the tables in the tippling houses. The work, he knew, was hard and dangerous. From William Bent and Ceran St. Vrain, Cadet Chouteau and others, he had learned that the easiest way to a fortune was as a trader, not standing hip-deep in ball-freezing water to retrieve a drowned beaver caught in the jaws of a five-pound steel trap.

The distant muffled thunder of hoofbeats broke

Stonecipher from his reverie. He stood on tiptoe, craning to get a better glimpse of the eastern horizon. A blot, then two, then three, appeared, bobbing through the gamma grass, heading straight toward him. Jake raised his rifle, shook it in a signal. The blots grew closer, took on shapes. Less than three minutes later, Joe Perkins, leading Jake's horse and the pair of mules, hove into full view, riding at a breakneck gallop.

Jake frowned. Joe's horse was lathered and blowing hard.

Perkins reined in at the knoll, his chest heaving, eyes wide as saucers. "J-Jake, w-we got about, hah, ten minutes, buh-before a pack of Utes show up here, hungry for hair."

"How many?" asked Jake with calmness.

"I, hah-ah, counted six." Joe fought for breath. "Hah, about five more'n I figured on handlin'."

"They chasin' you, Joe?"

"They wasn't at first. But they are now."

Jake looked at his horse, the mules. They too were sleek with sweat, foamy with yellowish lather. "Light down, and let's hobble them animals," he said.

"Ah, what are we goin' to do, Jake?"

"Ain't nothin' but to wait for 'em now. Them horses and mules can't go another foot, and we got to pertect our goods."

"Them are Utes, Jake. They's painted and got blood in their eyes."

Jake grabbed his horse's halter, shook the lead rope from Joe's frozen hand. Joe dismounted, gulping in great draughts of precious air. He followed, leading his horse, as Jake headed toward the willows. They had the animals hobbled inside the willow thicket within a few minutes.

"We'd best get ahind that knoll,' said Jake, and he started back through the swath in the gamma grass. Joe jerked his .52 caliber J. Henry rifle from its boot and still panting, followed Stonecipher to the knoll.

"Here comes one of 'em," said Jake as he knelt down on the west slope of the mound. "But he ain't no Ute."

Joe crawled up alongside the older man. "Nope," said Perkins, "he ain't got no paint on his face."

The rider drew closer.

"Arapaho buck," said Jake.

As the two men watched, the Arapaho's pinto foundered. The Indian hit the ground running.

"He don't have no rifle," said Joe. "Not even a knife."

The Utes broke over the horizon. They began yapping like a pack of coyotes. One of them saw the Arapaho and let out a high-pitched yip. He gestured toward the enemy with his bow, and the other Utes whooped and fanned out behind their leader.

"They'll get that buck," said Joe. "And maybe forget about me'n you."

"Damned if they will," said Stonecipher. He raised up, brought the Hawken to his shoulder. He cocked the hammer, picked out the closest Ute, a brave who had his lance raised to hurl at the fleeing Arapaho's back. Jake ticked the set trigger, fingered the front trigger. He led the Ute, squeezed off the shot.

The Ute brave threw up his arms. The lance flew from his hand, tumbling through the air. His pony ran out from under him. He landed in the tall grass and lay still. The other Utes wheeled toward the puff of white smoke that hung like a cloud over the knoll.

Joe picked a target, fired his Henry at a charging Ute. The Ute crumpled and fell from his pony. His bow snapped as his body crunched down on it.

Jake wondered if he'd have time to reload the Hawken. As he poured powder down the barrel, he knew he wouldn't make it. Three screeching Utes angled toward him, began drawing their bows. He dropped his rifle, drew his knife.

Joe was trying to reload his rifle too. His hand was shaking, and he couldn't keep the powder horn to the muzzle. Powder spilled everywhere. One of the Utes shot an arrow at Joe. It sizzled past his ear, he turned white, and started to run.

The Arapaho saw this and picked up a stone, dashed toward the Ute who had shot at Perkins.

Two Utes fired arrows at Stonecipher, but their aim was off. Both braves leapt from their horses and began stalking Jake with their knives drawn. The sixth Ute stayed out of the fight, circled on his horse, bow at the ready with an arrow nocked to the gut-string.

The Arapaho grabbed the arm of the Ute who had shot at Joe and jerked him from his horse. He tried to brain the Ute with his rock, but the Ute rammed an obsidian blade into the Arapaho's side. The Arapaho staggered and fell. Jake stepped in, rammed his knife into the Ute's gut.

One of the other Utes ran after Joe, caught up to him, and knocked him down with a warclub. Joe hit the ground like a sack of meal. The Ute stooped down, drew his knife, and started cutting out a patch of Joe's scalp.

Joe screamed, and Jake pulled his knife free of the other Ute and raced up behind the warrior who was scalping Joe. Jake grabbed the Ute's hair, jerked him backward. Stonecipher's blade flashed in the sun as he razored it across the Indian's throat. Blood spurted from the neck wound. The Ute gurgled, fought for air, as Jake released him. The Indian pitched forward, fell on his face. A pool of blood began to well up in the dirt. Joe looked at the dying Indian and moved his lips but was unable to speak.

The remaining Ute caught up his horse, yelled something, and rode off, shaking his bow in defiance. As he passed by the Arapaho's pony, he drew his bow and sent a shaft into the animal's heart. The horse struggled to rise, then fell back. It kicked in its death throes for several moments. The sixth Ute joined the pony-killer, and the two of them disappeared over the eastern horizon.

"J-Jake, Godamighty, I been skelped," whimpered Joe. He dabbed at a trickle of blood sliding down the side of his face.

Stonecipher stepped up, panting hard. His hand and sleeve were bloody, and there was blood on his buckskin shirt. He looked at Joe's head. "You got a small cut there, a bump on your noggin, Joe."

"That's all?"

Jake picked up his rifle, measured approximately eighty grains of black powder into a small leather cylinder, poured it down the barrel. He put a patch over the muzzle, set a lead ball atop it. He started the ball down the barrel until it was just inside, then cut the patch evenly with a small sharp knife from his possibles pouch. He rammed the ball home with his wiping stick. "Come on," said Stonecipher. "We'd best look at that Arapaho buck."

Reluctantly, Joe got to his feet. He walked gingerly, tapped the cut in his scalp as if to reassure himself that his brains weren't leaking out. He picked up his own rifle, followed Jake to the wounded Indian.

The Arapaho lay in the flattened grass, pinching his wound shut with his hand.

Jake squatted beside him. "He has lost a lot of blood," said Stonecipher.

"Injun against Injun. No concern of our'n," said Joe.

The Arapaho's eyes fluttered, his lips flat against his teeth as if he were in great pain. He was a young man with black straight hair, eyes black as ripe chokecherries, a strong blunt nose.

Maybe he would pull through, Jake thought. He knew something of simple medicine, the good herbs, the beneficial flora. "Maybe we can fix this feller up," said Jake.

Joe fingered the cut in his scalp, touched the bump on his head. "Let him fix hisself up. Them Utes could come back, Jake. They could be gettin' up a war party with the rest of their band."

"This is our first contact among the redmen up here," said Stonecipher. "We do him a good turn, he might do us one."

"Hell, he'd kill us if he was able. One Injun's same as another."

"Maybe, but he come a-runnin' when we was in a fix. I don't aim to let the favor pass, him bein' down like this. I'm going to do some sewin'. Fetch one of them pails out of the dugout, fill it with water."

"Aw, Jake, shit."

"Do it, Joe. I'll need my awl and some sinew."

Joe shot Jake a disgruntled look and fought his way through the bent grasses to the boat.

Jake leaned over and looked at the wound. He sniffed it, didn't smell any intestinal matter. The blood was starting to dry hard and flaky. The wound was fairly clean. The lance had gone in straight, hadn't torn the skin much when it was pulled out.

The Arapaho watched Jake but lay very still. He did not wince when Jake touched the wound, but his jaw tightened, and the blood fled his lips.

Joe returned with the pail of water, a sewing awl, and a stick wound around with buffalo sinew.

"Get me some of that soft river mud, Joe," said Jake. "Don't get no sand in it."

"Aw, shit, Jake."

"Longer you take, longer we'll be here for them Utes to screw up courage to try for our hair again."

Joe went back to the river a little faster than he had the first time.

Jake washed out the wound. Quickly, he stitched it up with sinew. When Joe returned, he felt the mud, saw that it was free of sand. He packed the mud over the stitched wound. Joe watched, snorting his disbelief that Jake was going to so much trouble to patch up a wounded Indian.

"Cut me off a yard of that muslin in the boat," said Jake.

"Any damned thing else?"

"There's more to be done once I wrap this feller up," said Jake. He patted the mud. There were things in it, he knew, that would help with the healing. He didn't know exactly what, but he'd seen it work before. He touched the Arapaho's cheek. There was no fever yet, but he expected it would come. When Joe returned with the muslin, Jake cut several strips and wrapped the cloth over the wound and clear around the Arapaho's waist. He knotted it as tight as he dared. The bandages would hold for a while, long enough maybe for the mud to do its work.

"Now what?" asked Joe.

"Let's cut us some long skinny willows and make this feller a bed."

"Aw, Jake, for the love of Christ."

Jake ignored Perkins, spoke to the Arapaho. "Be right back. You stay put."

The Arapaho closed his eyes, made no sound.

Jake and Joe cut down two young willow trees, peeled them with knife and ax until Jake was satisfied.

"Joe, you load them panniers, get the horses ready. Hold out a couple of blankets."

"Who's goin' to pull the nigger?" asked Joe.

"I reckon I will, seein' you're so primed to do the chore."

"Waste of time," said Joe. "Just a damned waste of time."

Jake laid out the two poles, made a V of them with the narrow ends coming to a point. He began to rig a travois for the Arapaho. Jake had seen how the Indians at Fort William made theirs, and he carefully wove willow branches into a platform between the two poles. It was hard work and took a long time. He listened to Joe curse and wrestle with the goods in the boat. Every so often he looked over toward the Arapaho. The Indian seemed to be sleeping.

Finally, Jake stood up, viewed his handiwork. He was sweating. Hunger gnawed at his stomach. Joe finished hitching the canvas tarpaulin over the packs, grunted one last curse at the mules. "Help me tie the poles to my saddle, Joe."

"Joe this, Joe that."

They rigged slings for the poles, set them in place. Jake mounted his horse, rode up next to the sleeping Arapaho. Joe followed on his horse, leading the two packmules. He had his rifle across the pommel of his saddle. He fingered the hammer as he looked down on the Indian.

"Don't even consider it, Joe," said Stonecipher. "Help me get him onto the travvy. Likely we'll have to strap him in."

"He don't look too good to me," said Joe.

But Joe dismounted, and the two men lifted the Arapaho onto the travois. The Arapaho awoke with a start, his eyes glazed with pain.

Jake tucked blankets around the wounded Indian, knotted them together. "Now, he ought to ride right well."

"I hope he appreciates all the trouble we went to."

Jake fixed Perkins with a look. "I wonder, Joe, if you could stand the pain like he's got and not be a-bellerin' and caterwaulin' like a crybaby."

"Hell, I got pain, Jake. My head feels like somebody's a-hammerin' on it. I got plenty of pain."

Jake suppressed a smile and turned away. He hoped the rig would hold. He looked up to the mountains, felt a thrill at their closeness. He climbed into the saddle.

The Arapaho said something in his native tongue when Jake clapped heels to his horse's flanks.

"What'd he say?" asked Joe.

"Damned if I know. Maybe he's a-thankin' us."

"And maybe he's a-cursin' us," said Joe.

They set out, heading for the mountains, following the river. The Arapaho kept saying things neither Joe nor Jake could understand.

Jake realized by the end of the day that the fever had gripped the wounded Indian and that the Arapaho brave was plumb delirious.

≈ 2 ≈

Jake worried about the mules. And the Arapaho was still babbling and muttering in his delirium after two slow days of riding. The mountains looked close, but they seemed to get no closer. Jake carried a crude map he had gotten at Bent's Fort from a French trapper named Lucien Thibidoux. There was one particular stream that interested Jake. It was set perfectly, running out of the mountains into the Arkansas River. Joe, as usual, was impatient. He thought the Indian was slowing them down. Jake thought the mules were carrying too much of a load. They were dwarfed by the impedimenta, but he rested them often. Time meant little in such a place. But it was frustrating to look at the mountains every day and go to bed at night without having reached them.

On the third day, however, Jake was optimistic. There was a different smell to the air. When they made camp that night, he savored the tang as he stood at the riverbank. He could smell pine and fur and spruce, and the river made a sound that was different. Three pronghorn antelope stood like statues downstream, watching him. Two of them moved to the bank with stately grace and drank from the waters as the third stood guard. The water ran faster as it narrowed, and there seemed to be a steadiness to it, a fullness that had not been there before. The foothills were beginning to green out, and little wildflowers bloomed along the banks of the river.

They crossed dry arroyos and little feeder creeks that entered the Arkansas. Finally, the plain butted up against the mountains, and Jake found a beautiful creek, the one he had seen on Thibidoux's map. The creek was labeled *La Fontaine qui bouille*, and it was an apt description. The springwaters surged from the high country, cold as ice. When they hit the Arkansas, the waters boiled and steamed like a fountain.

"This be the place," said Jake, his face gaping with a wide grin. "Perfect."

"I don't see why in hell you want to build a trading post way out here. They ain't a living soul within a hunnert mile."

"There will be," said Jake.

"Bent ain't gonna like it none. St. Vrain neither."

"Bill didn't come far enough west with his fort. This is a better spot to build."

Jake saw it all in his mind. He rode up on a promontory where he could view the vast plain below. There was plenty of water, plenty of grass, and they would never run out of timber. Here was everything a man could ever need. As he looked down on the plain, he could imagine a crossroads, a junction where men and women could gather to buy and sell and trade goods. To the south lay Taos and Santa Fe; to the north, the fur trappers roamed the Rockies; to the west, the Pacific Ocean lapped against an unknown shore; to the east, by the Mississippi, stood the center of commerce, St. Louis.

"This Injun's yammerin' somethin'," called Perkins, breaking Jake's reverie.

Jake rode back down. The Arapaho was singing in his sleep. Jake could find no meaning in the words, but the

wounded brave repeated them over and over until
Stonecipher had them memorized. "We'll camp up on
that meadow," Jake told Perkins. "Tomorrow, we'll get
to work."

"A hell of a place," said Perkins. "Empty as a damned
bowl."

"It won't be for long."

Perkins had been working as a swamper in a water-
front dive in St. Louis when Jake had met him. The boy
had run off from home in Ohio, ventured west, working
his way at anything he could. He was a likable sort,
Jake thought, but he had the vision of a doodlebug. He
was restless, Jake had sensed that, anxious to go anywhere. But once there, Jake wondered how long he
would stick. He had been in St. Louis only two weeks
when Jake found him, and he was ready to jump the
minute Jake promised him adventure. There was hard
work ahead, and he wondered if Perkins would stick it
out. If he did, he could become rich. But he had not
promised Joe anything beyond a chance to build a life
for himself in a new place.

Jake had left home, Pennsylvania, two years before.
But, he had trapped the Ohio Valley, traveled to Nashville
in Tennessee, listened to the talk of beaver, mink,
marten, and seen the prices Easterners charged for
flint, powder, ball, traps, and such. He saw a chance to
make a fortune, not at the hard work of trapping but at
trading, and in St. Louis he had met a lot of people,
including Cadet Chouteau, and heard about William
Bent building a fort in the middle of the prairie.

He went there, saw how they made the adobe bricks,
how they stood their walls. He got a job there and
worked alongside the Mexican laborers. He looked and
listened, and learned a great deal. He questioned everyone he knew about the country beyond the new fort
and studied maps until his eyes blurred. If his hunch

was right, he had picked a grand place to build his
trading post, a perfect spot where no one else had
thought to come before him.

Jake set out a campsite in an alpine meadow above
Fountain Creek. There he gathered flowers and roots,
boiled them, fried them, baked them. He made teas
and broths, and fed them to the Arapaho. The wound
healed over, and the fever went away, but the brave was
still bedridden. To Jake's surprise, however, the Indian
could speak in two white men's tongues.

"*Qué pasa?*" were the first words out of the Arapaho's
mouth. "*Donde 'stamos?*"

"You speak English?" asked Jake.

"I speak English."

"What is your name?"

"Corno Rojo," the Arapaho replied in Spanish. "Red
Horn."

"I am Jake. This here is Joe. We are American."

"Good. I have much hunger."

"You want meat?"

"Buffalo."

"We don't have buffalo," said Jake. "Just some jerky.
I—I ain't had time to hunt yet."

"He can eat what we got," said Joe. He was as
surprised as Jake that the Indian could speak English.
"And it ain't much."

"I'll have to do some hunting. I've seen mule deer
every morning."

"I never seen 'em," said Joe.

"You would, you didn't sleep past sunrise every
mornin'," said Jake.

"Godamighty," said Joe. "It ain't one thing, it's
another'n."

"You can always go back to St. Louis," said Jake, "and
ride that broom. Or maybe Bill Bent will give you a job
at Fort William. He ought to be still a-buildin'. You

could go trappin' with Bill Sublette, freeze your eggs off in a beaver pond. There's plenty to do and other places to do 'em in."

"What's Bent gonna say when he knows what we're up to?" asked Joe. "Some folks say he don't like competition none."

"I expect he'll be madder'n a wet hornet."

"I hear tell he's got some kind of wall-eyed pizen temper."

"I got one of my own," said Stonecipher, spearing Joe with a fierce look.

Jake found a site for his trading post at a gravel ford half a mile west of Fountain Creek on the northwest side of a bend in the Arkansas. He laid out a rough foundation some two hundred yards from the river-bank, equidistant from the ford and southwest of it.

Stonecipher set stobs in the ground, connected them with string. He told Joe to follow the strings and dig the trenches. It was slow, tedious work, but it kept Perkins out of Jake's hair while he marked the timber for cutting, hunted and cured meat for their larder. Jake shot a mule-deer buck at dawn one morning, dressed it out. He built drying racks, boiled some of the meat in a large cast-iron pot. Red Horn gained strength rapidly.

One afternoon, Jake saw a herd of elk crossing the edge of the meadow, heading for high country. They made little sound, but they took his breath away. Some of the bulls had shed their antlers, but there was one with a majestic rack so big, Jake felt his heart pound in his chest, drum in his ears.

Jake spelled Joe on the digging but kept him busy building frames for the adobe bricks they would make. Jake cut timber, skidded the logs to the edge of the meadow with one of the mules, an obedient jack he called Zeke. The Arapaho watched the white men each day, said little to them at night when they returned, bone-tired, hungry as camp dogs.

"How come you know how to do so many things, Jake?" Perkins asked one day when they were climbing back up the hill.

"I always had the curiosity, and my pa told me to foller its track to wherever it took me."

"Hell, I got curiosity myself. I don't know how to do all them things."

"Well, I guess I got ambition too."

"What's that?"

"Means I want to make something of myself. I want people to remember I come by and left something for 'em before I moved on."

"That don't seem like much," said Joe.

"No, it don't," said Jake, and that faraway look crept into his eyes. "It seems like just about everything."

Another day, when Jake and Joe came trudging back into the camp, wet from a swim in the river, the Arapaho was out of his bedroll, cleaning the feathers off four blue grouse. He had already gutted the birds.

"How'd you kill them?" asked Jake.

Red Horn picked up a stone, made a throwing motion.

"Dumb birds," said Joe.

Jake imagined all of it in his mind: the stalk, the careful aim, the hurling of the stone. He vowed to try it himself one day.

"You cook," said Red Horn, pointing to Joe.

"Not me. I ain't no cook."

"You cook," repeated Red Horn.

Joe bristled. Jake picked up one of the plucked birds. "I can fix 'em," he said. "Joe, you get a bucket of mud, fetch it up here."

"I ain't takin' orders from no Injun."

"Joe, I'm asking you," Jake said quietly.

"What you want mud for, anyway?"

"We'll bake these birds and keep all the juices inside."

Joe grumbled all the way down to the river, kicked at rocks and flowers in his path. "Damned Jake thinks he knows ever' damned thing," he said.

Jake heard him and laughed. He and Red Horn exchanged knowing glances. "Him like woman," said Red Horn. "Much talk. No brave."

"He's brave enough," said Jake. "He helped out when you was runnin' from them Utes."

"Him run too."

Jake laughed. "You made your point, Red Horn."

Red Horn had laid out the hearts, livers, and gizzards of the birds. Jake built a cookfire, got a skillet. By the time Perkins returned, the Arapaho had finished plucking the birds. They were fat. Red Horn cut off the heads, poked holes in them, and sucked out the brains. Joe gulped and fought down the bile that rose in his throat.

Jake smiled and began basting the grouse with mud. He put the birds into the fire and began cooking the hearts, gizzards, and livers. The aroma wafted on the crisp, afternoon air.

"Red Horn plenty strong," the Arapaho said, after putting away two of the grouse himself. Jake and Joe contented themselves with one each, portions of the meats from the birds' innards. Jake made biscuits and a light gravy in the skillet.

"You fit?" asked Jake.

"I go," said Red Horn. "See people. Come back. Trade."

"Your people live far?"

Red Horn swept his arm to the north.

"Many sleep," he said.

"Take my horse," said Stonecipher. "You can bring him back when you bring your people to trade."

"Good," said Red Horn.

"Jake, have you plumb leaked out the last of your

brains?" asked Perkins. "You'll never see that horse again."

"Plenty trade," said Red Horn to Jake. "You want trade Arapaho? Arapaho mean trader. You make sweet whiskey. We trade good."

Jake grinned.

"Sweet whiskey?"

"No burn t'roat." Red Horn pointed to his throat, made a gagging sound.

Jake laughed.

"I'll sweeten ever' barrel," said Jake. "Put lots of sugar in it."

"Heap sugar," said Red Horn, and he laughed too.

Joe shook his head, sopped up the last of the gravy in his wooden bowl with a crumbling biscuit.

"Mmmf," said Joe, "you're makin' a big mistake, Jake. You'll never see hide ner hair of Red Horn again. Hell, we drug him up here, he can sure as hell walk back to where he come from."

"Shut up, Joe," said Jake amiably. "We've just got our first customer."

"Hell, we ain't even built a tradin' post yet."

"Tomorrow, we'll drag those logs down to the flat and start makin' bricks."

"Shit," said Joe, and stood up, glaring through the flames of the fire at Red Horn. "I was better off swampin' at the Bon Chance saloon. Warn't so damned lonely, neither."

"The people will come, Joe," said Jake, and he pulled out his pipe and tobacco pouch. He tamped the full bowl and lit the tobacco with a faggot from the fire. He drew smoke into his lungs, passed the pipe to Red Horn.

"Good," said Red Horn. "We smoke. We make plenty trade."

"We will," said Jake as Joe snorted and stalked off to clean his bowl at the creek.

"I want you to take a blanket and some knives with you, Red Horn. Show your people what I got here. Take anything you want."

"Good. Me take plenty."

"Joe won't like it none."

Red Horn grinned. He made sign with his hands. Jake read it well enough. He was saying that Joe was like a woman who talked all the time.

"He's just a boy," said Jake.

"Me heap man. You heap man. Him little squaw."

Jake leaned back against a keg of skinning knives and took the pipe when Red Horn handed it to him. He blew a plume of smoke into the air and patted his belly. Red Horn grinned at him, and Jake nodded. "You was singin' in your sleep, Red Horn. Over and over. Same song."

"Ummm."

"You remember it?"

Red Horn shook his head.

"I can't disremember it," said Jake. "Keeps goin' over and over in my mind. Up here." He touched his head.

"You sing," said the Arapaho.

Jake cleared his throat, tried to remember the exact pitch and tone. The words were hard to say. "*Nananina Nanakunithana, Nananina Neyachat-Chawaat, Cha anitana.*"

"*Anh,*" grunted Red Horn. "That old song. Cheyenne song. Arapaho song. Red Horn Club Society." He pointed to his chest. "Arapaho brave have heap dream. Him see two warrior, White Horn and Running Whirlwind. Both killed by Pawnee. They sing *Hichaachuthi* song."

"What does it mean?"

"Mean 'Look, I am White Horn. Look I am Running Whirlwind. We live. We live. Look, see us.' It heap good song for Arapaho brave. Red Horn dream good. Plenty strong."

It was a strange song, Jake thought. One to think about. He was glad he had asked Red Horn what it meant. He and Red Horn understood each other. They would trade, all right, Jake thought. And word of the new trading post would spread far and wide, through the mountains, across the prairie and clear down to Taos and Santa Fe.

Before he went to bed, Jake stood on the promontory and looked at the glistening river down on the flat. It was like a silver ribbon, a highway, and he felt its pulse like a heartbeat at his temple. The river would bring the hunters and trappers to him, the Indian traders, the buyers from the Mexican settlements. The river. It was the blood of the land. It was everything.

$$\approx 3 \approx$$

When Jake awoke before dawn the next morning, Jake's horse and Red Horn were gone. He had not heard them leave. It gave him a good feeling to know that the Arapaho was on his way back to his people. Now there was much to do. The sun rose slowly, lighting up the prairie, bathing the high peaks in a rosy glow. It was chill and the river gave up its smoky breath in a batting of fog that spread slowly over its banks like the steam from a stewpot.

"Joe, time to get up." Jake gently rocked Perkins, who lay in his blankets like a mummy.

"Damn, Jake."

"We've got a heap to do. Rise and break your fast."

Perkins poked his head out of the blankets, cocked an eye to the sky. "Hell, it's early yet, Jake."

"And it's going to get real late before we're done this day."

"Hell, I got the foundations dug."

"And now we've got to skid the logs down and get to making bricks."

"Bricks?"

"Adobe bricks."

"Hell, that's Mexican work."

"It's our work, Joe."

22

"Shit," said Joe.

Jake stoked the fire, added wood to it, and set the skillet to heat. After breakfast, they worked the mules, skidded the pine logs down to the building site, stacked them neatly out of the way. They trimmed and split several to use as frames to hold the bricks in place until they set. Jake hammered together a structure to be used to make the mud-mortar, dragged it to the river's edge. They worked all day in the warm spring sun, shirtless, and the bronze of their skins deepened until they looked like Mexicans from the waist up. It was nightfall before they quit.

"I thought you said we was goin' to make brick," said Joe after supper.

"Tomorrow," said Jake.

"How many brick we got to make?"

"I don't know. I've never built a fort before."

"I hope it's a little fort."

Jake laughed. "It'll be big enough to see," he said, and lit his pipe. He was pleased with the day's work, but he knew it would be harder tomorrow and the day after that. This was a job for several men, and they were only two. He wanted the fort that would be his trading post to be finished by the end of summer. He wanted a big room to display the goods, two smaller rooms for storage, and two rooms for sleeping quarters. In his mind, he measured the size of the fort, counted the bricks, set the log beams in place, put up the hitching posts, swept the dirt floors, and set his goods in order. He saw the bastions rise up, and he set the gates to the open courtyard. He put doors on the storerooms and the sleeping quarters. He built shelves, stocked them; he hung lanterns. Sometime near the end of the summer he would have to send Joe back to St. Louis with the mules to get more goods for the winter trading. He would be alone, and that would be the hardest part. Joe, for all his griping and such, was good company.

The next day, Jake and Joe cut grass, hacking it with knives instead of scythes. They laid the grass along the riverbank to dry in the sun. It was slow, painstaking work. The day after that, they did the same, and the day after that until Joe cursed the stiff hard grass and the sun and Jake.

"Damn, Jake," he said one night, "two weeks of cuttin' grass, and we've yet to make a brick."

"It'll be something to look forward to."

"Shit," said Joe.

When Jake figured they had cut enough grass, he brought out the saws, and they sawed up some of the pine logs into flat boards. Jake took his measurements and hammered together the frames to make the bricks. They would be, he decided, sixteen inches long, eight inches wide, and four inches thick. "A mite smaller than those used at Fort William," said Jake, "but a mite squarer too. We'll make the foundation bricks slightly bigger."

"How'd you learn all this?"

"I worked at Fort William."

"You mean you made bricks?"

"I did."

"I seen only Mexicans do that work."

"I did it," said Jake, and he set to hammering more frames for the foundation bricks.

At the end of the day, he checked the grasses and found them dry enough to use. He explained to Joe what they would do the following day.

"You mean we're finally going to make a brick?"

"We're going to make two or three hundred of them, maybe. And by the end of the week, we'll be doing four or five hundred a day."

Joe whistled. "I can't do more'n fifty or a hunnert a day."

"The Mexicans do two hundred and fifty a day on *frijole* beans and corn *tortillas*," said Jake.

"Well, I ain't no Mexican."

Jake looked at Joe. He had muscled out, was no longer the scrawny swamper he had met in St. Louis. "No, you ought to be able to make me three hundred bricks a day."

"Shit you say," said Joe.

Finally, the next day, they set to making bricks. It was backbreaking work, as Joe said, "fit only for Mexican laborers and nigger slaves."

Jake filled the mixing box with dried grass while Joe began filling it with water from the river. Jake shoveled dirt into the bin, began puddling the mixture with a paddle he'd made out of a pine board. When the mud and straw mixture was thick as mortar, Jake and Joe shoveled it into wooden frames, packed it solid. Jake leveled off the tops, then dumped the bricks onto a flat piece of bare earth to dry in the sun.

After several days, the ground around the riverbank was strewn with adobe bricks drying in the sun. Jake built another form for mixing mud and straw so that Joe could make his own bricks. The two men competed with each other, striving to outdo each other in the making of bricks. In the heat of the day, they stopped and swam in the river, cooled themselves at noon under the shade of a cottonwood tree. They saw herds of antelope watering downstream and grazing in the tall grass, their brown and white markings shimmering in the distance.

"Way too far for a shot," Joe said one day.

"You could sneak up on 'em, I 'spect," said Jake.

"Ever eaten antelope meat?"

Jake shook his head.

"Me neither. Heard it was tough as a boot, though."

"I heard it tasted like rancid pork," said Jake, and he

got two bricks ahead of Joe while he was daydreaming. Joe snorted and filled up his frames in a hurry, trying to catch up.

Jake began to build the fort. He and Joe decided one night that they needed a change of pace. Besides, the first bricks they had made were hard now, ready to set along the foundations.

"We'll work early and late a-building," said Jake. "Best to mix the adobe mud when it's hot."

"I hate the thought of totin' all them bricks up to the place you laid out."

"Might have to build us a barrow," said Jake.

"You got a wheel?"

"Make it like a travvy. We could stack the bricks on it and pull it up there."

"Shit," said Joe, but after lugging bricks in his arms, he began to cut willow saplings. Jake built a bigger travois, slung it on one of the mules. The next day, Joe got up early and rigged his own travois for the other mule.

They brought the bricks up as fast as they dried, and the building began to take shape. The foundation was thicker at the base to allow for erosion, the walls slanted inward as Jake had seen them do it at Fort William. Joe thought it was crazy, but he began to take a certain pride in the fort as it took shape.

Jake made the walls eight feet high. He built two bastions at opposite corners, like the turrets of a castle, and these were twelve feet high with rifle notches in them. Atop the walls, he sank cottonwood stakes in the still-wet adobe bricks every two feet. The mud dried around them until they were solidly anchored.

The days sped by, and they finished the exterior walls, the twin bastions at the southeast and northwest corners. Their muscles grew hard and supple from the work, and their bodies tanned. Both men wore only short buckskins, went barefoot. Jake gave up shaving once a week, and his beard began to take on shape and size. Joe shaved once a month, if that much, scraping the peach fuzz from his face with the edge of his knife. He looked in the metal mirror for signs of a man's beard, but always in secret, or so he thought.

"You'll get the curse soon enough," Jake told Perkins after he came upon Joe hiding something in his blanket.

"Whuh?"

"Havin' to shave ever' day or grow a brush like I got."

"Damn you, Jake."

Stonecipher laughed and walked away, stroking his beard with loving fingers.

With the bastions and most of the walls inside the fort up, Jake set to building a gate at the east entrance. He trimmed ten pine poles, each eight or nine inches in diameter, sharpened one end of each. He drilled holes and froed dowels to fit. Then he hammered five together in one bunch, the other five in another. With Joe's help, he built a log frame inside the front gate, with a crosspole twelve feet above. They hung the doors on thick leather hinges, built a crossbar latch on the inside.

"We might just as well move all our stuff and goods down here," said Jake when they were finished. "Pick yourself a room to sleep in."

"We goin' to live in the fort?"

"In Jake's Trading Post."

"Is that what it's called?"

"Always was called that, Joe. In my mind."

"I don't see no damned sign."

The next day, Jake made a sign, as bright and gaudy as anything Joe had ever seen, gluing colored beads onto the letters he had outlined. He hung the sign from the crosspole over the gate, using portions of trap chains screwed into pole and sign. It swung in the breeze, glinted blue, red, orange, purple, green, white, and yellow in the sun.

"They ought to be able to see that," said Jake, stepping back to admire his handiwork.

"It looks purely awful," said Joe.

Jake grinned.

They built another gate in the west wall and continued to make adobe bricks to finish off the interior rooms.

Jake built tables to display his wares, made shelves for the storerooms. He whistled ditties as he sawed and hammered, often driving Joe to the river to make bricks in silence with only the river's song in his ears. In the heat of the day, the two men swam naked in the shallows, floated in the current as they basked on their backs in the sun.

"Don't you think it's mighty peculiar we ain't seen no traders yet?" asked Joe one day when they were finishing the outside walls with a layer of adobe, spreading the muck with their palms like a couple of boys making giant mud pies.

"Nope," said Jake.

"I been studyin' on it, Jake. Seems to me you made a big mistake."

"How so?"

"When I come out with the mules from St. Louis, I heard talk of a shortcut to Santa Fe."

"The Cimarron cutoff. I heard of it."

"Well then, at Fort William, they was a road cut south at Timpas Creek to Santa Fe. I didn't see nobody once't I follered the Arkansas to meet you."

"You saw a road, didn't you?"

"Sure enough. Wasn't nobody on it, Jake."

"Too early."

"Too early?"

"Jedediah Smith, Bill Sublette, and Dave Jackson

were fixin' to leave St. Louis in April, a month after I left. They were waitin' for Tom Fitzpatrick to come in from rendezvous and buy supplies. They were goin' to Santa Fe across that Cimarron desert."

"So?" asked Perkins.

"So they couldn't have made it to Santa Fe until late June, early July. I figure they'll be passin' by one of these days, headin' north."

"What month is this?"

"July, I figure," said Jake. "August maybe. I haven't been keepin' track."

"Me neither," said Joe, but the empty spaces were beginning to get to him. He kept trying to figure out what month it was, but the mountains told him nothing. They seemed the same. It was warmer, the sun hotter—that was all he knew for sure.

Then one day when Jake was building a fur press inside the fort and Joe was trying to catch fish in the Arkansas, they had their first visitor from the east.

Joe came running into the fort, half naked, barefoot, his hair tumbled by the wind and seared to straw by the sun, gasping for breath. "Somebody's comin', J-Jake, sure enough," he stammered. "Man on a damned Injun paint, a-pullin' a mule."

"Where?"

"Right up the river road, right smack out in the open. Come see for yourself."

Jake followed Joe outside, stood on tiptoe to look at the man riding up the crude road along the river. The man was singing. He rode a painted pony, pulled a Mexican mule behind him. He wore no shirt, but a wide-brimmed hat that shaded his face. Jake couldn't understand the words, but the man was singing right enough. And he appeared to be drunker'n seven hundred *pesetas*. As the rider drew closer, the words he sang became clearer.

"Oh, I left my Doney Gal in Donegal,
Went on down to London Town.
Left her there in the prettiest gown,
The prettiest gal in Donegal, my Doney Gal.

He broke off the song, gave a whoop, and lifted his jug high in the air.

"What's he singin'?" asked Joe.

"Damned if I know. Looks to be an Irisher, red hair and all."

The man rode up close, and Joe saw that he did indeed have red hair. It streamed from under his beaver felt hat, seemed to flow onto his jaw and chin like copper wire. His eyes were hazel, flecked with green and gold, and his button nose was red as a beet. He filled the Santa Fe saddle with a torso and chest as full and round as a barrel, as though he had no waist at all. Two rifle butts jutted from beaded Indian scabbards. He wore buckskin trousers and beaded moccasins, carried a large knife on his wide belt, a tomahawk and pistol as well. His chest dangled with two powder horns, and he carried a possibles bag slung from his saddle horn, shortened up so that it was in easy reach. He looked like some kind of red-haired Viking madman, his bare chest scrawled with wiry copper hair, skin bronzed by the sun.

"Well, now, am I drunk or is that a fort standin' where I pissed in the open last spring? Are ye traders or scalawags, pilgrims or brigands? I'll fight with ye or drink with ye, gents, so make up your minds so's I know whether to swaller or start shootin'."

"We're traders," said Jake.

"You're the first white man we've seen up here," said Joe, his voice quavering.

"White man? Why, I'll brook none of your insults, you young pup. I'm half squaw man, half he-bear, a son of the mountains, a child of the wilderness. I'm Will Burke, and I eat Christians and pilgrims for breakfast."

"I'm Jacob Stonecipher." Jake stepped toward the rider, held out his hand.

"And who be thisun a-callin' me a white man?"

"He's Joe Perkins," said Jake. "Light down. We'll have a drink with you."

"By the derrydown gods, you will, eh?" Will Burke squinted, tapped his earthen jug. A look of slyness crept into his eyes. "And be either of ye man enough to swaller rattler's milk an' tiger piss? There's fire in this jug, an' lightnin' an' thunderbolts an' Rio Grande river water full of dead rats an' terbacker soaked in pizen."

Burke rode up to Stonecipher, thrust the jug in his face. It sloshed on Jake's hands as he grabbed. He figured it to be three-quarters full.

Jake drank from the jug, felt the liquid burn his throat as it blazed down to his stomach, he gasped for air as the thick fumes strangled him. The whiskey struck his belly like molten lava. He gasped, struggled to keep his stomach from belching the firewater back up his throat.

"Haw!" yelled Burke.

Jake's eyes watered, and he gulped in air.

"Let me taste it," said Joe. Jake handed the jug over to him eagerly.

Joe tipped the jug as he brought it to his lips. The whiskey hit him like a jolt of lightning. Perkins staggered under the impact. The liquid boiled in his stomach, made it contract and buck. The fumes burned his eyes. His throat felt as if a strip of it had been ripped out, leaving only a raw wound. He blinked and fought down the hot bile that rose in his throat. He gagged, sputtered, spat.

Will Burke roared. "Waugh! Son of a buck, the

creature's too much for ye, lad. It'll turn your innards inside out and gorge 'em up till you wished you was dead."

Jake managed a weak smile as he watched Perkins teeter around in a little circle.

Joe handed the jug back to Jake.

Jake gave it back to Burke.

"Lily-livers, the both of ye," said Burke. He took a swallow from the jug and never batted an eye. He wiped a paw across his lips, belched contentedly, then swung down from his horse, his powder horns rattling against his bare chest. His horse and mule stood, reins and rope dangling. They looked weary, hung their heads, stood hipshot in the sun. "So ye built ye a fort, did ye? Be a-tradin' with the Injuns?"

"With anyone," said Jake, awed by the burly red-haired man who stalked toward the entrance of the trading post. Burke didn't seem at all drunk, but Perkins was having seven kinds of fits trying to keep the white-hot whiskey down.

"Good spot, maybe," said Burke.

The gate was open. Jake followed Burke inside, saw him check the rooms, the goods. Stonecipher waited for him by the fur press.

Burke plopped in the shade of a roof Jake had built, leaned against the log support. He set his jug down beside him.

"Where you bound?" Jake asked.

"Yonder, up the Fountain."

"You know it, then?" Jake squatted in the shade.

"Nope. Too many niggers up on the Yallerstone and the Big Horn, too goddamned much politics. I'm a free trapper, and by God, I won't have no truck with Sublette and his bloody bunch. American Fur and Rocky Mountain Fur are buckin' heads and swarmin' over ever' goddamned beaver pond from hell to breakfast. I figgered

I'd stay south, close to Taos. Was goin' there when I got word that Jed Smith got kilt by Comanches. He was a mighty good man."

Jake studied the man. He recognized him as a true mountain man. For in Burke's gold-flecked green eyes that sometimes darkened to a murky brown there was the wild far-off look he had seen in the eyes of men like him in St. Louis and at Fort William. He had heard tales of Jedediah Smith, too, and knew Bill Sublette but not his brothers. They were a strange breed of men, hardy and brave, independent as a Santa Fe mule, mean as any dockwalloper he'd seen on the Missouri levee.

"Where'd you get your goods?" asked Stonecipher. "You look as though you don't need none from me."

"Didn't know you was here or I'da saved a good mule a heavy burden. Traded me some at Fort William, some I got in St. Louis. I butchered a cow at the Cimarron, jerked the meat I didn't eat, traded the rest to some Utes for lettin' me keep my hair. They took two jugs of this lightnin' from me too. This is my last. When it's gone, I'll have no more till spring."

"We'll make whiskey here. I'm sending Perkins back to St. Louis for more supplies in a day or two."

"You got the right goods, Pilgrim. Whiskey and beaver are the coin of the realm, all right. You could do well here, the Utes don't skin ye, the Rappyhoes don't thieve you blind. We come up this away once't from Taos, headed up to South Park, then onto the head of Wind River where it comes out of the mountains."

Perkins came into the fort, steadier on his feet than he had been. When Burke offered him another pull on the jug, Joe shook his head. He smelled of fresh vomit.

"Set, then," said Burke to Perkins.

The mountain man seemed right at home. It seemed to Jake that he had already known him a long time.

Although he had roared when he first rode up, he seemed content to sit in the shade and sip his whiskey, talk about the things he had done. Until Burke had come, Jake didn't realize how lonesome he had been for news of the outside world. Now he was hungry for gossip, news, no matter how old or secondhand.

"You think I have a chance here as a trader, then?" asked Jake.

"Good as any. Sublette'll be comin' through here pretty soon. He set out for Santa Fe, him and Kit Carson and about forty men. Should be a-comin' through here 'fore long. He'll mark your bein' here, and so will ever' man jack of his brigade. You make up some whiskey, an' you'll draw 'em here like flies to sugarwater."

"I could build a still, I reckon," said Jake.

"Another swaller?" offered Burke, picking up the jug.

Jake thought about it. Here, he sensed, was a friend. There was something about Will Burke that he liked. He smiled, took the jug from Burke. This time, the whiskey did not burn so much going down.

"See?" said Burke. "You're gettin' used to it."

Jake grinned.

Joe retched again, and Jake thought he was going to throw up.

That night, Will Burke and Jake Stonecipher got roaring drunk as Joe looked on helplessly.

But the bonds of friendship between the trader and the trapper were forged in that sharing of the worst whiskey Jake had ever tasted in his life.

≈ 4 ≈

Will Burke seemed a different man the next morning. He didn't say much, but tended to his stock, put up his goods inside the trading post. He bought some mirrors and extra knives from Jake, packed them away. He rode up into the hills that afternoon, came back at dusk with a mule-deer buck across his saddle. He dressed it out, cut up the antlers to use for knife handles and buttons.

That night, Will cooked the best parts of the meat over a fire he built himself, invited Jake and Joe to have supper with him. He never mentioned a word about the night before, except to thank Joe for drinking the last of the firewater. After he said that, he gave Jake a knowing wink, and that was the end of it.

The next morning, Jake fixed breakfast, served it on a table he had built. They sat on barrels Jake had cut away for chairs, padded with elk hide.

"You want to go huntin', Jake?" Burke asked, putting away the last of a biscuit.

"I've got a lot of work to do."

"You also got ye a pretty fair herd of goats. Shame to let 'em go to waste."

"Goats?"

"Them antelope."

"Are they good to eat?"

"Injuns don't eat 'em much," Will replied, "less'n they be out of buffler. But you cook 'em right, and the meat'll go down, stick to your innards. 'Sides, you need to be puttin' meat up for the winter. The muleys and elk are feedin' high this summer. Won't be down for another month or two."

"You're right, Will. I hadn't thought about the winter. I've got enough staples, but we're shy on meat."

"We'll walk out on the prairie, get us a goat or two. Once't I show you how, you can get 'em anytime you like. The meat cures up right smart."

"We won't take the horses?"

"Nope, too distractin'. You foller me. We'll get us some meat."

"Joe, can you handle things here? Finish off those shelves I was makin'?"

"I can do it," said Joe. The look he gave Jake behind Will's back indicated that he thought they were both crazy.

"Get your rifle, Jake," said Will. "Load it and prime it."

Burke took one of his rifles, the longer-barreled one, like none other that Jake had ever seen. The stock was studded with tacks. It was not a full-stock rifle, but the barrel was at least forty inches long. It was slender, fashioned in the Kentucky style, and appeared to be .58 caliber or better. The barrel was some pitted and the stock worn down in spots, but it was a fine-looking piece.

Jake and Will set out from the trading post across the prairie. Behind them, the mountains lay like emerald lizards in the sun, the high peaks glistening snowy and majestic in the thin, clear air.

After they had walked an hour, Burke stopped. "They'll be just over that next rise," he whispered. "Smell 'em?"

Jake shook his head.

"Grass is shorter yonder, and they got water from a little feeder crick. You mind what I do and do the same."

"All right." Jake felt a tingle of excitement. Will was older than he was. He figured to be a man in his midtwenties or early thirties, expert at surviving far from civilization. That mule deer Burke had brought in had weighed better than 140 pounds, and Jake never tasted meat as good. He was anxious to learn whatever Will could teach him.

"Come on, then."

Before they reached the knoll, Will went into a squat, then lay flat and crawled the rest of the way. Jake stayed right behind him. When Burke stopped, he stopped. They topped the rise, and Burke looked back, motioned for Jake to crawl up to him.

Jake inched up to where Will was waiting. Burke pointed to the east. Jake lifted his head slightly. His heart caught in his throat when he saw them. They seemed so close, and there must have been fifty or a hundred pronghorn antelope grazing right out in the open. Several animals stood as sentries, scanning the land in all directions while the others grazed.

Jake knew they were farther away than they seemed to be, but even so, he had never been so close to so many at once.

Will tapped Jake on the shoulder. He pointed to his lock, indicated that the pan was primed. Jake showed Will his rifle. Will nodded in approval. Then Will reversed his direction, turned over on his back, lay flat.

Jake did the same.

Will looked over to him and grinned. Then he did a strange thing.

Burke lifted his legs in the air and moved them back and forth in a scissoring motion.

Jake felt like a fool. But, he lifted his legs and began

moving them back and forth. When Will stopped, Jake stopped.

Will's head was up slightly, so he could see. Jake took a peek. A few of the antelope had started toward them. Will scissored his legs again. Jake followed suit.

The curious pronghorns trotted in close to investigate.

"Now," whispered Will Burke, and sat up, bringing his rifle to his shoulder, cocking on the rise. Jake snapped up, pulled back the hammer.

Will picked out a big buck, fired. The antelope dropped. Jake shot at one that could not have been more than fifty yards away. It bolted, but fell dead after running about a hundred yards. The other antelope bolted and rejoined the main herd. Several antelope lifted their heads and looked toward the two men.

"Just leave 'em," said Will. "We'll bring a few of them goats back after we reload."

Will lay down and began measuring out powder. It was hard work, but Jake watched him and managed. He seated the ball with the wiping stick, poured fine powder in the pan. When both men were ready, they started kicking their legs in that odd scissoring motion.

They shot five more antelope.

"They're pretty dumb, I guess," said Jake.

"Nope. It's just they're mighty curious. I'll show ye another trick." Will took out a piece of red ribbon, tied it to the muzzle of his rifle. Both men sat down. Burke raised the barrel of his rifle, wigwagged it. The ribbon fluttered.

Two antelope trotted up after about a half hour of this, and the men shot them both dead.

"We'll gut 'em out, go back for the mules, drag the meat to the fort," said Will. "No use'n our shootin' no more today."

"I've never seen anything like that," said Jake.

"Stand you in good stead when you're hungry," said

Burke. "Don't let 'em see your trick too much. They got memories, like anythin' else."

Joe helped bring the nine antelope back to the trading post. He was dumbstruck as seeing so many dead animals. When Jake told him how they did it, he knew for sure that Stonecipher was pulling his leg.

That night, the three men worked late cutting up the nine antelope. The next day, they built drying racks and stripped the meat, hung the strips to cure in the sun.

"You can pick berries in a month or so, up in the mountains, and make yourself some pemmican," said Burke.

Will kept looking up at the mountains all that morning. To Jake, he seemed restless. They walked to the river together late in the morning. Will was still pensive, as if he had something powerful strong on his mind.

Burke was looking downriver, and Jake was filling a wooden bucket with cook water when the trapper asked an odd question. "You ever see Liggett come by here?"

"Liggett? Nobody by that name's been by here. *Nobody's* been by here," said Jake.

"What about in St. Louis? Did you know a man named Liggett? Ned Liggett?"

"No, can't say as I ever knew anyone named Liggett."

"Well, no matter," said Burke.

"He a friend of yours? If I see him . . ."

"No, he ain't no friend. You just forget I ever spoke his cursed name," said Burke.

And Jake wondered who Ned Liggett might be, but he knew better than to question his often taciturn friend about the matter.

Will walked up to the Fountain at noon, carrying his rifle. He seemed to be a man carrying a heavy burden. There was something in those silences of Burke's that made Jake sense the man was looking back over his shoulder. He did look out over the prairie a lot, and Jake wondered what he did when he went up into the foothills.

"He's an odd sort," said Joe.

"I don't know. I like him."

"He's crazy."

"Maybe. Maybe we all are."

"Not me," said Perkins.

"Joe, I want you to leave for St. Louis in the morning. I'll make out a list of supplies we'll need for winter. Some goods to trade in the spring. I'll want you to buy another mule, a packframe, panniers."

"You got credit?"

"I've got cash."

"Be a long trip," said Joe.

"Be back before the snow flies. You won't have time to dawdle."

"God, it'll be good to see people again."

"What are me and Will?"

"I reckon I mean a city," said Joe sheepishly.

"Stay away from the tippling houses, Joe."

"Don't you worry none about that, Jake. I got my taste of whiskey the other night."

Jake laughed.

Will Burke didn't return until the sun was going down. He seemed lighter in step, happier than when he had left. He whistled an Irish ditty before supper, and afterward he got up from the table and dug out his pipe. "Join me in a smoke, Jake?" he asked, taking a wood splinter and poking it into the fire. When it was well lit, he started for the gate.

"Joe, will you clean things up?" said Jake.

"Don't forget to make out that list," said Joe. He too seemed happier than he had been in a long time. As Jake and Will walked out of the trading post, he started whistling that tune Will had been working on earlier. He was way off-key.

The trapper and the trader walked down to the river. The Arkansas was lower than it had been when Jake had first arrived. They'd had no rain in weeks. It was a cloudless night, and the stars seemed close, spangling the river with glittering diamonds. An owl hooted from a spruce tree in the foothills. A lone coyote yapped far out on the prairie.

"I'll be leavin' in the mornin'," said Will as he lit his pipe. Jake tamped the bowl of his own pipe. Will handed him the burning stick. When his pipe was lit, Jake threw the stick into the river. It hissed when it struck the water and winked out.

"You don't expect to spend the whole winter up there, do you?" asked Jake.

"I will."

"You'll die of exposure, Will."

"Not this coon," said Burke. "I figger I got me a good month after I get to where I'm goin'. Be huntin' and settin' up winter quarters, puttin' meat by. I got me in mind a place where the beaver's thick and the snow thin."

"You ever been up there?" Jake cocked a thumb toward the mountains.

"Nope, but I know mountains. There's places a man can winter and places where he'll freeze like still water."

"You've been trappin' a long time?"

"Likely, Jake. Since twenty-three, I reckon. First went out with Jedediah from Fort Kioway. We went to the Crow villages, run into Andy Henry and his bunch. We wintered with them red niggers in the Wind River valley. In the spring, we went into the Green River country and found a passel of beaver; cotched me a bunch."

"You can't trap in the winter, can you?"

"I can trap some, when the pelts is prime."

"But you don't have to go up there now, stay through the winter?"

Will puffed on his pipe, said nothing for a moment or two. When he spoke again, his voice was soft, his tone almost reverent. "I worked in the brigades until twenty-seven when the Blackfeet come ridin' hell-bent into our rendezvous at Bear Lake. I was there with Beckwourth and Sublette. We had a hell of a fight, and we skelped a lot of Blackfeet. But I got my fill of bein' a hired man. It were a hell of a year, twenty-seven." He paused as if he meant to say more about something that happened to him that year. Instead, he drew a deep breath, let it out as if to wipe out his thoughts.

"Next winter," Burke continued, "I went up into the Absorkas an' hunted alone. Best time I ever had. I didn't have to do for none but myself. Free trapper's the best, Jake. You hire out, they can make you cook, cut wood, hunt, stand guard, load the packhorses, unload 'em. You're working for the booshway, not yourself, beggin' your pardon."

"I guess I am a booshway."

"A trader, yep. Reason why I wanted to talk with you, Jake. I got my own outfit. I just need someplace to sell my furs for the highest price."

"I'll buy 'em," said Jake. "Name your price."

"You might not like it none," said Will.

"If I don't, I'll tell you."

"Five and two bits, guaranteed."

"Done," said Jake, and he stuck out his hand.

"Done," said Will. In the dark, Stonecipher could see the man's shadowy grin.

They walked back to the trading post in silence. Jake knocked out his dottle before going inside the walls. His tongue felt as if it had been bitten.

"I'll be gone before first light," said Will.

"You and Joe will be leavin' about the same time. I'll say good-bye in the mornin'. It's goin' to be quiet round here with both of you gone."

"That's what I like about the winters up in the high country," said Burke. "It's mighty quiet, an' a man can think. I got me some books in my pack and plenty of candlewax to burn."

"Do you know exactly where you're goin', Will?"

"I know and I don't know."

"What do you mean?" asked Jake.

"I'll know the place when I find it."

Jake thought about what Burke had said after the trapper went to bed and Joe was sound asleep. Stonecipher sat at the table he had built and wrote out his list by lamplight. The way Will talked, the mountains were no hardship in winter but a peaceful haven for a man who liked his pipe and his books, his freedom. But even as he thought about it, Jake knew that not every man was like Will Burke. Not even every hundredth man. He was as rare as any he'd ever met, and he was glad they had an agreement to trade with each other. He sensed that Will Burke had some troubles in his past, that he sought the lonesome places in the mountains for some deeper reason. Burke was a man who shunned civilization, he felt. Jake could understand why a man like Burke preferred the wild places. He had the heart of a wild creature, and he had that same look of wariness in his eyes that Jake had seen in wild creatures. A wariness and a restlessness that surrounded him like a shadow. But he liked Will Burke. He liked him a lot.

Now, Jake thought, I have made two friends out here in the wilderness. Red Horn and Will Burke. He wondered if the two men would ever meet, and if they did, would they like each other? It would be interesting to see.

Jake put away his list and blew out the lamp. In the distance, he heard a wolf howl, and he shivered at the mournful sound as a breeze gusted off the river.

Will Burke rode out before Joe left for St. Louis. There was a thin slit of cream on the eastern horizon, but the mountains were still dark.

"That's the last we'll see of him," said Perkins.

"I reckon he'll be back," said Jake. He handed the list and a sack of coin and banknotes to Joe. "I made a drawin' of a handbill I want you to have printed up, twenty of 'em. Take 'em round and post 'em in the grogshops for me. I allowed for price changes, and there's some coin in there for your expenses too. Just post those bills for me."

"Aw, Jake."

"Want to let folks know where we are."

"Shit," said Joe.

Perkins mounted his horse. Leather creaked like whispers, and the two mules balked when Joe took up the slack in the lead rope. "Be seein' you, Jake."

"Be careful," said Jake as Joe started out. It was chilly, and he wished he had brought a blanket to wrap around him. Maybe he would make a capote or two while Joe was gone, one for himself, one for Perkins when he got back.

Stonecipher watched Joe ride away into the pale dawn. He turned, saw no trace of Will Burke. But he heard the clack of his horse's hooves on stone somewhere in the dark.

He heard that sound for a long time after Will was gone, long after the sun came up and brightened the empty trading post, splashing tawny light on its adobe walls, chasing the shadows back toward the west and the looming snow-peaked mountains.

Soon, he knew, the aspen leaves would turn to gold,

the cold mountain winds would sweep down on the plain, dusting the prairie with snow.

That day, Jake went up into the hills and began to cut wood for the winter. When he came down that evening, he heard a young elk whistle, and he knew that autumn was not far off. That night, he locked the gate early and built a big fire out in the open. He stared into the flames for a long time, wondering where Will Burke was at that moment and if he would ever see him again.

≈ 5 ≈

The mountains drew him into them. The moment he crossed Fountain Creek, Will Burke knew he could go on, westward instead of north, up the creek. The map he carried showed the Arkansas River continuing on, deeper into the Sangre de Cristo Range, cutting through a gigantic gorge south of South Park. There was a big creek running into the Arkansas some thirty miles from where Jake had built his fort. The creek had no name, but it rose somewhere to the southwest in the shadow of the Wet Mountains.

Will was in no hurry. He had learned long ago that the man who went too fast into the wild country never went into it, never saw what he should see, never learned what he should learn. One had to go into the mountains slowly and be careful. A man could die so easily if he was not careful. A horse could go lame and have to be destroyed. A man could break his leg and die of starvation. What might only be an annoyance in a city, a sprained ankle or a mashed hand, could prove fatal in the wilderness. Will rode up the Arkansas slowly, and he noticed every detail of the country.

He savored the crisp, clear air, the endless green-tiered walls of the mountains on either side of the summer-lazy Arkansas. He saw game at every bend of the old Indian trail, no recent sign of man. With each step of the horse, he felt a great weight drop from his shoulders. Jays, both Stellar's and the frosty northern breed, haunted his camp both nights, and he took delight in feeding them scraps, watching them fight over a bit of hardtack, a scrap of meat. Their shrill taunts were company. He was at home, with the furred robbers for company until the sun went down and the land turned chill around his small campfire.

The country was as wild and untamed as any Burke had seen. The Arkansas was a bolder river up here in the high country, swifter, more powerful, not as graceful, but raw, muscular, with the force of gravity pulling on it and its banks trying to confine it, holding it in for that last rush to the flat prairie. The river ran richer here than down on the flat, and he saw trout jump in the pools, silver flashes in the sun, like sparks thrown off a knife sharpener's wheel. The air reeked of balsam, fir, spruce, and pine, air untainted by smoke or the breath of a city's crowds. The atmosphere grew thinner as Will threaded his slow way, higher and higher, deeper and deeper into the savage beauty of the Rockies. He knew his head would ache until he became accustomed to the altitude.

Late on the second day, Will found the creek that fed into the river. He figured he had ridden thirty miles on the tough little pony with its spotted coat of reddish-liver and black patches. A feeling of elation surged through him when he saw the mouth of the creek, clear water spilling into the Arkansas, mingling its waters in the turbulent river's.

He made camp several hundred yards upstream on the creek, vowing to follow it in the morning. He walked a wide circle, his flintlock cradled in his arms, before laying out his bedroll, checking for tracks, ani-

mal or human. Satisfied that he was alone and likely to
remain that way, he gathered stones for a fire pit, set up
his camp well away from the stream.

It was a trick he had learned from observing the
empty Ute camps up on the headwaters of the Rio
Grande del Norte high in the mountains. The Ute
never pitched camp within the sound of running water
but preferred the high flat ridges that gave them a view
for miles around. They sometimes had to walk a long
distance for water, but it was safer that way. They could
hear an enemy approaching long before there was any
danger. The Ute survived by being able to see and hear
any enemies that might search them out.

Burke smoked his pipe in the cool silence of evening.
Far off, he heard the faint murmur of the creek. But he
had long ago learned to listen to the undertones, the
sounds beneath sounds, in the forest. He had a habit of
identifying each sound, whether a branch scraping against
another, dried autumn leaves rustling in the wind, or
the trickle of a spring, so that any alien sound instantly
alerted him. He knew the difference between a deer's
footfall and the careful step of a man, could separate the
sound of a horse from that of an elk. His ears were
attuned to every sound now, and a man would have to
be quieter than the Canadian lynx to sneak up on Will
Burke.

He heard an elk bugle just before the moon rose, and
there was an answering call from several miles away. In
the clear, thin air of the mountains, sound traveled far.
He felt himself settle even more into the country, felt
the mountains become part of him. There was a thrill to
it, one he could never explain to anyone else.

As Burke sat there in his aloneness, looking at the
stars and the sliver of moon, the scent of evergreens in
his nostrils, he let himself become part of it all—the
stars, the sky, the towering granite mountains, the

gentle slope behind him, the trees in shadow all around. There was a blessed peace upon that corner of his universe, a solemnity he felt deep in his heart. He felt the shedding of his civilized self, the shucking of nerves and armor that he no longer needed. He became attuned to a different rhythm, a cadence of the wild places, a harmony of breeze and rustling spruce branches that seeped through him and peeled away all the baggage of the long trail from Fort Laramie.

The smoke he drew from his pipe was sweet in his mouth and warm in his lungs. He listened to the sounds of the forest cooling down—the crack of a pine limb, the faint breath of trees as they moved with vagrant gusts of air springing from some invisible source far away.

Tonight, Will vowed, he would not think of those bitter days when he trapped in Ashley's brigade. He had fought the memories off with whiskey and the companionship of Jake Stonecipher, but he knew they would haunt him again, when he least expected it. For now, it was enough to listen to the muffled scratch of squaw wood in the pines, the soft creak of the pony's hobbles as it grazed along the creek.

When he finished his pipe, he tamped the dottle out of the bowl, put it away in his possibles pouch. He walked to his bedroll and crawled in, fully dressed, moccasins and all. He closed his eyes, setting his senses to rest yet listening to every sound until they faded away in sleep.

Will broke camp early the next morning.

He made his way slowly along the creek, eyeing the ridges, the contour of the surrounding mountains.

The deeper into the mountains he rode, the more excited he became. Game trails crossed and crisscrossed his path like mysterious lacework. He saw no tree blaze, no moccasin track, no scrap of human trash, no stacked stones, no blackened campfire wood, no mark of man. Yet he knew that men's tracks were underfoot, Ute or Arapaho, or both, perhaps Pawnee or Apache as well.

The valley widened after he rounded a bend in the creek. Its slow movement made his blood quicken. Then he began to see branches and trickles from other sources. His excitement increased as he followed the main branch. More and more trickles appeared. Well before noon, he saw his first small beaver dam across a lean sliver of stream, and by late afternoon, he rode in the middle of a brushy marsh created by beaver, rode in wide-eyed wonder at all the aspen stumps, the dams, the large beaver houses.

He rode still higher, and when he came to the forks of two streams, he knew he had found a trapper's paradise. Beaver waddled among the trees and slapped hard tails in warning when he came upon one of their ponds. Burke wanted to shout in jubilation, but he held back superstitiously. He didn't want a soul to know what he had discovered.

He rode still higher, straight up from the place where the two other large streams joined the main one that fed into the Arkansas River, and found a flat ridge where he could build his camp. His pulse raced as he looked back down at the wide beaver-infested valley. Willows grew in profusion; there were aspen, pine, spruce, and fir on the slopes, clear to timberline. He sighed deeply, dragged a quart of thin air into his lungs. He felt good. He had found the place he sought, and it was all his. The beaver were growing hair. Their coats would be prime in a month.

Plenty of time to set up camp, explore his surroundings, make ready for the trapping season. He would run six traps a day, try to check them twice. Set more than that, and he would lose pelfries, wear out his welcome.

He would start at the deepest ponds, the ones farthest from camp, work his way back up the marshy meadow. In all his years of trapping, he had never seen such prime country for beaver. He had seen plenty of cubs that day and enough full-grown beaver to make his hair prickle.

Burke began felling timber for his home. He cleared out an area under an overhang of rock, so he had only three walls to contend with and half a roof. He topped the pines, trimmed them, skidded the logs through the timber up to the outcropping. He didn't bother with squaring off the logs but cut his notches and laid them snug. He rigged a rope-and-pulley system, used the mule to hoist the top logs into place. When he was finished, he chinked the gaps with mud and straw. He hacked out a door, cut a hole in it for a latchkey, hung it using strips of cured buffalo hide for hinges. He built a simple fur press, began to cut willow branches to use for beaver frames. He laid them by for later use inside the simple hut. He cut a smoke hole near the overhanging ledge, dug a fire pit. There was no time to make a proper chimney, nor did he have pipe for such a luxury. There would be a draft from the door, he reasoned, and the smoke hole ought to keep the cabin reasonably smokeless on cold winter nights.

When the cabin was finished, the old melancholia began to worm its way into his mind. He looked at the crude cabin and saw an empty home. A wave of sadness, like gray clouds of winter sliding into a mountain valley, engulfed him slowly, rising as subtly as a high stream when the snow melts. He began to think back to the days when he first came westward with Ashley to the South Platte, trapped the upper Missouri. His memories threaded with bitterness as he recalled his youth, the woman he had loved with all his heart.

As a young man, a dreamer, he had joined one of the

brigades in St. Louis, learned the trapper's trade in the Rockies. In March of 1827, Will became one of the men Ashley hired to go to the mountains at $110 a year. In that first year, he fought the Blackfeet, took a Cheyenne woman, Running Fawn, who had been captured by the Crow when she was but a lass. She had escaped during the fighting at South Pass, and Will, just seventeen in that year, had been smitten with her. They stayed in Bear Lake until time to trap, and he took her with him to Willow Valley.

Running Fawn kept his lodge for him through the winter, and he fell deeply in love with her. He was too young to know that other men would envy him such a prize. He was blind to all but her and took her with him to rendezvous on Sweet Lake. At the gathering on the south end of Bear Lake, Burke learned that there would be no supply train that year. Bill Sublette and Dave Jackson had brought out supplies in November that did not reach rendezvous until summer.

There was another fight with the Blackfeet that year. A hundred braves or more attacked Bob Campbell's party about sixteen or eighteen miles north of the lake. The first Burke heard of it was when a Spaniard and another brave man galloped into camp, their horses lathered, and told the trappers of the situation. By the time Burke and the others got to Campbell, the Blackfoot war party had disappeared. While he was gone, one trapper, Ned Liggett, stayed behind and made advances to Running Fawn. She told him about it, and he confronted Liggett.

"Hell, I'll buy your squaw from you, Burke," said Liggett.

"She ain't for sale," Burke told him.

"Baw! I'll bet you'd take ten skins for her." At the time, beaver pelts were selling for three dollars per pound.

"I wouldn't take nothin' for her, Liggett. Stay away from my lodge."

He had thought no more about the matter until the day he came back from a hunting trip and Running Fawn was not in their lodge. He asked the other trappers about her, and finally Jim Beckwourth told him what had happened. "Liggett got hisself drunk and spoiled your woman, Will," said the big mulatto trapper.

"Raped her?"

"That's what they'd call it in the States."

"The sonofabitch. Where'd he go to?"

Beckwourth shrugged.

"I'm goin' after him," said Burke.

"Best you forget about the squaw," said Jim. "Liggett's mean, and he's tricky."

Burke went after Liggett, heedless of the warnings some of the other trappers offered. Liggett was treacherous; he was smart, and he was dangerous. He had twenty pounds and ten years on Burke. Will tracked them to South Pass and found them down on the Platte in late summer.

Running Fawn was almost dead from a brutal beating, and Liggett was grunting over her like a hog in the slop. Burke put a ball through Liggett's brain. He tried to nurse Running Fawn back to life, but she died in his arms.

Running Fawn was dead, but she shimmered in the shadows of his memory like a distant star seldom seen.

Burke did not return to rendezvous, nor did he seek the company of other trappers. Instead, his hatred for Liggett turned into a bitterness he held toward all of his breed. There were times when he thought that Liggett was not dead, that he was following Burke, waiting to shoot him. It was irrational, but he could not shake the thought. Liggett had run away when Burke found him plumbing the half-dead Running Fawn. The shot was clean, he thought. He saw Liggett pitch forward and fall into the river. He never saw him come up as the current swept him away, and he ran to his woman and took her into his arms. In his heart, he knew Liggett was dead, but his mind played tricks on him.

Will left the brigade and drifted for two years, back and forth from the mountains to St. Louis, where he could get five dollars a pound for his beaver. He returned often to Running Fawn's grave on the Platte, but finally the river took a bend and covered over her resting place. He finally outfitted at Fort Laramie, determined to use the map he had bought there to trap the upper Arkansas. He was told he would have no competition, that it was too wild even for the Indians.

One day he would learn that this was not so.

Will built a crude shelter for the horse and mule. He had a small supply of grain that he would use during the winter, but he belled both animals and let them graze in a grassy meadow within earshot. He brought them in every night so they'd know where home was, and soon they got in the habit of coming back in the evening on their own.

The weather began to change. Burke heard an elk bugle one morning, tracked it, and brought it down with a single shot at two hundred yards. He had located it in a stand of pines by seeing its steaming breath. That afternoon, the sky skudded over with clouds, and when he awoke in the morning, there was frost on his blankets.

That same day, Burke cut a pair of strong willow limbs, trimmed them to about eighteen inches apiece, and made a squeezer in case he had to make his sets on mushy beds. He held the sticks parallel to each other and tied one end tightly with a thick leather thong. He carried six traps to places he had scouted in the willow-bordered streams, the deep ponds, and the marshy runways that threaded the high meadow. There was a crisp tang to the air when he set out, and the sky skudded over with gray clouds that brought the faint promise of snow on the vagrant downdrafts that kissed his bearded face, made his cheeks rosy as young ripening apples.

≈ 6 ≈

Burke waded down a leg of the creek where there was beaver sign aplenty. He had seen beaver running the waters and didn't want to leave scent. He found a spot where a shelf dropped off from the bank in a gentle slope. He set the trap under the lip of the bank on a hard bed. He depressed the springs by standing with a foot on each spring, extended the trap chain to its full length to a deeper point in the stream, stuck a float stick, a pole of deadwood that would not tempt a beaver to gnaw it for food, through the ring at the end of the chain, and tied the chain ring to the stake with strong cord. He drove the stick hard into the bottom. If a trapped beaver managed to pull the stake loose, the deadwood would float, and he would find his drowned beaver.

When he had set the trap, Burke cut a willow wand, scraped the bark off, smeared castoreum on the end of the switch, and rammed the stick into the soft bank. He adjusted the willow branch so that its alluring end dangled six inches above the trap. He waded far downstream before he walked out onto dry ground.

He made his sets far enough apart so that the beaver would not be wary of any particular area but close enough so that he could tend all six traps in a day, perhaps twice a day if he was lucky. When he was with the brigades, Will had had a helper. By the time he finished his last set, he felt the weariness in his bones. He shivered from the cold as he hiked back to his camp. He would not check his trapline until the next day when he was rested.

The mountains had turned smoky, mist rising from the bog, clouding through the trees. Will shivered in the sudden chill, felt a numbness in his feet. There was an eerie hush as the light began to fail. Landmarks disappeared in the fog, and for a moment, Will lost his bearings. He continued to climb, angling left by dead reckoning toward his camp. As he topped a familiar knoll, he thought he saw a man standing at the edge of the woods. It was only an impression, but he couldn't shake it from his mind. He fingered the lock on his rifle and wondered if he ought to cock it.

He stared into the murky shadows of the evergreens and felt the hackles rise on the back of his neck. "Liggett," he whispered, and knew that his ghost had returned.

Something moved, and Will was sure it was a man. He took another step, looking for cover in the scattered brush of the marsh—an alder bush, a scrub juniper, anything. He heard something crack, and his heart leapt in his chest. Fear tightened his throat, and his mouth went dry.

Burke stomped over to the place where he had seen the man. He made a lot of noise, which helped to quell the fear roiling his stomach. There was nothing there. No tracks, not a sign that anyone had been there. He was almost disappointed.

That night, after he had put the horse and mule up, taken their bells off and hobbled them, he stalked around his camp, looking for any signs of an intruder. He used a pine torch to light his way and carried a pistol at the cock. Inside his shelter, he heard night noises and jumped at every one of them. But the animals stayed quiet, and when he went to bed, he cursed himself for jumping at shadows, seeing things that were not there. He listened to the cabin tick in the nightcool for a long time before he went to sleep. He didn't remember his dreams in the morning, but they nagged at him from the back of his mind while he boiled coffee and fried fatback in the skillet. The smoke hole worked well enough, but he had not kept the fire lit during the night, and there was frost on the log walls near the ground.

He turned the horse and mule out, watched as they ambled toward the meadow, bells clanking. They were hobbled, but loosely so they could run if a bear or painter came on them. He didn't want them running down the mountain and leaving him stranded.

He got four beaver that first day. There was a foot in one trap. The beaver had dragged the trap into shallow water and gnawed through his leg at the joint. The other trap was empty, and he smeared castoreum on the stick, stuck it closer to the trap. He reset the other five, set to skinning out his catch.

Will got back to his camp at midafternoon. He laid out his beaver, picked up the first one. He smiled at its weight, the sleekness of its pelt.

"Prime," he said, and slit its belly open. He made cuts along the inside of each leg, cut off the feet. He cut off the tail for his supper, set it aside. He tugged the pelt from the carcass, laid it on a flat piece of bare ground. He took his tomahawk and scraped the inside of the hide clean of fat and flesh. He did this with the other three beaver, then bent their pelts on a hoop of willow withe tied at the ends into a hoop. He stretched each pelt and sewed it to the hoop with elk sinew. When he was finished, he had four flat, round plews that would dry evenly and quickly. When each was dry, they would resist insects pretty well.

"Well," he said to himself afterward, "I'm in business," and he filled his pipe and watched the sun burnish the afternoon sky, gilding each cloud, smearing their underbellies with orange and pink and purple. When the horse and mule came up that evening, he set out a handful of grain for each. He built a fire in the cabin and kept it tended so he wouldn't kink up when he arose in the morning. He knew it was going to be a good day. The sky had blazed red when the sun had set.

He trapped for a month, watched his plews dry in the sun, stacked them on logs so the air could get to them after they were dry, built a little fence around the drying place to keep the night animals away from them.

The days grew lonely and long.

Sometimes he would hear Running Fawn call to him. When the high winds came into the valley, he would hear her in the undertones that murmured in the spruce boughs. She called him Bear Face because of his heavy beard, and he heard those words in Cheyenne when the stream waters trickled just so over the green moss and rocks. Or he heard her in the creak of wood in the night, the harsh whisper of wind under the eaves of his log hut, the sigh of alder thickets when the vagrant breezes laced them with zephyrs in the late afternoon. At such times, he ached for her, and he could see her face in the clouds, in the intricate arrangements of pine needles, in shadows that played in the bright waters that trickled through the marsh like silver ribbons in morning sunlight. And sometimes he could feel her touch on the back of his neck, her lips brushing against the lobe of his ear. He would turn around and expect to take her in his arms, but he felt foolish and empty when she wasn't there, and he knew there was never anyone there, that she had gone forever and had only left her tracks across his memory like the dark prints of a fawn in the snow.

The weather began to change. Some afternoons, he saw clouds sail over the mountain peaks, big and fluffy as sheep on a hill and white as milled flour. They would roll away, and he would hear thunder on the plain and know that Jake Stonecipher was watching rain dance on the flowing Arkansas and hearing it pelt the roof of his trading post, turning the earth to mud. A month after Will had built his shelter, there came the first snow of the season, and he felt a longing for Running Fawn that was worse than any that year.

The snow started falling when he was returning with six prime beaver pelts, all skinned out and laced to willow withes. The flakes fell slowly at first, then thickened, getting bigger and bigger until he knew they would stick and he would have to make a pair of snowshoes if he was to tend his sets in the morning. He lit his pipe that night, set grain out for the horse and mule, and saw snowflakes dance down the hole in the roof and melt in the smoke of the fire. He had not seen Liggett's ghost in days, but he thought of him that night and wished God would give him the chance to kill him all over again, slowly and up close where he could watch him writhe and die on the tip of his blade.

When he awoke in the morning, the earth was shawled in ermine, and it was quiet and lonesome up on the mountain. But it was clean and white, the trees dark beneath the mantle of snow. The snow was not deep, and he put off making snowshoes that day because he wanted to tend his traps and get back early.

He rode the horse down to the marsh and let him feed on high grasses while he turned the mule out on hobbles and let him forage where he might. There were only two traps sprung, and one held a mink, the other a marten, so he made the sets farther down, toward the river, and rode back early, skinned out his pelfries, and made snowshoes until the sun went down.

It snowed some that night, and he tried out the snowshoes the next day; it was like learning to walk all over again. Will laughed when he fell down and rolled in the snow, and he saw a mule-deer buck jump out of an alder thicket and toss clumps of snow up in the air as he gamboled into the woods and disappeared.

Then the sun came out again, and the snow melted. Will watched huge cloud formations blunder over the mountain and shadow the valley before moving on to the plain beyond. But the air stayed crisp and cold, and one morning he shot the mule-deer buck that had been night-feeding in the marsh. He braintanned the hide and dug out his moccasin patterns from a pouch he kept in the bottom of his saddlebag. He found his awl and a stick wound with sinew, and got out the books he had brought along to read by candlelight when the snows were deep.

When he finished running his trapline early, Will would load up his rifle with birdshot and hunt mountain partridge. They were easy to find, and he shot them on the ground. They made a savory addition to his diet of elk, venison, and rabbit. When he had cleaned and plucked them, he made mud from the snow and earth and encased their bodies. He baked them right in the coals, peeled off the mud, and ate them with his bare hands.

Then came another big snow, and it too melted in a few days, but there were patches that never saw the sun, and these stayed to remind him that he had not been touched by winter yet and he had better work hard on the good days because he was going to miss some when the wind blew down from the north and brought the really big snowstorm.

He figured the month to be October when he went

down to check his first trap one morning. It had begun to snow early, just little flurries, and he wanted to get finished early. He had added another trap to his line and moved farther down the marsh so he wouldn't trap out the upper streams.

He knew something was wrong long before he reached the first trap. He heard something, sensed something, or just felt odd about the way the air tasted and smelled.

He stayed to the tree fringe, looking out every so often, stopping to listen, looking for anything different. Still, when he saw them, he didn't expect it. They were so close, he almost gave himself away. They didn't make much noise at first, and they were behind bushes. But when he stalked closer, using the trees for cover, he saw them—four Ute braves riding up a meandering stream that coursed through the marsh. They weren't painted, seemed to be a hunting party. His heart caught in his throat when they stopped and one of them pointed to his beaver set.

"Damn," said Burke, but he made little sound, just an exhalation of air with a soft curse attached to it.

Burke heard the muffled tones of the guttural Ute voices as they stared at his beaver set. They gesticulated with their bows and argued for three or four minutes before they split up and ranged the marsh, looking for more beaver sets. Will stayed hidden until they had passed him twice, once going up toward his cabin and again when they rode out of the valley, spread far apart on their ponies, quiet as ghosts.

He began to breathe easier after they had gone, but he knew they would be back. They had full quivers, and he'd bet they had more horses down by the river. He imagined that they were camped down on the flat somewhere and had been hunting game to feed their wives and mothers and children. A small party, to be sure, but there were probably more where they had come from, and he wanted to be ready when they returned.

Two days after he had seen the Ute there was another snow, and Will figured it was the month of November. It snowed for three days, off and on, and he worked his trapline with snowshoes. He took the horse and mule down to grass in a sheltered valley and ran off a herd of fifty elk or so when he rode in. There, he figured, the animals could find shelter and forage for at least a couple of weeks. It was a long walk on snowshoes to his trapline, but he harvested five beaver and two mink.

It was dark before he finished making new sets, and he had to crisscross a trail since the climbing was too hard on a straight path. He was weary to the bone when he built his fire that night and too tired to fill his pipe. He listened to the wind moan and wondered when the Ute would return and if they would wear some paint on their faces next time.

Burke checked each day for tracks in the snow, pony tracks, and after a week of seeing no sign, he began to think the Ute had just been passing through. Perhaps, he thought, they were just a ranging hunting party, coming into the mountains one last time before going on to warmer climes. He let his guard down because the trapping was hard and it was bitter cold working the sets in the chill waters. Each beaver he took seemed to weigh more than the last, and when he brought the horse and mule up after the sun had thawed some of the snow, he was glad he didn't have to carry the pelts on his back and trudge through heavy drifts on foot.

As he rode up to his cabin that day late in November, he wasn't thinking about the Ute at all, had all but forgotten them. His brain was numb with cold, and his fingers felt as if they had been burned in fire. His feet were dead asleep, and he had been wiggling his toes to keep blood circulating through them.

Then he saw the man at his cabin. He knew it wasn't Liggett, but he couldn't help himself. "Liggett!" he shouted.

He shot the Ute without thinking. Somehow, Burke was able to cock his rifle, and his powder was dry. He took quick aim, and when the white smoke cleared, he saw that his ball had shot true. The buck lay in a bloody pool next to the cabin, and one of Burke's pistols lay in the snow a few inches from the Ute's dead hand.

Will dropped the mule's lead rope and clapped his heels into the horse's flanks. He rode at a lope the hundred yards to where the Ute lay crumpled up in the snow. The ball had taken out a chunk of the brave's ribs where it exited. There was a lot of blood, and some of it was pink and frothy. There was blood trickling from the buck's mouth and a small hole through his coat just below the shoulder.

"You sonofabitch," Burke panted. "You was tryin' to clean me out." He kicked the dead buck, and with shaking cold fingers, he reloaded his rifle, primed the pan.

He looked at the dead Ute's face a long time. "No, you ain't Liggett," he said to the corpse. "But you might have been."

The brave had loaded beaver packs onto his pony and was preparing to leave with the stolen pistol when Will had shot him. He dragged the dead buck into the trees, out of sight.

He was trembling when he was finished, from the cold and from the enormity of what he had done. "Where in glorious hell are your damned friends?" he asked the dead buck, and he peered hard all around as if expecting the earth to erupt in Ute at any moment.

The horse and mule regarded Will with baleful looks as he unloaded the beaver packs from the Ute's pony and tied him to the stock shelter. He hobbled the horse and mule, put them inside the shelter, and set out grain for them.

"I made a big mistake," he told the horse. "Killin' that damned buck. Now I got to go out and hunt down his friends. Maybe Liggett sent 'em."

The other Ute would want his scalp now that he had killed one of them. He could not afford to wait for them to come to him. They would have the advantage. No, he would have to hunt them down, every one of them, if he was to stay alive.

And maybe Liggett was among 'em, damn his hide. Burke shivered again. But not from the cold.

≈ 7 ≈

Burke took two rifles with him, his Hawken .50 caliber caplock and a Nathan Kiles flintlock in .33 caliber. He tucked a .45 caliber caplock pistol in his belt, wore a 'hawk and his knife. He took plenty of powder and ball in his possibles bag, stuck in some jerky and a tinderbox, flint, and steel for making a fire. He didn't know how long he was going to be gone, but he wanted to be ready to live on the trail if he must. He carried a pint of birdshot too, just in case he ran across blue grouse. He could eat jaybird if he had to; it wouldn't be the first time.

He mounted the Ute pony, rode him around for a few minutes to get used to his ways. The pony responded with touches of the knee; the grass bridle worked well, with its Spanish bit, rawhide reins. It was an odd-looking piece of tack, but the pony had been well trained.

Burke backtracked the Ute brave as the sun crawled down the sky, throwing his shadow far ahead of him, making the snow glisten like mother-of-pearl.

For a long stretch of brush, rock, and boggy marshland there was only a single set of pony tracks. Then he found a place, far down the meadow, where the four bucks had split up. The one Burke had killed had ridden up the mountain, following the treeline. Will felt the hackles rise on the back of his neck when he realized the Ute must have seen him as he passed. A mile back, he saw where the Indian pony's tracks had crossed his own, made that morning. So the Ute had known where to go, where to find the pelts. He had no doubt that the Indian had planned to come back with the other three braves and kill him, take Burke's guns and goods.

He followed the tracks of the three braves. After a mile, one set of tracks wandered off from the other two. Burke reasoned that the one buck was going off on his own in a wide circle, opposite the track of the one that had been at Will's cabin. He concentrated on the other two tracks. They were still fresh, no more than three or four hours old. He knew there was a danger of that one buck backtracking on him and coming up on his rear, but he was prepared for that.

Will didn't follow right behind them. Instead, he crisscrossed them at intervals, always checking his backtrail. He didn't hurry, but he kept his horse moving, always moving. An hour later, he came upon a clearing on a high tor ringed with spruce and pine. What he saw there made his heart grow cold, his belly swirl with fluttering wings.

Skeletons rotted on scaffolds, grinning hideously at the sky, the sockets in their skulls empty. Tattered buckskins flapped disconsolately in the breeze. Beads rattled against poles. The bones of slain horses lay beneath the funeral beds of the dead or were scattered beneath the snow, sticking out like so many fractured grave markers.

"So that's why they come up here," Will whispered, and he found the tracks of the two braves. They had skirted the Ute burial ground, but there was one place where they had stopped their ponies and made smoke.

He saw dottle in the snow, tiny dark holes where hot ashes had burned through.

The tracks angled back up to the second ridge below his cabin on the eastern side. They continued to look fresher. There was a place where the two bucks had stopped to relieve themselves, and Burke gained more ground on them. At another spot, they had found elk tracks and had begun to follow them. Burke followed the track more tightly now. His backtrail seemed clean as a hen's egg.

He came upon the two Ute braves dressing out a large cow elk. They looked up, skinning knives clutched in bloody hands, one of them with blood smeared on his mouth. He belched when he saw Will. Both braves looked toward their bows and quivers, which were leaning against a pine a dozen yards away.

"Which one of you be Liggett?" Will asked as he cocked the caplock rifle. He brought it to his shoulder as one of the bucks started to rise. He centered the blade front sight on the buck's chest and squeezed the trigger. He dropped the leather thong of the rifle around the saddle horn, let the rifle swing down to the horse's shoulder, and unslung the flintlock. He removed the tiny piece of grouse quill in the touchhole and cocked the weapon.

The second brave crawled toward his bow. The first lay in the snow, pumping blood from the hole in his chest.

Will took careful aim, held his breath, and pulled the trigger. The flint struck the frizzen, showered sparks in the pan. The rifle bucked against his shoulder. A cloud of white smoke billowed from the barrel, and Burke heard the round ball smack flesh. The Ute let out a grunt and rolled onto his back, mortally wounded.

Burke rode up slowly. The first buck was dead, the

second dying. He looked closely at their faces. Neither was Liggett. Will sighed in disappointment.

He took his pistol from his belt and dispatched the second brave. He reloaded all three weapons, cut off a haunch from the elk, and cut it up so that he could fit the pieces in both saddlebags. He noticed the heart and liver were missing from the cow.

Burke knew he had spent too much time at the killing place. He kept hearing things. His nerves jumped at every sound, every silence. "Maybe that other'n is Liggett," he said under his breath, and rode away.

The sky was the color of lead, and the temperature was dropping. There was, he figured, about two hours of daylight left. If he rode back to where he had last seen the fourth Ute's track, he would lose it in darkness. He headed back toward his cabin.

To his surprise, Burke found the track of the fourth Ute as he was circling the ridge, looking for an easier way back to his diggings. When he neared the burial ground, he gave it a wide berth. That's when he saw the other track. He recognized it. The pony had a damaged frog in his right forehoof and left a distinctive track in the snow. The pony favored that hoof, which left a muddled track that was half filled with snow.

The tracks were very fresh, easy to follow. They led Burke in a circle, then doubled back. He lost the trail once in a thicket but found it by circling to the place where it came out. The brave was clever. He rode his pony to places where the wind had blown the snow from rock, and this was the hardest riding of all. Will's horse was weary, and it was growing colder by the minute. Burke kept checking his backtrail, but he saw no one. It began to snow, a light fall that cut down the distance he could see. Finally, Will had to lean close to the ground to follow the track.

He felt stupid when he saw that the Ute, after all the

twisting torturous backtracking, was now headed straight for Will's cabin. Or had been an hour before. Burke was still shaking from having killed three men. He had tried to brush it off, but now he had to admit that it bothered him. He had shot the first Ute for stealing. The other two had done him no harm. He had killed them for the simplest of reasons: He was afraid they might kill him.

His heart pounding, Will checked his caplock to make sure the cap was still seated. The tracks were very fresh now, but they angled off once again, away from the cabin. It was getting darker, harder to see. On a hunch, he rode on a different angle, came upon the tracks again. The Ute was circling him, trying to come up on his backtrail. If it was the Ute. Now, with darkness coming on, the snow falling faster, Burke wasn't so sure. Maybe it was Liggett, come back to kill him. The tracks melded into his own, made previously, and headed back toward the cabin.

Will made up his mind. He headed for the cabin, uncertain now of his bearings. If he was right, he had one more ridge to cross. But he knew it would be stupid and dangerous to ride right up to his shelter. Instead, he took a roundabout course, heading off to the northwest to come up behind his dwelling.

He heard only the sound of his horse plodding through the building snow. The wind came up and dusted his tracks in the trackless forest. He came to the last ridge, and it was hard going. He had to ride around rock outcroppings and backtrack to find a path the horse could manage. He gained the crest of the ridge and kept on his heading. When he reached the fringe of the trees, he saw that he had come up behind the cabin. He saw no sign of the Ute.

He stopped the horse in the trees and looked for a long time. "Where in hell are you, Liggett?" he said softly.

The horse nickered, and Will knew he had to move. He rode on, following the treeline around the high meadow. He circled until he had rounded the edge of the clearing. He rode into the woods, heading for the place where he had dragged the Ute who had been stealing his furs.

As he drew closer, he heard a low keening sound. Will halted his horse, dismounted. He moved slow, holding his rifle well away from him, clamping his pouch and horn with his elbows so that they wouldn't rattle. He tied the reins to a bush, began a careful stalk. He moved from tree to tree, stopped to listen. The muffled keening grew louder.

"What was Liggett saying?" he asked himself, for by now, Burke was sure that Liggett had returned. "Come back to get me," he whispered soundlessly.

Burke drew close to the place where he had left the dead brave. The light was dim, but the buck was still there. Will stepped cautiously toward the body. He stopped, listened.

The keening had stopped.

Will's pulse quickened. His ears pounded with the throb of his heart. He moved closer to the dead Ute.

In the hazy light, the corpse looked like Liggett. Maybe he had killed him, after all. This time, if not the first time. In his mind, he saw Liggett fall into the Platte and float away.

Burke sucked in a breath. "You're even talkin' to yourself," he said softly. "Whoever's there is stone dead."

He wanted to look at the dead man's face one more time. He stepped carefully toward the body, his rifle at the ready. A stand of pines blocked his way. He went around a tree and saw the body less than ten yards away. It appeared to be as he had left it.

Maybe the other Ute, or Liggett, had ridden away to

seek shelter for the night. Or maybe he had imagined it all. Maybe those tracks he had followed had belonged to this dead brave. It was puzzling, but he could figure it out when he had a fire going, his pipe lit.

Burke's mouth went dry, and he tried to swallow. He let out a breath and took a step toward the body on the ground. Snow had dusted the Ute's features into a white frozen mask.

"He's dead, all right," Burke said, and then he stiffened as a scream pierced his ears. He saw a shadow and felt a jolt as his rifle spun out of his arms, thwacked into a tree. He turned as another bloodcurdling yell blasted his eardrums.

Something struck Burke in the head, and lights danced in the darkness of his brain. The man hurtled into him, so close Will could smell the rotten stench of his breath. He went down, his attacker's weight crushing him. He lashed out with his left arm, grabbed hair, and hit the ground with a jarring thud, the wind knocked from his lungs.

Will rolled out from under the man, scrambled to his feet. The attacker's sleek oily hair had slipped from his grasp. Will wiped his hand on his buckskins and grabbed the handle of his knife. His breath burned in his lungs as the man drew himself into a crouch and jumped to his feet.

This was Liggett, he knew, come back to kill him. In the darkness, he could not see the man's face. But he saw the flash of Liggett's knife as he waded into him. Burke sidestepped the lunge and slashed at the man's face. Liggett ducked and, catlike, whirled to lunge again.

So this was how it was to be, Burke thought. No guns, just the knives, the iron in their hands, the sharp blades. The breathy silence of combat. Just two men, alone, facing one another a final time.

"Liggett, you sonofabitch," gasped Burke, and he

barreled toward his enemy, knife poised for a fatal thrust.

In close, he could see the man's face. He was made up like an Indian, like a Ute, but Burke was not fooled. He thought he could see the man's eyes, even in the darkness. Liggett's eyes, he was sure.

The man spoke as he sucked in his belly, avoided Burke's rush. Burke could not understand his words. Guttural mumbles that made no sense.

"I been waiting for you, Liggett," panted Burke. "I knew you'd come up on me by and by."

The Ute, Liggett, grunted and began to circle, arms outspread, the knife moving, moving, always moving, making little thrusts, slashing empty space, diving up and down in the man's hand. Steamclouds streamed from their mouths as the two men circled each other warily, each waiting for the opportunity to pounce, to charge in for the kill. They were like dancers, the snow dusting them, flakes crashing softly on their grim faces, sticking to their eyelashes, clinging to their hair, Burke's beard.

Neither man spoke now. Burke held his knife in a tight grip, hunched forward, dancing lightly on the balls of his feet.

The Ute made a feint, then leapt toward Burke. He was fast, and Will barely got out of the way. He ringnecked the brave and tried to stab him in the side. The Ute wriggled away and went down. Burke dove at him, but the man scooted out of harm's way.

Will shot a hand out, grabbed the fur sleeve of the Ute's coat. The Indian grabbed Burke's arm. The two men rolled and tumbled, slashing and stabbing. Burke felt the Ute blade slice his arm, but there was no pain, only the urgency to kill Liggett once and for all.

Burke shook the brave off and got to his feet. His lungs burned with fire. The Ute stood up, breathing hard. The two men squared off and stood there, catching their breath, staring through the gathering darkness at one another.

The Ute began to chant, and his knife began moving again. Back and forth, up and down, in and out. Burke knew the man was stoking up his courage, getting ready for the final rush, the killing lunge.

His lungs cooled, and he set himself, waiting. "Come on, Liggett," he growled. "Make your move."

The Ute broke off his chant and half turned as if to walk away, then whirled and charged. The Indian's knife rose in the air and swept downward, slashing like a scythe.

Burke did not step away but ducked to the side. The buck's blade swished by, narrowly missing Will's face.

Burke drove in, hunched low, driving the blade upward. He sank his blade in the buck's side, felt it ease into the flesh, graze against a rib bone.

The Ute made a sound, like sighing, and went down, his eyes misting over with the glaze of death.

"Die, Liggett, damn you," snarled Burke. He pulled his knife free.

The Ute cursed Burke in broken English. "Piss bastard sumbitch."

Burke fell on the brave, hammered his blade into the Ute's heart. Again and again.

He plunged it in a half-dozen times until he realized he was screaming and that the brave was no longer saying anything. There was blood all over Burke's hand, all over his face and coat.

The trapper rose from the bloody carcass of the Ute. He was drenched in blood. He looked down at the mutilated chest of the slain warrior, the last of the light fading into the blackness of pitch.

"I *knowed* you was Liggett," he panted. "I knowed you was him all along."

Will staggered away from the dead Indian, still clutching his blood-smeared knife. His arm began to throb with pain. But there was a warmth inside him, a feeling of goodness that made him unmindful of his wound. He felt clean and whole, weightless, his shoulders light and unburdened. He zigzagged through the snow to the cabin, opened the door, and lurched inside.

He lay a long time in the darkness, listening to the horse nicker outside. The wind died down to gusty whispers, and the cabin creaked where the roof rested on the beams. Burke squeezed his arm, held the wound tight until the bleeding stopped. "Liggett's dead," he murmured. "Liggett's finally dead."

A great peace settled over him, and the pain in his arm went away.

Burke rose up and began to build a fire in the darkness. He hummed an old song of the sod he'd heard his father sing when Will was a boy, a lilting song of boats and whaling, and although he could not remember the words, Burke could still hear his mother playing the dulcimer while his father sang the song in his rich Irish tenor.

When the sparks caught in the tinder, Will blew on them until the faggots blazed. He laughed aloud as the cabin lit up and the shadows skulked off into the corners. He laughed, but there were tears running down his cheeks and brimming in his eyes. He looked down at the dried blood on his hands and threw back his head. He shouted in triumph, shouted for the sheer joy of it, and sobbed and shouted until he was hoarse and the tears dry on his face, his beard dry from the heat of the fire and all the blood dried and caked on him like armor, like new new skin grown in battle, grown in the darkness of night as the snow fell and made everything new and fresh and whole and clean.

*　　*　　*

In the spring, Burke descended from the mountains. He had cached most of his furs, knew he must return to pack them out. He had trimmed his beard with his knife and splashed his face with water from the Arkansas before riding down to the plain.

He felt vital and alive, tough as a chunk of sun-cured hickory. He threw gristle to the jays as he nibbled on elk jerky, laughed as they fought over each morsel. The pines, spruce, and firs wafted a heady scent to his nostrils. He filled his lungs with the good air and licked his lips, parched for a taste of whiskey after a winter of deprivation.

A young man, a Mexican from Santa Fe, stood in the shadows of a stand of spruce high above the river, looking down at the trapper. He made no sound, for he did not want to be seen. He watched as Burke, whistling and singing snatches of ditties, rode downriver, his packmule laden with beaver pelfries, his horse carrying a load behind the cantle. The Mexican made note of the man's passing, and when Burke had disappeared, continued on his way. He carried with him surveying instruments, maps, and a battered journal that he carried in a pouch so that it was always within easy reach.

Jake's adobe fort glistened in the sun. Burke read the sign above the gate as he rode up: *JAKE'S TRADING POST*. Along the river, Arapaho tepees bristled like upside-down cones, each one covered with crude designs and pictures. He saw children playing, women washing at the riverbank, men lying in the grass, passing an earthen jug among them. One man was dancing soundlessly, and Will figured he'd had his fill of the burning cup.

The gate to the fort was open. He hitched up outside, strolled inside on wobbly feet. Returning to the flat was like returning from the sea; it required a different set of legs.

The post was stacked high with beaver plews, and he saw marten and mink pelts. There were buffalo robes dripping from sturdy wooden tables and men strolling past the fur press toward a room full of hearty laughter and the clink of tankards, a sound sweet to Burke's ears.

Jake Stonecipher looked up from a stack of pelts he was grading on a table in the shade.

"Looks like you're in business," said Burke.

Jake nodded. He stepped from behind the table, came close. He looked square into Burke's eyes. "You find what you was lookin' for, Will?" he asked.

"Some. I found me some of it."

"You want to do some tradin'?"

"I seen them Rappyhoe niggers outside a-smackin' their lips. Don't give me none of that sugar whiskey. I want some what boils when it goes down, boils out snake pizen."

Jake grinned. "Welcome to civilization," he said.

≈ 8 ≈

There was another who had seen the country of the upper Arkansas, and he knew that someday he would live there. He had gone there long before Jake Stonecipher, Joe Perkins, and Will Burke had come to the edge of the mountains to live and work on the land.

His name was Francisco Serrano. Everyone called him Paco. He was a poor boy, born in Santa Fe when it was still part of the Spanish Empire. When the Santa Fe Trail opened, he, like many others, knew that Mexico must win its independence from Spain. When that happened in 1821, he was overjoyed, and he loved to sit in the cantinas and listen to the stories of mountain men and their tales of riches in the mountains.

Although he was young, he knew that someday he would be one of these men. He longed to go into the Sangre de Cristo Mountains, named after the precious blood of Christ because of the way they glowed red in the sunrise. He wanted to trap beaver, marten, lynx, and mink. He made friends with the American traders and learned the English tongue. He read books in Spanish and English when he could find them.

Some of the trappers hired Paco to read to them when they suffered from nights of hard drinking in the cantinas. The priest at the little parochial church on the plaza in Santa Fe learned of the boy's ability and let him come into the rectory and read the valuable journals and books the *frey* kept in the sacristy under lock and key.

Francisco Serrano knocked politely on the rectory door.

"*Quién es?*"

"Paco," said the boy.

"*Entra.*"

Paco took off his straw hat and lifted the latch. The heavy door swung open. Frey Alfonso Quintín looked up from his desk. He was a corpulent man, shaped like a wine barrel. Bushy eyebrows masked inquisitive nut-brown eyes. His pudgy face belied a keen intelligence; thick sensuous lips that proclaimed him as much a follower of Bacchus as of God were stained with sacristy wine.

"So you have come to talk about the river again, have you, Francisco?"

"The valley, yes."

"Well, I may have something that will interest you. I found it just this morning."

Paco could scarcely contain his eagerness. He twisted the straw hat in his hands. He was a thin intense boy of fourteen, with darting nervous eyes, a thick shock of black hair, dimples, gleaming white teeth, smooth olive skin. He was always scrubbed because his mother insisted he be clean, although they were poor.

"What is it?" asked Paco.

Frey Quintín reached toward the back of his rolltop desk, pulled out what appeared to be a book. But its pages were curled and tattered, and it had only a flimsy, well-worn leather cover. "This is a journal, my son,"

said Quintín, "written by Juan de Ulibarri. He was
from this village of Santa Fe. But he traveled to the
place you speak of, this creek that is called the
Fountain. He went there a long time ago, in 1706.
He wrote of the big river, which the Indians called
the *Napestle*, and which the white men call the
Arkansas. He said it was four times as large as the *Rio
del Norte* and meandered through the best and broadest
valley in New Spain. He said the land was very fertile,
abounding in cottonwoods, plums, cherries, and wild
grapes."

Paco's eyes glittered like polished agates.

"I would like to see this valley," Paco said to the
priest.

"Perhaps you will, someday, my son. But I have
read the journal of another, an American soldier, who
visited there in 1820 when you were but a boy of ten
years."

"Who was this man?" asked Paco, breathless with his
search for knowledge.

"His name was Stepen Long. He was a major in the
army. He camped very near the place where Juan
Ulibarri had crossed the Arkansas River, a few miles
above the mouth of the Fountain. His chronicler wrote
that the river bottom was beautiful, but Long did not
like the place. He called it dreary and disgusting. He
said that the valley was a desolate plain covered with
withered grasses."

"How can this be so, Father?" asked Paco. "One sees
beauty, the other disgust."

"It all depends on one's point of view," said the
priest.

"I think it is beautiful there," said Paco stubbornly.
"It must be beautiful."

Frey Quintín laughed. He lifted a small silver chalice
to his lips and gurgled down the wine in the cup. He

had red lines on his cheeks, and Paco's father said that was from saying the mass too often and drinking more than his share of wine. Paco thought the priest was wonderful.

"Ulibarri saw the valley as a garden, possibly because he was used to this dry land to the south, or perhaps he was from such a place in Spain. The American came from a country where fields had to be cleared of timber, where rivers flowed deep and strong and where there was much rain."

The priest handed the battered journal to Paco. The youth took the delicate packet, held it reverently in his hands. He stared at the scarred leather, numb with pleasure. "May I . . . ?"

"You may take the journal. It is a gift. Someday you may write your own."

"Oh thank you, Frey Quintín. A million thanks."

"It is nothing, my son. Go now. Go with God."

Paco tucked the journal under his arm and crushed his straw hat down on his head. He turned and left the room, forgetting to close the door behind him. In seconds, he was racing across the plaza toward home, his heart thumping like a grouse's wing drumming on a hollow log.

Paco drew maps from the journals, kept them until the day when he left Santa Fe, alone, and journeyed to Fountain Creek, which the French had named *fontaine qui bouille,* the fountain that boils. This was in the year before Jake Stonecipher built his fort, when Paco was eighteen years old. He had saved his money, every *peseta,* every *peso,* and bought rifle, pistol, knife, tomahawk, traps, a horse and mule. He was, by his standards, a rich man.

The young Mexican rode into a land of incredible beauty. He crossed through the Cumbre Pass and followed the old Indian trail to the Arkansas River. He ascended the river to its junction with Fountain Creek. The land around that place was flat and barren, but nearby the Rocky Mountains soared more than a mile into the sky and brought a thousand miles of Great Plains to an abrupt and breathtaking halt.

The Arkansas and Fountain were both shallow streams at that juncture in the mountains, bordered with bulrushes and coarse grass, thinly timbered with cottonwoods and willows, hemmed in by stark bluffs of sandstone. Beyond the bluffs, to the west, Paco saw a vast expanse of desert sand, naked as an ocean beach, leading to foothills stippled with dwarf piñon, scrub oak, and pine. To the east, he saw the arid beginnings of the Great Plains, gouged by deep gullies and dotted with sparse clumps of grass, sage, and greasewood, yucca and prickly pear, prairie-dog towns, and anthills, jackrabbits, horned toads, lizards, and rattlesnakes.

At their mountain birthings, the Arkansas and its tributaries were torrents in the spring. When they reached the plains, they grew tranquil and began to deposit pebbles and sand along the banks. As the rushing waters began to lose momentum, they meandered and formed islands in ever wider and shallower beds. In dry years, the water sank below the riverbeds and disappeared in underground channels for miles at a stretch.

When Paco first looked at the valley of the Arkansas, he saw what Ulibarri had seen—a garden, a paradise. He saw, in a moment of visionary precognition, irrigation systems twenty meters wide and a hundred kilometers in length, extending out from the river for a good fifteen kilometers. He saw farms and green fields, crops of wheat, oats, alfalfa, seed-flowers, sugar beets, tomatoes, chili peppers, orchards with trees sagging under the weight of apples, persimmons, pears, and apricots.

Young Serrano saw that the mouth of the Fountain was the western limit of the short-grass country, where foot-high gramma grass sent up its oblong shoots like brown *banderas* and curly buffalo grass grew in clumps only three to five inches high. He knew from reading books and talking to travelers that despite their sparse and dry appearance, these short grasses would provide good pasture for buffalo, sheep, and cattle. Even then, in August, he saw that the grass was curing and would retain its strength and nutrition all winter.

Paco roamed the mountains like a blind man suddenly given the gift of sight. He followed his maps and studied the journals and notes he had made. He rode to the Fountain and knew that the buffalo did not come to its mouth. The great herds of bison grazed on the more abundant grass to the east and northeast of the Fountain. He had listened carefully to the travelers, the mountain men, had asked them searching questions about this unknown land to the north. And in all of the books and journals he had read, nowhere had he seen mention of Indian villages, and that was a relief to him. Paco was terrified of Indians. He had listened to those stories too.

Yet he found traces of men who had settled near that juncture of the Fountain and the Arkansas. The men were no longer there. Maybe, Paco reasoned, they would come back someday.

This was a good place, he decided, as he followed Fountain Creek through the mountains. In places where the water boiled beneath the rocks, the stream kicked up a spray, and he saw rainbows in the mist. The mouth of the Fountain was nestled deep in a hollow pocket, closed in on three sides by timbered slopes. To the south were the high east-stretching mesas of the Raton Mountains; directly west lay the rugged Front Range and the Wet Mountains, thrown up like barriers and

separated by the deep and cramped Royal Gorge of the
Arkansas River; to the north rose the majestic Platte-
Arkansas Divide, a pine-crested ridge jutting eastward
onto the plains for twenty kilometers or more. It was a
natural trap, Paco knew, and buffalo gave the place a
wide berth. So did the Indians. The buffalo stayed out
on the open plains where the gramma grass was thicker,
the Arkansas easier to ford, and paths straight and on
the level.

Paco roamed the country all that autumn and went
back to Santa Fe before winter. In the spring, he
followed the rivers and their creeks. He saw few signs
of man, no hunters or trappers. Once he came upon a
high bench where Ute had stayed, far from running
water so that in the silence they could hear any enemy's
approach. He found obsidian arrowheads, fire-blackened
stones, a few clay utensils. He left the mountains again
before winter settled in and went back through the
Ratons the next spring. It was then that he saw the
trapper leave the high country. He followed Burke until
he saw the fort, then turned back into the mountains,
not yet ready to reveal his presence.

But his heart fluttered in his chest. He had been
right about this place. Men were already setting up a
trading post, and a trapper had worked one of the
streams that fed into the Arkansas. Someday the mountains would be filled with men, and he wanted to be
there when they came.

Paco found where Will Burke had built his shelter.
He saw too the bones of dead men, their winter clothing ripped apart by predators and scattered in the
woods. He shuddered as he discovered that they were
Ute, and he reasoned that the trapper must have killed
them when he was under attack. He made note of it in
his journal and rode on, heading back toward Santa Fe,
drinking in the beauty of the mountains. He followed

one of the creeks to the Wet Mountains, descended into a huge valley. He camped at the northern fringe, safely in the trees. In the morning, he was glad that he had done this, for when he awoke, he heard the breathy voices of Indians, husky and guttural, floating across the valley.

Seven or eight Arapaho braves, a hunting party, rode straight toward Paco. Quickly he saddled his horse, packed his saddlebags, checked his rifle. He tried to stay in the trees, but the Indians spotted him. They all yipped at once and fanned out to cut him off. Paco rode out of the trees and kicked his horse into a gallop across the broad valley.

Their ponies were fleet, and Paco turned when he heard the hoofbeats getting louder. He stopped his horse, took aim at the lead rider, and fired. The Arapaho screeched and threw up his arms. His trade musket flew out of his hand and tumbled through the air.

The braves faltered, but now that Paco was in the open, they changed course to catch up with him. They fired their muskets from long range, and Paco heard the balls whistle harmlessly past his ears. He kicked his horse and reloaded on the run. He shot another brave and reloaded again, giving the horse his head. He poured another handful of black powder down the barrel, rammed a patched ball home. He primed the pan, cocked the hammer, closed the frizzen, then turned the horse and halted him. He took careful aim and pulled the trigger. His flintlock rifle spoke true once again. The Arapaho yelled insults at him and turned their horses to reload their smoothbores.

Paco reloaded quickly and continued south. The remaining Arapaho were hunting him, he knew, so he stayed to the high country, drifted through unfamiliar terrain, holding the sun to his right shoulder. When he was able to stop and rest, he looked at his maps. At his back there was a high peak and farther south the Sangre de Christo Range.

He rode southeast to a creek called Cucharas on one of his crude maps, followed it to the gentle hills west of Spanish Peaks, two towering sentinels rising abruptly from the plain. He knew from his reading that the Comanche called these peaks *Wah-to-ya* and the Spanish spelled it *Huatolla*, the breasts of the world.

Paco rode up Cucharas Creek, followed another creek westward, deeper into the mountains to throw off the pursuing Arapaho. There, in a high mountain meadow, he saw a herd of elk feeding in deep grasses, and there he found growing a most beautiful blue flower, its petals a pair of long graceful spurs. He dismounted and knelt down to look at the flower closely. He leaned over and smelled it.

Here, he thought, rocking back on his haunches, in a place like this, is where I will make my home someday, with the high mountains behind me, the vast empty plain stretching to meet the sky.

Paco stayed there on a high crown of land, a meadow between stands of pine where elk foraged unafraid. He had a long view of the trail he had followed and knew that he would have plenty of warning should his pursuers overtake him. He spent a month exploring the whole region, and the Arapaho never came. He stayed and watched the storms form in the mountains or out on the plain, and he felt like a king. Here he found sign that the grizzly bears and deer were thick in the timber by day, fed in the starlit meadow by night.

But this was not the place. He realized he had already seen such a place, very like this one, on the other side of the Wet Mountains. And he had seen no track of the Arapaho or the Ute in that place.

He rode back to the place where he had seen the trapper's camp, followed one of the creeks, the middle one, almost to where it rose, and there again he found a meadow with the pretty blue flowers and game, and he knew that this would be the place where he would one day live and build a home.

He set stones in a line for the foundation of his house, and he named the creek Adobe; he measured off a section of five thousand hectares and drew lines on a piece of buckskin, using a hawk's quill and juice squeezed from a juniper berry. He prowled the three creeks and drew them on his crude map. He drew lines to represent the Wet Mountains and when he was finished, he drew in a deep breath and surveyed once again the land he already owned in his heart.

Finally Paco rode out of the mountains, to the trail that led over Raton Pass. Above Taos, three brigands of the road, New Mexicans, fired a shot over his head. Paco fired back and killed one of their horses. They cursed him in Spanish, and he reloaded and started to chase them. They picked up their insulted brother and rode away. The other two had only crude clubs, and there was no time for the one who had shot to reload. Paco sent another shot after them and laughed when they galloped even faster to escape him. "*Pendejos*, cowards," he said.

In Santa Fe, Paco went to see the official who handled land grants, applied for five thousand hectares, and paid the fees and appropriate bribes. He marked off the boundaries from the Spanish Peaks westward, deep into the mountains.

"It will take a year, perhaps, before the government will tell you if you may take title to this land," said the official.

"I will wait," said Paco. But in his mind he already owned the land.

He stopped to see his parents, to tell them good-bye again.

"Where do you go, my son?" asked his mother.

"Back to the mountains."

"What do you do there?" asked his father. Their names were Elena and Fernando Serrano. They worked for a *rico* who owned a large sheep ranch. His mother cooked for the shepherds, and his father was one of them. They lived in a little adobe hut in the hills, out of sight of the landowner.

"I look and I find out things."

"You do not trap. You do not make any money," said Fernando.

"I will. I have many things to do."

"Go with God, *mi hijo*," said his mother.

"You make some money, eh," his father said, and Paco embraced him, then his mother. He heard a sob catch in her throat, and when he left, her eyes brimmed with silent tears. He felt a great weight lift from his shoulders.

"You need a wife!" shouted his mother.

Paco mounted his horse, turned, and looked back at her. "I am going to see Consuelo in Taos," he said and galloped away before his mother could ask him a thousand questions that he could not answer.

His heart made thunder in his ears when he thought about Consuelo Velez. He had met her at the August Fair in Taos the previous year, in church. She had invited him to the *baile*, and he had danced with her. They had kissed when he had tricked her chaperone by letting some coins fall to the ground. When the *dueña* bent over to pick them up, he stole the kiss. Consuelo was delighted.

Paco did not stop in Santa Fe but rode on toward

Taos. He had much to tell Consuelo now that he was a man and about to become a landowner. He still had *pesetas* in his pocket, and there was a question he wanted to ask her.

He wondered if Consuelo would think him crazy.

≈ 9 ≈

Paco rode beyond the settlement of Taos, just north of the village. The sun was setting, burnishing the western sky with gold. The smell of young wheat filled his nostrils. As he passed the adobe buildings blushing pink in the afterglow, his stomach growled with hunger. The faint aroma of corn tortillas and beef assailed his nostrils. Dogs barked, and he heard the sounds of children playing in the dirt streets, a mother calling for her son. A mule brayed, and a few people waved at him as they carried water from the river in buckets strung from yokes on their shoulders.

Alonzo Velez had built his adobe north of Taos on a little knoll where he could look down at the wheat fields, see the road out of Taos for a long way. Paco's heart quickened when he saw the little house shimmering in a rosy glow atop the hill. He wondered what Consuelo was doing, if she knew he was coming. He did not see any of the family but knew they must be inside. Consuelo came from a large industrious family. Her father, Alonzo, was a maker of adobe brick. Her brother Antonio was a muleteer. She, her sister, Felicia, and her mother, Paciencia, worked for a merchant-trader. Another brother, Lafcadio, was a trapper.

Consuelo was smart. She could read and write, and

kept the books for her employer, Don Ignacio Mendoza y Llave. Her position brought her in contact with a number of Americans, Spaniards, French, and Mexicans who traveled from the upper Missouri and from St. Louis to Taos and Santa Fe. Sometimes she met the businessmen who came up from Chihuahua to trade and sell their goods, to buy things to take back to their province. She heard all the latest gossip, the rumors, the stories of great hunts and fights with Indians along the Arkansas and the Rio Grande del Norte.

He turned off the main road into the little dirt trail rutted with wagon tracks. As he climbed the grade, he saw the door to the adobe open.

Consuelo appeared. She waved to him and then hiked her skirts, started running toward him. Paco waved back and grinned as he touched heels to his horse's flanks. He galloped toward Consuelo, saddlebags flapping against his horse's flanks.

When he drew near, he slid from the saddle and landed on his feet, running. The horse slowed. Consuelo rushed up to him, and he took her in his arms.

"Paco, Paco," said Consuelo. "Oh, I'm so happy."

"It is good to see you," he said, then took her in his arms. She was soft, and her breasts thrust against his chest. He peppered her face with kisses, and she dove at him with her lips, attacking his cheeks and chin, nibbling at his ear. Finally their lips met, they kissed, and Paco turned warm all over.

"Are you staying? Can you stay? Where are you going? Where have you been? Have you got a present for me?"

He could not answer all of her questions at once, and she kept asking them as they hop-skipped up the trail to the house. She pulled on him, trying to drag him along, and he pulled on the horse's reins, dragging the horse behind them. They started laughing when he tried to answer her, and they were still laughing when they stopped at the hitchrail her father had built out front for the men who came to do business.

"Wait," he said as he wrapped the reins around the crosspole. "Let's not go in just yet. I have much to tell you."

A goat bleated, and he heard a copper bell clank as the small herd her father kept moved up the hillside.

"You look so serious, Paco."

"I am serious. Come." He pulled her hand, and they walked away from the house together.

"What is it?" she asked.

Paco pointed to the Sangre de Cristo Range, snow-capped peaks stretching as far as the eye could see, jagged peaks dominating the western skyline. "I have found a place in the mountains where it is very beautiful," he said. "Up there, beyond the pass. There is plenty of game there—beaver, elk, deer, even the big bear. I am going to build a home there someday, near a spring, far from the settlements and the fighting."

"It is too wild in the mountains," said Consuelo. "No woman would live there with you."

"One will," he said.

"She would have to love her husband much."

"She would."

"Her father would have to give his permission."

"Yes," said Paco, "but when he sees how much land I have, he will give his daughter willingly to such a man."

She squeezed his arm, and Paco felt warm inside. Something fluttered in his stomach, and his knees quivered like jelly. He and Consuelo went into the house, and her mother, Paciencia, fussed over him. When her father came back that evening, Paco sat down to supper with them.

Paciencia and Consuelo served the warm tortillas, strips of beef shredded from *el pecho* of the cow, the breast, *frijoles*, goat's milk, the chilies ripened in the sun. Consuelo told her parents about Paco's dream, and he wanted to throttle her.

"So, you would live in the mountains," said Alonzo. "Why would you not live here in Taos, or in Santa Fe, where there is trade, money to be made, the *bailes*, the companionship of good people?"

"There is something about the mountains," said Paco, "something about the way I felt when I was up there. It was as if I was the only man on earth. It was like I was very close to God. At night, the stars were so close I could almost reach up and touch them. And the streams, the clear mountain streams, were so beautiful they seemed to have been made special by God. And the game, there's so much game there, a man would never go hungry. So much water a man would never go thirsty. And there's this river, this mighty river, that runs down out of the mountains, and it seems to be alive.

"It's just a place I want to go and where I want to live, and I want Consuelo to be my wife and have the same joy I do living in such a place. I want to build a big house there and raise cattle and sheep. But I don't want to be under the domination of the government. I want to live as a free man."

"Well," said Alonzo, biting into a tortilla stuffed fat with beans and beef and chili peppers, "that sounds very much like a dream, like a dream you have and it's sometimes hard to bring other people into the dream, like Consuelo."

"Wait'll you see it," said Paco, wiping his plate with the torn flap from a tortilla. "Wait'll Consuelo sees it. I think it's going to be a fine place to raise a family, and I think there will be much business. I think there will be lots of money to be made. I believe America is going to be a rich country. And I believe they will someday live in Taos and Santa Fe and all along the Rio Grande."

"No, they will never do that," said Alonzo. "There is too much blood already spilled on this land for the Mexican government to let the *gringos* settle here. The river is flowing in blood."

"But it is no different than it was when Spain had its boot on our necks," said Paco. "There are Comanches and soldiers, and I think these Americans are very strong. Already there is a fort up on the Arkansas River, a small fort, but it is a beginning. And I think there will be other forts, much trading. I think the Americans will just come and keep coming until they drive out all the bad people."

"Well, maybe they are bad people themselves," said Alonzo, winking at his wife.

Consuelo sat there, eating very quietly and daintily, not wishing to make a sound. She looked at Paco with wonder, and her face was radiant, glowing like the candles that lit their table.

"I do not know," said Paco, "but I have this feeling, this strong feeling, and I have seen one man going into the mountains, an American, and he brought out many furs. And I think he will go back again and others will follow him. There are riches in the mountains, riches we can't even see, riches we can only dream about and hope someday to find."

"Well, maybe you will find it, Paco," said Alonzo, "but there have been a lot of men go into the mountains and a lot of men who did not come back. So I worry about you, my son."

"Do not worry, Alonzo," said Paco. "Nothing will happen to me. I feel at home up there. I feel like it's a place where I've always wanted to be, and in my heart, I feel it's a place where I've always been."

"*Ay, carraijo!*" exclaimed Alonzo, slapping Paco on

the back. "This one is truly a dreamer. Paciencia, bring us the bottle of *aguardiente*. We will have a drink and then smoke a pipe outside where it is cool."

"You will stay the night, then?" asked Paciencia. "You may sleep in Lafcadio's bed."

"Oh, yes," answered Consuelo, and her mother gave her a dark look, but there was a soft smile at the end of it.

"Yes, thanks, a million of thanks," said Paco, and he drank the brandy with Alonzo. They went outside and filled their pipes with American tobacco that was fragrant and sweet in the lungs.

"I have asked for a grant of land," Paco told Alonzo. "I want to marry Consuelo when I have the deed."

"It will be very hard in the mountains," said Alonzo. "For a woman, much harder than for a man."

"Not in this place," said Paco. "It is most beautiful."

"And you are a young pup who dreams of being a wolf."

"Well, I am going to live up there," said Paco stubbornly.

"I will have to think about this to see if you are crazy or not," joked Alonzo. "You might be a little crazy, you know. I have seen men come out of the mountains and talk to themselves and say nothing. I have seen them go to the cantinas and drink too much *mezcal*, too much Taos whiskey, and they don't ever want to go back to the mountains again. Maybe someday you will be like one of these men, eh Paco?"

"No, Alonzo, I will never be like those men. They do not feel what I feel. They do not see what I see. I cannot wait to get back again."

When Alonzo went inside, Consuelo came out, and Paco put his arm around her waist. They looked at the mountains and the stars, and he whispered sweet *piropos* in her ear; she giggled and gave him compliments as well.

"The mountains, they are beautiful tonight," said Consuelo. Below, lamps glowed in the windows of the town, and beyond was the dark sea of land and the peaks of the Sangre de Cristos white with snow. "You love them, do you not?"

"I feel, when I'm up there," said Paco, "like a boy standing on the shoulders of a giant. The mountains are so big, and I'm so small. But if I'm standing up there, I feel big too. It's as if the mountains are coming into me and making me feel big. It's hard to describe. It's hard to talk about such things. I don't know if you know what I mean."

"I think I understand about feeling small in such bigness," said Consuelo.

"Well, it's not like that exactly, Consuelo. It's hard to talk about when you're not there. The way I feel up there. It's like I'm part of the sky, and part of the earth, and part of the sunlight and the stars, the moon. And I don't feel like an ordinary man up there. I feel as if I was brought to the mountains to do something immense, something very big. I think the mountains do something to a man. Maybe to his dreams. I think I cannot get the mountains out of me even if I can get out of the mountains."

"I think I know how you feel," said Consuelo, and her voice was very soft as she squeezed his hand in hers until his love for her filled him and spilled over and he kissed her impetuously.

"Consuelo!" called Paciencia. "You must come inside the house now."

"How does she know?" asked Paco.

Consuelo laughed and kissed him quickly, then drew away before their fires grew any stronger.

They went back inside the house then and said their

good-nights very chastely and properly. Paco lay awake
a long time, looking at the stars outside the window.
They seemed so far away, and the adobe walls of the
house made it hard for him to breathe. When finally he
slept, it was with a great peace in his heart, for he knew
he would go back to the mountains on the morrow and
leave the towns behind him.

When Paco left the next day, he told Consuelo that
he would bring her back a pretty blue flower when he
returned. "It was so beautiful, I did not want to pick
it," he said, "but it would be pretty in your hair."

"We have blue flowers," she said.

"Not like this one," Paco laughed. Before he mounted up, Alonzo gave him two white Jalisco burros.
"Bring me back some furs, and these fine animals are
yours," said Alonzo.

"I will, I will," said Paco.

Then Alonzo came close and whispered to him dark-
ly. "Remember, my son, with a woman there is much
delight, but there is also much trouble, and deep
sorrow."

"Not with Consuelo," said Paco, smiling.

But Alonzo only shook his head sadly and turned
away when Paco stole a kiss from his daughter. She
waved to him as he rode away, and Paco knew he was
stricken with Consuelo. He had fallen in love, and
Alonzo's warning was forgotten as soon as the young
man rode into Taos and bought traps and such for a
winter in the mountains. He was still lighthearted when
he rode over Raton Pass toward Spanish Peaks and saw
again the country that had stolen his heart.

Stonecipher began to furnish the rooms of his dream.
Perkins returned with the goods Jake needed, and they
began to build on the fort. They began to get many
visitors, Indian and white men. Some men told him

that he would fail there, that the land where the fort stood was claimed by both the Ute and the Arapaho, that the Cheyenne had camps at Big Timber, downriver on the Arkansas.

Jake argued that his fort was the closest point in U.S. territory to the village of Taos. Taos would provide Stonecipher not only more customers but also flour and whiskey as trade goods. He made his own whiskey, but he could not keep up with the demand. He had already learned that the Indians would trade furs for sugar whiskey, and soon there was a fine level wagon road down the Arkansas and along the Santa Fe Trail to Westport where the steamboats made the regular run on the Missouri River to St. Louis.

Whenever he wanted to think, Jake walked to the river, strolled along its bank. Often he thought that this was the only peaceful time in his life. There were worries aplenty and decisions to be made, and there were times when he felt that his life was changing so fast that he could not keep up with it. He was changing as the river changed, slowly, imperceptibly. The river was his gauge, his barometer, his measuring stick. He never failed to see something that made him take notice and wonder if he had made the right decision. And always the river would tell him that life was fleeting and short but sweet to the taste.

One day when he had finished with some new settlers, Stonecipher left the fort and walked far down the river to be alone with his thoughts. Something caught his eye, and he stopped short, peered at the dark specks rising from the prairie grasses. Jake looked at the blackbirds wheeling over the river, their dark bodies shining in the sun. They whisked downstream, sought the cattails, the privacy of reeds and shadow, away from the hated magpies that stole their eggs. This river, he thought, was their home as much as it was his.

Jake smiled with satisfaction.

When he returned, the settlers' wagon was just nearing the Fountain. Joe Perkins stood outside the fort, a sheaf of papers in his hand. "Where you been?" he asked. "I got some figures what don't tote up right."

Jake shrugged and pointed toward the distant wagon, come that day from Taos. "Look at 'em, Joe," he said to Perkins. "Settlers come to stay."

"Mexicans," said Joe.

"People," said Jake.

First the men had come up from Taos to trade, and later they brought their women and children. They built adobe huts near Jake's Trading Post along the Arkansas, and others moved up on the Fountain. Jake hired some of the women to build some adobe ovens for the fort, one in the courtyard, another in one of the rooms. The women made the big adobe ovens, shaped like beehives. They came to the fort and baked bread, parched corn, and burned lime for the whitewash their men used on the walls of the fort and on their adobe dwellings. The oven was called *un horno*.

Soon Jake built additional storehouses and rooms for families to stay in overnight or longer, places where traders and weary travelers could rest and become part of the life. Americans came to the valley too, and a few settled along the various creeks, set up homesteads downriver, less than a day's ride from the fort. Joe didn't like any of it, but business was good. Although he grumbled, he seemed content until word came from the north that the Ute had killed a family up on a place called Jimmy Camp Creek. A settler named Henry Janss rode into the fort one day with the news.

Janss was a big rawboned man, a loner who drifted from camp to camp, worked as a hunter who brought fresh game to settlers. He was visibly shaken as he related the story of the Ute raid. "Them was good

people," said Janss as he swallowed a drink of hard
whiskey Jake had served him. "Them Injuns massacreed
ever' one. Blanco gutted 'em like toads."

" 'Blanco'?" asked Jake.

"Chief Blanco. He's a Ute, meaner'n a timber rattler,
hates whites like a hound hates skunks. Wears a damned
red shirt. A wool shirt, at that. Ever since one of his
braves was kilt two year ago, he's been lookin' for the
white man what kilt him. Meanwhile, he's stealin' hogs
and cattle, horses, from any settlers can't defend theirself."

Joe Perkins swallowed as his face blanched. He looked
at Jake, who ignored him.

"How do you know this?" asked Stonecipher.

"Blanco brags about it. Some whites he knows has
been with him. That's all he talks about. Brave was kilt
somewhere near here, I reckon."

Perkins swallowed again.

"What was the name of the family?" asked Jake.

"Carpenter. John Carpenter. Wife name 'uz Tess.
Three kids. Built 'em a 'dobe house up there. I hunted
for 'em, same as I do for a lot of folks settlin' in these
parts."

"Well, that's too bad," said Jake.

"Blanco knows about this here fort," said Janss. "He
don't like it none."

"I'm not afraid of him," said Jake.

"Well, I sure as hell am," said Perkins.

"Blanco's pretty sneaky," said Henry. "Bides his time.
I'd keep my eyes peeled was I you."

"We'll do that," said Jake, and forgot all about it after
Janss left to talk to settlers up on the Fountain about
bringing fresh game to their tables.

≈ 10 ≈

Late in the summer of Jake's second year on the Arkansas, Red Horn rode in with several Arapaho braves, leading a string of horses, a young maiden with him. It was warm and bright that day, and the fort shone white in the sun.

"Friend," said Red Horn, solemn as stone, but bright-eyed and handsome on his fine spotted pony, a lone eagle feather jutting from his shining black hair. "Bring horse. You take."

"For me?" asked Jake.

"You take," said Red Horn.

There were six horses that the Arapaho offered Stonecipher, and every one a beauty. Four mares and two geldings, sleek and strong, fat with summer grasses. Jake beamed and accepted the gift, offering tobacco to Red Horn and the three other braves in return. The young bucks eyed the fort warily, but when Joe Perkins brought out the sugar whiskey, they all dismounted and tied up their ponies. They passed the bottle among them; Red Horn spoke to the maiden and she dismounted. She held her head down so Jake could not see her eyes, only the top of her head, the braided black hair. She was small and young, and wore a beaded buckskin dress bleached white, her moccasins Arapaho-made. She seemed light-skinned, although she was tanned from the sun.

"Woman for you," said Red Horn.

Jake's eyes widened in surprise. Joe grinned like a possum in the pigpen.

"Aw, Red Horn," said Jake, embarrassed.

"You take squaw. Good squaw. Plenty wife. Work good."

"Who is she?"

"Name Leaf Shadow," said Red Horn. "Shoshone slave woman. Cheyenne take woman from Shoshone. Make slave. Red Horn trade two horse for woman."

"I don't know," said Jake. The woman still hung her head, as if she were ashamed. "How'd she come by that name?"

Red Horn grinned, used his hands to make sign. "Cheyenne name. Leaf move, make no sound. Sun make leaf shake on ground. Night take shadow away. Sun bring shadow back. Shadow make no sound. Leaf Shadow no make talk. Make work. Good squaw."

Jake looked at the woman, wondering what to do. There were few women in the territory. Most he'd seen were Mexicans or Indians.

"Take her, Jake," said Perkins. "Wouldn't be polite to turn Red Horn down."

Jake had thought of women, a lot lately. Some of the Mexican women had made eyes at him, but their men kept close watch on them. He had thought of going to St. Louis and looking for a woman to help him, but he just hadn't had time. Now he looked more closely at Leaf Shadow. He was struck with her quiet beauty. He tucked two fingers under her chin and lifted her head. Her dark brown eyes flickered with a look of wariness, and he could see pain in their depths. "Can you talk, woman?" he asked.

The woman did not reply. With her finely chiseled

features, almond-shaped eyes, thin straight nose, she did not look like the other Indian women he had seen. She was thin and small-breasted, with nicely curved hips but none of the paunch of the squaws he'd seen around the fort. She looked at him now, stone-faced, her lips pursed tightly, something haughty in her expression.

Red Horn laughed. "Squaw no talk," said the Arapaho. "Dumb." He touched his head, cupped one hand, and turned it over, the sign of an empty bowl or cup.

"I will take her," said Jake impulsively. Red Horn grinned, slapped his friend on the back. "Good," said the Indian.

Red Horn made sign with his hands, and Leaf Shadow nodded to him. "You take," he said. "Make work."

"Haw," said Perkins.

"Shut up, Joe," said Stonecipher.

Leaf Shadow followed Jake to his still-unfinished quarters inside the fort. She owned nothing, Jake figured, beyond the clothes on her back. He signed that she was to work with the other women and make his house ready. His sign was crude, but the woman nodded dumbly.

Jake stepped outside, called to one of the Mexican women making tortillas on the dome oven. "Luz, come here," he said.

Luz Delgado was married to one of the masons, José Delgado. She finished two tortillas, tossed them, steaming, into a cloth-lined basket, and scurried to Jake's room.

"This woman's name is Leaf Shadow," said Jake. "Put her to work. She doesn't talk, so you have to use hand-sign with her. I don't even know if she's got a tongue."

"*Pulde a hablar? Tiene la lengua?*" asked Luz.

Leaf Shadow just stared at her.

"This one is dumb," said Luz.

"I know," said Jake. "Just put her to work."

Jake went back outside to visit with Red Horn and learn the ways of the Arapaho, ask him of the Ute led by Blanco, and see if his tribe meant to trade as he had once said they would. There was something about the woman that bothered him, and he didn't know what it was. She seemed half wild, but scared too, and it was the wildness that bothered him, the haunted look in her eyes, the unspoken memories of a girl who had lived with the wild Shoshone, the Southern Cheyenne, and the Arapaho, now handed down to him like a piece of unwanted furniture. Maybe he would talk more of her with Red Horn, yet he didn't want to question the gift. But he wanted to be on his guard. Would she cut his throat while he slept? Would she run away? Was it necessary to beat her, or should he tie her up at night, lock her in a room where she could harm no one? Jake had many questions, and yet he was fascinated by this dark-skinned creature in a white buckskin dress.

≈ 11 ≈

Luz showed Leaf Shadow how to grind the dried corn, mash it into powder, make the little cakes, and flatten them on *el horno*, bake them so they would keep awhile, and stack them in the baskets. Luz, a burly woman with Yaqui and Spanish blood in her veins, did not like the sullen girl, but she was surprised at her intelligence, her quickness in learning how to do things.

That afternoon, Luz and Leaf Shadow began with the floor in Jake's new room. He had added this one to his bedroom, saying he would make an office of it. It adjoined his bedroom, which had a little stove where he could boil coffee and warm his whiskey on cold winter nights. They stripped the soil of grass, crawling around on their hands and knees until nightfall. Luz inspected the floor, lit the candles in the wooden and glass lamps on the wall.

She chattered constantly in Spanish as if Leaf Shadow could hear and understand. "In the morning, we will sprinkle water on the floor and sweep, sweep, sweep," said Luz in a staccato stream of Spanish. "And you will sprinkle water on it two or three times each day and sweep, sweep, sweep, you understand?"

Leaf Shadow did not answer, and Luz grunted, grabbed the girl's arm, jerked her from the room.

Luz showed Leaf Shadow how she prepared Jake's supper and her own man's in another room with a fireplace and chimney.

Jake came in while they were cooking over the little fireplace with its quarter-round hood raised above the hearth. He smelled the beans and buffalo meat, and his belly roiled with hunger. "How did you do with the girl, Luz?" he asked.

"She is strong enough to work."

"I looked at the room. It looks pretty nice."

"There is much to do, Señor Jake. Much to do."

"Good. Can she cook?"

"We will see," said Luz enigmatically. Leaf Shadow did not look at him, and he took out his pipe and saw to it that the gate was locked for the night. The squealing of pigs subsided, and he knew that Luz's husband, José, must have fed them. Horses whickered in the stable, and a few men laughed as they drank and swapped lies with Joe Perkins in the drinking room. The smell of corn tortillas was heavy on the summer air, and mingled with it, always, the scent of the river, the heady musk of it lingering on the night air like steam, like the smell of a man's own blood.

Jake put his pipe away when the women brought the food to his room, the room where he slept. Leaf Shadow carried the large wooden tray. He sat on a folded buffalo robe, a poncho spread out on the floor in front of him. Luz showed Leaf Shadow where to put the dishes. In the center of the poncho, Luz set the soup, steaming in an earthen bowl. Alongside it the Mexican woman placed another bowl filled with the thin mush called *atole*.

"*Ponga, ponga*," said Luz with every bowl and plate she placed, and the Indian girl showed no sign that she understood. But Leaf Shadow served the basket of hot tortillas and set down a bowl with a mixture of chili peppers, corn, onions, venison, and beans. Lastly, she put the plate with the roasted portion of buffalo hump before her new master.

"Ah, she learns quickly, this one," said Luz, clucking like a mother hen.

"You tell her to sit down while I eat. She can eat after I'm finished," said Jake.

"*Sientese, sientese,*" ordered Luz and made a squatting motion. She pointed to a bare spot on the floor nearby.

Leaf Shadow sat down, crossed her legs.

"Good," said Jake. "Now go feed José before his stomach makes too much noise."

The Mexican woman laughed and closed the door as she left.

"Well now," said Jake, "you have done your first day's work for me, and soon you will eat. You watch me, and maybe someday we will share a meal together."

Leaf Shadow spoke not a word, but watched as Jake dipped into the bowls with a tortilla doubled between his fingers and cut meat from the buffalo hump with a knife. He spoke about Red Horn and how he had saved him from the Ute and told her of the trades he made that day while he ravished the food before him.

Leaf Shadow never made a sound, but she seemed to be listening. She watched his every move, and Jake thought that was a good sign. Maybe one day she would speak. Maybe Luz could teach her at least to speak Spanish. He had no patience to teach her English, and it didn't make much difference anyway. There was still that wildness in her, and he was wary of her. He wished he knew what tribe she belonged to, but Red Horn said that she was Shoshone, although she was light-skinned. Her hair was light too.

"You will sleep on a buffalo robe in that corner," said Jake, pointing to a rolled-up robe across the room. "I will sleep with my pistol by my side, so do not try to cut my throat."

He laughed to himself, because he knew she didn't understand a word he said. When he finished his supper, he motioned to her. She crawled over to the poncho, and he signed to her that she should eat. He lit his pipe while she ate, then left her to walk the fort one more time before going to bed. When he returned, the food was gone, and his buffalo robe was laid out neatly for him, Leaf Shadow on the other buffalo robe.

He looked at her in puzzlement for a long time. "Sleep," he said, and he tilted his head and clamped his hands together to show her what he meant. She lay down on the buffalo robe. Jake blew out the candles and lay in the darkness, thinking about what a strange day it had been.

In the days that followed, Luz showed Leaf Shadow how to grind corn on the *metate*, how to dry the strings of chili peppers and onions that she hung on the inside wall of the fort where the sun shone most. Each day, Leaf Shadow sprinkled Jake's new floors with water two or three times and swept them until they were hard and dustless.

Luz and Leaf Shadow plastered the inside walls with adobe, then whitewashed them with *jaspe*, a compound of selenite that they burned in the oven to cure. They mixed the cured selenite with water, then spread the gypsum on the walls with their bare hands and brushed the walls gently with sheepskin. Since the whitewash came off on clothes or skin very easily, Luz covered the lower half of the walls with material cut from bolts of brightly colored calico Jake had bought from a Taos trader.

Each night, Jake reviewed the progress the women had made. Leaf Shadow now prepared his supper unassisted, leaving Luz to cook only for José. Jake spoke to Leaf Shadow, expecting no answer as she cooked on his little stove and served his food on the poncho.

"One day soon," he told her, "I will have José build me a table and chairs so we can sit down like civilized people and eat our supper."

Did Leaf Shadow nod? He could not be sure. But he wished she could speak, for he found that he liked her presence. He became used to her, looked forward to seeing her at the end of each day.

And one night she bathed before him, her lean body gleaming copper in the candleglow, and he felt a stirring in his loins. She seemed very chaste, but that only added to the mystery of this silent woman who made his room bright and cooked his supper for him. When he went to bed that night, he couldn't get her out of his mind, and he tossed and turned as his blood raged in his veins.

The next night, Jake told Leaf Shadow to eat with him. He was embarrassed about it at first and talked constantly. "No sense in you waitin' until I've finished my meal. Hell, we're both civilized here, ain't we? I don't hold with slavery, Leaf Shadow. Why, you're more like a companion and all, and I like the way you keep my house. I reckon you're probably a good woman under all that savage skin. Mighty pretty skin too. You are a mite prettier'n you might think. Pretty for a squaw, anyways. You ain't no young girl, neither, but you ain't old."

Leaf Shadow ate daintily, dipping her tortilla only after he had dipped his, and her eyes followed his every movement. She took small bites and chewed her food more thoroughly than he.

"I reckon I wished you could talk, Leaf, but you can't and that's that. Seems to me, though, a man and a woman ought to be able to talk to each other. 'Specially if a man takes a liking to a woman and might want to bundle with her in his blankets. Now, I'm not saying that I do, mind you," he said, pointing a tortilla at her for emphasis, "but I might, and you might too. But if a man and a woman don't talk and don't know how to talk and just start making sign, why it might look like the man was ordering the woman to lie in his blankets. And if that woman was a dumb slave, why she might just obey him, and he'd never know if she wanted him for himself or was just doin' what she was told to do."

He looked at her face for any sign of comprehension, but as always, she wore no expression. She just looked at him openly with those deep brown eyes of hers, and he was glad she couldn't understand what he was saying.

"God, woman, there are times when I plumb think of you naked and want to touch your bare skin, feel your breasts, and I think I will except you might take a knife to my gullet. I don't know what them Shoshone and Cheyenne did to you, but I ain't never took advantage of no woman, and I ain't goin' to start now."

Leaf Shadow chewed silently on a chunk of venison, regarded him with empty doll-eyes.

"Christ, all this sounds silly now, don't it?"

He grinned at her. He leaned over the poncho and made a funny face.

Leaf Shadow smiled, but it was only a brief flicker on her lips. But it was something, Jake thought. A sign. He played the buffoon for a few minutes more, but she turned her face away, and he knew that she had tired of the game.

"Good food," he said, patting his belly. "Can you say 'good food'?"

Leaf Shadow just stared at him, a blank look on her face.

"Well, if you ever want to crawl into my blankets, woman, you just holler, hear?" He then made all the filthy signs with his fingers, the dirty signs the trappers used and had taught to the Indians. He slapped his palms together, rammed the middle finger of his right hand through a hole made by the index and thumb of his left.

Leaf Shadow's gaze did not waver. If anything, she seemed to lift her chin higher, jut it out further as if defying him.

Jake spoke loudly and knew that he had let his anger get the better of him. He hated himself for making the dirty signs. It was a stupid thing to do. He rose from the buffalo robe and found his pipe on the fireplace mantle. He filled it, lit it with a candle, and stalked angrily from the room.

When he came back to the room that night, Jake was filled with remorse. There was only one candle lit. The room was dark. "I'm sorry, Leaf Shadow," he said. "Leaf Shadow? Are you here?"

He looked at her buffalo robe in the corner. She was not there.

"Damn," he muttered.

As he started to undress, his eye caught a movement. There on his buffalo robe lay Leaf Shadow. She was all curled up, her legs drawn up to her belly. As he shucked his clothes, she straightened out her legs and lay flat on her back. He blew out the candle and swore softly in the darkness.

Leaf Shadow was waiting for him, and when he took her in his arms, he felt a surge of energy shoot through him like a lightning bolt. She was soft and warm and pliant in his arms. "You don't have to do this, woman," he whispered, but he wanted her, and he did not stop.

He found her in the darkness, and all of his pent-up emotions overflowed as he took the silent woman, took her in silence, took her shamefully as if he were her master and she his slave.

≈ 12 ≈

Joe Perkins noticed the difference in Jake. The change. Jake walked around in a dreamy state during the day, couldn't wait to get to his quarters at night. Jake did not joke with the trappers and traders so much, and he posted guards on the fort walls, even though the trappers told him the Ute would not come during warm weather.

"They'll come when it's cold and you're too tired to put a rifle on the walls," Joe told Jake. "That's what they all say."

"I don't give a damn what they say," Jake snapped.

"That woman's got you by the balls," said Joe.

"You shut up," said Jake.

"Ain't no nevermind to me, Jake. Hell, I seen men turn fuzzy-headed before over a piece of tail."

"There ain't much choice, now, is there, Joe?"

"No, I reckon there ain't. You keep her like a pup in your room every night, it's bound to happen."

"Well, I'll get over it," said Jake. He knew that Leaf Shadow had him blanketed. He couldn't think of anything but her, and he wondered if he hadn't ought to go to St. Louis and fetch him a regular wife. Someone who spoke English and didn't stare at him like she was mocking him. At times, he felt shame for what he was doing, but when he lay with Leaf Shadow, she made him forget everything. He didn't care if she couldn't talk. She could do other things, and when they were alone at night, she took him away from the fort and made him forget about Ute and trading. Joe was probably jealous, for good reason. He had not been to Taos for a while, nor to St. Louis, and was probably getting randy as a buck deer when the does were in season.

Jake went, as always, to the river for solace in the evenings and when he needed time alone with his thoughts. He watched the rolling waters and lost himself in their imperturbable depths. He looked at the flowing waters as if trying to find meaning to his life, to decipher the Arkansas's deepest secrets. In the splash of a leaping fish, the random roil of a swirling eddy, he saw indications of hidden things, hints that life was not superficial but complex and powerful, and there was no seeing into its future.

The long summer days dwindled into winter, and Jake sent Joe to St. Louis before the first snows. Will Burke came up from Taos and stayed three days, then rode up to the three creeks for another season of trapping. To Jake he seemed less wild than before, and he did not drink so much whiskey that he lost his reason. The settlers brought wood in for the winter fires, and Jake saw the day when the fort was empty except for Leaf Shadow and Luz Delgado, who came in three times a week to make tortillas and grind corn.

Leaf Shadow, more mysterious than ever, had become indispensable to Jake. He thought that he might be falling in love with her. She shared his blankets every night, and she kept him warm in the cold hours before dawn. She was eager and compliant when they made love, and he thought, even, that she might love him.

"You ain't a bad woman," he told her one night after they had made love.

"Nor are you a bad man," said Leaf Shadow in perfect English.

Jake was dumbstruck. "You—you talked!" he said. "How do you come by speaking the English tongue so all of a sudden?"

"I am a white woman," said Leaf Shadow. "I made a vow never to speak to my captors. I would only speak if I was returned to my own people."

"What's your name, then?"

"Sarah. Sarah Reynolds. I was only twelve when the Shoshone killed my parents, my two brothers, and my aunt. They let me live, took me away. They made me a slave. Two years ago, the Cheyenne took me away from the Shoshone."

"I will call you Sarah, then."

"I would be much obliged."

For a time, Sarah and Jake were very happy. He said he would marry her someday, perhaps in Taos or Santa Fe.

"Make it soon," said Sarah. "I am carrying your child."

≈ 13 ≈

Jake watched in wonderment as Sarah swelled with child. She urged him to marry her, but something held him back.

"Wait'll after the baby is born," he said.

"I want my child to have a name," she told him. "His father's name."

"He will, he will," said Jake, but he broke out in a cold, clammy sweat at night when he thought of being a father. Of being married. His own parents had not given him much incentive. Jake's father was a stern, cold man, stoical as a stump. His mother was illiterate, had no ambition. She had worked the fields alongside her husband, left Jake to be raised by a nanny. Neither his father nor his mother had ever shown him any affection. As soon as he was big enough to walk, they had worked him, from chopping kindling and carrying wood and water to washing dishes and mending socks. That was why he had run away from home as soon as he got up the gumption. His mother and his father both beat him and used up so many willow withes on his back, cuffed him so many times, he knew he had to leave or he would strike them back. There had been moments when he'd wanted to kill his father, nights when he had cried in his bed, not because his mother

116

had whipped him so bad but because he hated her for it.

He looked at Sarah closely during her pregnancy, wondering what kind of mother she would be. He looked for signs of cruelty in her, signs that she was like his mother. And he wondered about himself, too. What would he expect of a son? Would he want him to work like a slave as he had been made to do?

No, Jake knew he would not be like his father. Still, he feared the challenge. Maybe he would bend too far the other way and not be much of a father at all. His thoughts confused him, but he noticed a change in himself, and he did not like it much.

Sarah became very heavy, and she began to sleep on her own bed because she said she was uncomfortable with him.

Jake was hurt by this. "You don't want to do it, that's fine with me," he told her. "I just don't see why you got to sleep by yourself."

"It's very uncomfortable, carrying your baby," she said. "It's hard to find a spot in the bed where I can sleep. I just don't want to make it any harder on you."

"Well, I feel spurned, woman," he said, and knew it wasn't the right word, just the first one that popped into his mind.

Sarah laughed, but after that, they drifted apart. She spoke very little to him, and he couldn't think of anything to say to her. He just watched her swell up like a gourd and waddle around the fort with that baby inside her until he was almost ashamed to have her sleep in the same room with him. Her hair lost its luster, and she never used vermillion on her cheeks anymore.

Luz spoke to him one day when the birth of the baby was near. "She is too small, Señor Jake," she said. "And the baby is too big."

"What are you talkin' about, Luz?" he asked. The woman had cornered him while he was currying his horse in the stables. He had planned to ride up to the pueblo that day to see how the building was coming. Sarah was still in bed. He had heard her groaning in her sleep all night.

"I think when your woman gives light, she will have a very bad time. Maybe you ought to go to Santa Fe and bring a doctor here."

"How soon?" he asked.

"Very soon," said Luz. "A week, maybe two."

"I will talk to Sarah about it."

"She does not know. She is still a little girl in many ways."

"I don't know what you mean, Luz."

"She did not have the childhood," said the Mexican woman. "She had only twelve years when the Snakes took her. She became a woman then. But she did not grow up."

"I think I know what you mean."

Sarah did not want him to ride to Santa Fe and fetch a doctor. "It would be too late. The baby has dropped down, and he's pushing to get out," she said.

"Luz says you will have a difficult birth."

"Stay with me, Jake. I'm frightened."

"All right. If that's what you want."

But Jake was not there when Sarah went into labor, and by the time he returned from a buffalo hunting trip with Joe Perkins, it was too late.

≈ 14 ≈

Sarah screamed in pain.

In seconds, she saw Luz run into the bedroom, her bronze face etched with concern, her eyes wide. "Is it time?" Luz asked breathlessly.

One look at Sarah, and she knew that the baby was coming. Sarah lay on her back, her legs wide. Her hands flanked her abdomen, palms down. Agony contorted her face. She bucked under a sudden convulsion.

"Oh, oh, oh," moaned Sarah.

"Hold on. I will return," said Luz.

Sarah's face glistened with sweat. She heard the Mexican woman barking orders in Spanish. She recognized the words. *"Agua caliente, pronto, andale!"* In a moment, Luz was back, her sleeves rolled up, the collar of her blouse tucked down inside, out of the way.

Quickly, Luz stripped Sarah out of her dress. She gave her a broom. "Esqueeze the handle of this," said Luz. "And push. Bear down hard. *Ay de mi*, it is coming."

Sarah felt as if she were being torn apart. Shoots of pain lanced her spine as she strained to push the baby out of her womb. She felt Luz's hands spreading her legs apart, and it felt as if they were being pulled out by

the roots. Another contraction convulsed her, and she
screamed. Sweat washed her face.

"*Bien, bien,*" said Luz. "*Ya viene el niño. Ah, venga,
venga, pobrecito.* He is coming, Sarah. Push, push.
Esqueeze and push."

"I—I can't," she stuttered, but she bore down and
tried to blot out the agony. Brightly colored lights
popped and flashed in the darkness of her brain. The
cords stood out on her neck, and her legs quivered
spasmodically as Luz pulled on the baby's shoulders.
He felt so big, so big, tearing her apart, pulling out all
of her insides.

Each moment seemed like hours of unremitting torment. Agony, agony, and her own screams shattering
her eardrums, echoing in the adobe room, smacking
against the walls like wet mud. She grunted and strained,
wanting to eject the baby before he killed her, wanting
to spew it from her belly before she died.

"*Allá, allá,*" breathed Luz, and the baby slithered
through the portals, eyes closed, hair plastered down
with an egg-white scum, face wrinkled, puckered like a
fist, and still, so still that Luz felt her heart stop. The
umbilical uncoiled as she dragged the infant onto the
bed. The dark ochre of afterbirth trailed the baby,
oozed onto the blanket.

A girl rushed in with a pan of water. Another followed,
carrying a large steaming kettle. They stopped, looked
at the baby as Luz snatched it up, whacked it on the
buttocks.

"*Llore, llore!*" Luz pleaded.

Sarah gagged as a wave of nausea flooded her, stirring
the bile in her stomach, roiling the goat's milk she'd
had for breakfast. Her abdomen quivered, and the
muscles in her legs twitched as she began to relax after
her ordeal. The pain between her legs started to subside, but it still felt as if someone had touched her

tenderest parts with a red-hot poker. Her breathing was less labored now, the strain of the birth lessening with each filling of her lungs, each gentle exhalation.

Something was wrong with the baby! she thought. What is Luz doing with my baby?

Luz slapped the baby, turned it over in her hands, shook it like an *olla*. Shook it, shook it.

"*Ay, Dios!*" the Delgado woman sighed. "*Ayudame, Jesus, Madre de Dios.*"

But the baby was not breathing. Luz turned it over, opened its tiny puckered mouth. She put her lips to the infant's and blew into its lungs.

Sarah tried to sit up. The two maids set their vessels down on a table and rushed to her side. They held her down, but there was no struggle.

"My baby," said Sarah. "Give me my baby."

"*Está muerto,*" said one of the girls.

"*Cállate!*" ordered Luz. She opened one of the baby's eyes. It was dull glass, in death.

"Luz, what's the matter?" Panic rose in Sarah's voice. She knew what was wrong. Something clutched at her heart. Something tore at her insides. Something quivered deep in her womb. She felt empty, drained, turned inside out. She saw the wrinkled babe in Luz's strong hands, saw it as the dead thing it was, and her throat constricted as she fought back the tears.

Stillborn, she thought. My baby is stillborn. A heavy weight settled on Sarah's chest, and she couldn't breathe.

The two girls looked at her with pity in their eyes. They looked at each other and shook their heads.

"*Tráigame un cuchillo,*" Luz said to one of the girls. "*Andale.*"

One of the girls dashed from the room. She returned with a butcher knife.

Luz spat and grabbed the knife from the girl's hand. Quickly she cut the withered vine of life from the dead baby's belly. She ordered the girls to wash Sarah and clean away the afterbirth. The girls sprang to work with alacrity, dabbing Sarah off, washing her abdomen. They carried away the dead matter on the bed as Luz gently washed the baby's head and face.

Sarah began to weep.

Luz carried the baby over to its mother, placed it by her side. "I'm so sorry, Sarah," whispered Luz, her voice a raspy husk in her throat. "God wills it."

"No, no, Luz," said Sarah, and she looked at her dead son and crumpled up, the tears bursting forth, flooding her face. "No, no, *no*," she said, strangling on her words.

Luz could not bear it. She turned away and dabbed at her eyes with the damp washcloth. Her body shook as she began to cry.

Sarah touched the baby's tiny face, traced a finger over its dead lips. "Luz," she said. "Why? Why?"

Luz came over to the bed. "I do not know, Sarah."

"But he was alive. I could feel him kicking."

"Yes, he was alive. He did not strangle. Maybe his little heart..."

"My fault," said Sarah.

"No, you must not say such a thing. It is the will of God."

Sarah closed her eyes as a spasm of intense grief shook her. If God did this, she thought, then he's cruel. "Oh, Luz, I can't bear it. Can you..."

"I will take the little boy and dress him in the little clothes you made. I will have a man make him a little casket. We will light a candle for him and say a novena. We will pray for his soul."

Sarah closed her eyes as Luz lifted the baby and carried him from the room. She lay there, her eyes shut tight, listening to the fluttering whispers of female voices out in the *placita*, and then it was quiet for a long time.

Where was Jake? She wondered if he knew that his son had been born dead.

She slept, and when she awoke, she smelled flowers in the room and the oily aroma of a votive candle. There on the mantel was a small statue of the Virgin Mary and a candle burning. Wildflowers sprouted from an earthen vase. There was a coverlet over her, and she knew Luz had tended to her while she had been asleep. It was dark outside, and quiet, and she wondered how long she had slept. She was still sore, but the ache was dull and far away.

Sarah heard the heavy wagons enter the fort. She shivered in dread. A few minutes later, she heard Luz's keening voice, Jake's terse questions rumbling in the lower octaves. Sarah's jaw hardened as she clenched her fists, trying to quell the impulse to scream, to cry out. She needed Jake, needed his touch, his caress, his understanding. There was an undercurrent of anger beneath her grief at the loss of her first child. Anger at Jake for not being there. Anger at herself for unnameable sins of omission and commission. What could she have done to save the baby? What had she done to cause it to die?

Jake's frame filled the doorway. He hesitated for a moment. Sarah tried to sit up, but she was too weak.

The candle on the mantel flickered, and Jake's gaze shifted there for a moment. "Dark in here," he said.

"Oh, Jake!" she whispered, trying not to cry.

He walked toward her, hesitatingly. Stood by the edge of the bed. She unclenched her fists, held out a hand to him. He did not take it.

"What did you do to the baby?" he asked, his voice coarse, the words like a lash strapping her face.

"I—he—he died," she said.

"Goddamnit."

"It doesn't do any good to curse."

"You must have *done* something," he said lamely.

"I—I'm sorry, Jake," she said. "He—he was so tiny."

"Luz told me. I wanted him. I wanted a son."

"Aren't you sorry for me, Jake? Aren't you sorry for him, for both of us?"

"I don't know. There must be something wrong with you, Sarah."

She struggled to sit up as her anger boiled over, surfaced like a flame emerging from coals. She winced at the sudden pain, managed to pull herself up to a sitting position. The soreness throbbed through her; a sharp pain stabbed her loins. "Why? Why do you say this? Why do you hurt me?"

"Goddammit, Sarah. That baby, that boy, should be alive now, suckling at your breast. But he's dead, and I have no son."

"Why is that my fault?" Sweat broke out on her forehead, and she clenched her fists, trying to drive down the pain.

"You—you," he stammered. "The Shoshone. What they did to you. They must have ruined you."

She recoiled from him, aghast at his accusation. She held on, sitting up when she wanted to fall back on the bed and close her eyes, shut him out of her mind. "Ruined me? What do you mean?"

He was silent for a long moment. "When they took you," he said slowly, his voice low, laced with gravel, "when you were a girl, they must have . . ."

"Oh, is that it? Is that what's on your mind, Jake? Is that what you've been thinking all along?"

"You wasn't no virgin, Sarah."

"Were you?" she snapped.

"I reckon not."

"You want to know what they did to me? Is that

what's bothering you? Is that why you wouldn't marry me? Yes, it must be. Well, I'll tell you, Jake. So you'll know and can put your mean mind to rest. Is that what you want?"

"No," he croaked.

She leaned toward him. Never mind the pain. Never mind the ache in her heart. "I was twelve years old, Jake. The Shoshone took me to their camp. It was a large village. It was night, and they danced and gabbled and bragged about what they did to my folks and the others they killed. They put me in a lodge and bound my ankles and my wrists. Two women burned me with burning sticks and laughed when I screamed. They stripped me naked and put their fingers inside me and pinched the nipples of my breasts."

"D-don't," he said, bowing his head.

"No, you bastard. You asked for it. You're going to hear it."

"I don't want . . ."

"The bucks came in after that. Young and old. They all took a turn at me. I screamed the first time, and the man laughed and broke my maidenhead. I thought I was going to die. I wanted to die. I begged them to stop. But they took me, one by one, all night long, and some of them slapped my face and punched my belly. Maybe they tore something inside me. Maybe they tore everything inside so the baby couldn't live. Maybe that's why the baby was born dead. Maybe it's all my fault because I let those men do those things to me."

"Jesus. Sarah, I—"

"No, Jake, you got what you wanted out of me. You found out the ugly truth. Are you happy now, Mr. Stonecipher? Now that you've laid blame, are you happy?"

"No, goddammit, I'm not happy. I—I . . ."

"Just get out," she spat. "Get out and leave me

alone. Don't say another word or I'll scream so loud you'll have to kill me to shut me up."

He backed away, stunned by the savagery of her tone. She watched as he ducked through the doorway. He closed the door, and she heard the latch click. She heard his footsteps on the hard-packed earth, and then she heard nothing.

Sarah fell back on the bed, exhausted, the pain throbbing in her loins. Her body, drenched with sweat, quivered as if she'd been whipped.

"That was a long time ago," she whispered to herself. But the memories danced in her mind, shadows around a fire—hideous, faceless, dark.

She closed her eyes to shut out the tears, but they leaked through the lids and coursed over her cheeks. The sobs came then, out of control, and she didn't know if she was crying for the baby, for Jake, or for herself. It didn't matter now. She was broken inside. If the Shoshone hadn't broken her, Jake had. Jake had broken her, dug out her shame and held it up to her and thrown it back in her face. The shame, the memories, the terrible memories.

"My baby," she sobbed. "My baby."

The sounds of her weeping filled the room, and she was hollow inside. Hollow. Hollow as her empty womb. Hollow.

≈ 15 ≈

As the settlements along the Arkansas and the Fountain grew, Paco began to plan for his future. The government granted him the five thousand hectares of land and more besides. Paco was surprised to learn that he owned the land where Fort Stonecipher (for that was what they were calling it now) was located. He said nothing, however, since his plans for a home were in the mountains where the three creeks rose in a valley blooming with blue flowers.

He built a cabin of pine logs, married Consuelo, and took her to the mountains. Her father and brothers rode up with them to carry all the supplies and wedding gifts to their home. They brought a cookstove, lamps and lanterns, chests, lumber, blankets, sheets, pillows, and tools.

When they were gone, Paco took Consuelo on a ride to show her the land they now owned.

"It's very beautiful," she said wistfully, and Paco, in his joy at her words, did not notice that Consuelo was already feeling the first pangs of loneliness.

"I will winter cattle down on the plain," he said, "bring them here for the summer. We will sell them for much money."

"We are so far away from everyone," she said.

"Soon there will be many people up here," he told her. "As our ranch grows, we will need families to help us. Maybe your parents and mine will someday live here with us."

"Oh, I hope so," she said, and for a time, she held on to that dream.

Paco gradually brought in cattle and a few goats, some pigs. He trapped the streams that Burke did not but kept his eye on the American. It gave Paco some satisfaction to know that he owned the land where the American trapper earned his money, but in those days, there was plenty of room for everyone, plenty of beaver, marten, fox, mink, and game for the table.

Each August and October, he and Consuelo rode to Taos and visited with her family, then rode on to Santa Fe to see his mother and father. He was sad to see that his parents were growing old, and he was not yet rich, but he promised them he would someday be an important man.

He learned that the white men called the pretty blue flower columbine, and that was the name he chose for his ranch. He devised and registered a brand that consisted of a circle with two small curved slashes growing out of the bottom that resembled large commas. He explained to Consuelo that the circle was the columbine, the slashes its graceful spurs. He drove his beef to the plains each winter, sold some off each spring when the calves were weaned.

Paco hired *vaqueros* to tend his cattle herd and hired a woman to serve as maid and companion to Consuelo. The woman, Lupe Sanchez, was strong and wiry, a widow who was barren. She was perhaps forty years old and smoked a little corncob pipe. Consuelo enjoyed her company, but she missed her family in Taos, missed the *bailes* and the laughter and jokes of women her own age. Still, Paco was a good husband, and she loved him very much. Often he came home tired and dirty, and she filled the wooden tub with hot water and bathed him, rubbed the tiredness out of his shoulders. Then they would make love, and life would bloom for her like the blue columbines that dotted the summer meadow.

Paco began to raise horses too, and Consuelo felt that he was taking on too much, but he seemed driven to make money. When he was gone for a long time driving cattle or horses to market, she pined for him, and the flowers in the meadow began to fade as she heard only the raucous call of magpies and jays taunting her, driving her to the edge of madness. When she went to bed alone at night, she cried into her pillow and beat her fists against the mattress. At such times she hated Paco for leaving her alone, but she knew that he was not the enemy. It was the ranch and the loneliness and the emptiness inside her. She longed for a child, but Paco's seed did not fertilize her egg, and she began to wonder if the widow Lupe's barrenness was contagious.

Jake Stonecipher filed for title to all the land surrounding the fort from a point east on the Huerfano River, west to Greenhorn peak, north to Newlin Creek, thence east to Fort Stonecipher. Unknown to him, this was land already granted by the Mexican government to Paco Serrano. But it was disputed land and had not been claimed by the United States until Jake filed on it. In his request, Stonecipher claimed townsites for the fort itself, a settlement on the Arkansas where the three creeks joined to one that drained into the big river, and another where the Huerfano flowed into the Arkansas. This was enough for the American authorities to grant him legal claim to a sizable portion of land on American soil.

In effect, Jake became an unofficial governor of lands claimed by both Mexico and the United States. His

documents, at the time, were just as legal as those
granted Paco by the Mexican government. Jake did not
know then that the United States had its roving eye
fixed not only on Santa Fe and the entire territory of
New Mexico but on Texas as well. When Jake received
title to his land, he knew nothing of these things. But
he, like Paco, envisioned an empire.

Jake Stonecipher had expanded his enterprise on the
Arkansas. When Will rode in, he was surprised to see
how many adobe houses now surrounded the fort. Work
was just beginning on the *pueblo* between Fort Stonecipher and Fountain Creek. Men swarmed over the
foundations, and Mexican masons were busy making
adobe brick.

Jake's masons were building a new wall on the fort,
extending from the old one on three sides.

"What's a-goin' on?" Will asked Jake when he rode
in, pulling his horses and mules behind. "Looks like a
damned city."

"Light down, and I'll buy you a cup," said Jake,
grinning wide as a barn door.

Over whiskey, Burke learned that Jake was taking in
other traders and their families, letting them build,
buy, or rent a house within the new walls.

"They'll all be independent," said Jake. "No corpora-
tion or partnership. Just a bunch of good people getting
together for the common good. Like that *pueblo* goin'
up. We got folks who can keep milk cows, chickens,
pigs, and such, farm the bottoms, and make do."

"Too many goddamned people," said Will, but the
whiskey warmed him.

"Can't give you much for your furs, Will. Market's
plumb dried up."

"Three dollars?"

"Dollar and a half the pound," said Jake.

"Two."

"For you, then, two dollars."

"Done," said Will, glad to get the business over with. He had more important things to discuss with Jake Stonecipher, and this seemed the best time.

They were alone, but Jake seemed anxious to leave the small room that served as a saloon. They were its only occupants at the moment. Will took out his pipe, poured himself another drink. Jake waved him away when he offered to refill his cup. Will stuffed tobacco in his pipe, scratched a spark in it with flint and steel, puffed it to life.

"You got somethin' else on your mind, Will?"

"Maybe. I saw me a chunk of land up in the hills, wanted to know if you owned it, maybe might sell it to me."

"Well, I don't know. Why up there? Mighty poor pickins, seems to me. Ain't no call for beaver and such no more."

"Jake, I got the mountains in me. Can't get 'em out. You got a map of your holdings?"

"I do."

"Maybe I can show you the property, you think about it."

"I'll get it," said Jake, and left the room.

The adobe made the room cool, and Will drank his whiskey slowly, puffed on his pipe until Jake returned with his map. Jake spread it out on a small crude table, and the two men huddled over it. Will's eyes fixed on the three creeks. They were all in the boundaries of Jake's land.

"Looks to me like you got land where Serrano's built him a log house," said Will.

"I heard there was a family living up there. See 'em bring their cattle down every spring, run horses down the mountain to St. Louis every so often."

"You don't mind?"

"Not yet," said Jake, pulling at his chin. "I never met the man."

"Well, it's something to think about."

"Where's the property you want to buy?"

"That middle crick there. Adobe, I call it. A stretch of that. I'll mark it out for you. First, though, I got to go to Santa Fe."

"We've got everything here you need," said Jake.

"Maybe, but I got to ride over the pass, see me a real city."

Jake looked at his friend for a long moment. Burke avoided his gaze, and Stonecipher knew that Will was holding back something from him. "Suit yourself, Will. I've got work to do. Take as much whiskey as you want. I'll check your furs, give you what they're worth."

"You ever marry that white squaw?"

"Nope," said Jake. "Wasn't no point to it after she had that stillbirth. Woman don't seem the same since. I reckon she'd like to marry up with me, but I might want to have kids someday. Sarah looks to be gettin' old before her time."

"Don't the time fairly fly," said Will, and he leaned back in his chair as Jake left him alone. He studied the map, memorized it carefully. He paid particular attention to the boundaries, the landmarks.

The next day, Burke left for Santa Fe before dawn. He didn't want to answer a lot of questions he was sure Jake would ask.

≈ 16 ≈

Burke wanted to linger at Stonecipher's before he went back to the mountains so that he could be around Sarah Reynolds. Something about the woman reminded him of himself, the ghosts he carried in his heart. He sensed that she was like him, essentially a loner, an outcast from regular society. He felt a kinship with her that was so tangled up in his mind, he could not express his feelings. Over the years, he had seen her become part of the fort, yet remain strangely aloof. She was there, but she was not there.

At times, in the mountains, he found himself thinking of her, wondering what she was doing, what it would be like to talk to her. Now that he was about to leave again, he found himself reluctant to go away without at least speaking to her. It took him a long time to figure out something to say to her, some way to open a conversation with the shadowy woman.

Finally, he had found the courage one day. He spoke to her, complimenting her on the dress she wore. "Looks to me you made it yourself," he said, "and if so, you've a mighty fine eye for beauty."

"Why, thank you, Mr. Burke, and so do you yourself."

Will blushed, but something tugged at his heart, and whenever he could, he watched Sarah in secret—the way she walked, the way she moved—and when she spoke, which was rarely, he thought she had a most pleasant voice, deep and sweet; there was a comely lilt to it that lingered in the ear like the song of a night thrush.

Finally, though, Will could no longer stand to be around Sarah and not be able to talk to her about anything more than the weather and her cooking. Although she was not married, he still considered her Jake's property, and he would not take liberties with another man's woman. And he knew he must ride back to Adobe Creek and work his claim. After a week, he was as fidgety as a cat in a hailstorm.

"Jake," said Will the day he was ready to return to the mountains, "I'd like to buy that piece of land from you."

"Land?"

"Up on one of the cricks, where I showed you."

"I'll get the map," said Jake. Will stood outside Jake's door at one of the trader's empty tables. Jake returned with the map and spread it out.

"This chunk right here," said Will, using his finger to draw a crude rectangle on the map.

"That's not very much land."

"It's enough," said Will gruffly. "Place to put me a cabin and hang my hat. Build me a little corral for the stock."

"Why? Why there?"

"Now, that ain't rightly none of your business, Jake. I got me reasons."

"That gold chunk hangin' from your neck?"

Will flushed crimson. "That don't have nothin' to do with it," he lied. "Just name your price."

Jake wondered if he was right about the gold. A Mexican who had come in from Santa Fe two days ago had told Jake about the talk there. They were saying an

American trapper had come in with some gold and had gotten cash for it. The trapper's description sounded a lot like Will Burke. The talk was that the American had found the gold somewhere in the mountains.

"Will, that little piece of land will cost you three thousand dollars," said Jake.

Will almost choked. "Three thou—"

"Might be valuable someday. If it's prime enough for you to want it, must be worth at least that much."

Will's neck swelled like a bull elk's in rut. His face purpled as every vein filled with a rage of blood. He balled his fists, and for a moment Jake thought he was going to be struck. But he held his ground and let Will's anger subside.

"You write out a paper I can take to Santa Fe," said Will. "Here's five hundred now, and I'll pay you the rest by next spring. Fair enough?"

"Fair enough," said Jake. He smiled. If Will had asked, had told him why he wanted the land, he might have just given it to him. But he enjoyed playing the trapper like a trout, watching him squirm and dance on the end of a line.

"Land's mine, then."

"Soon as you pay for it. I'll write you a receipt, and we'll record the transaction in Santa Fe."

"Meanwhile, it's mine to do with what I want."

"Until spring," said Jake, amused at Will's determination.

"You'll get your goddamned money come spring," said Will. He fished in his possibles pouch, counted out five hundred dollars in gold coin.

"I'm not worried about it," said Jake, taking the money. "Don't get in such a fret about the rest."

"I ain't in no goddamn 'fret' about it," fumed Burke. "But you make a powerful stab at a man when he's give you nigh all he's got in his poke."

"I'll draw you up a paper before you go," said Jake, trying to mollify his friend.

"I'll be buyin' me some supplies too."

"Oh? What will you be needin'?"

"A shovel, pick, some lumber, nails, a big light fry pan."

Jake tried not to smile. He smirked instead and turned his head so that Will could not see his amusement.

"And—and I'll take some whiskey with me and maybe some sweet candy. Some blankets and such. Horse blankets. Wool, if you've got."

"Pick out what you want. I've got wool saddle blankets. And good whiskey. I'll give you your paper in a few minutes."

"That'll be right fine," said Will, still swollen with belligerence. He stalked off to prowl the traders' stalls.

Jake went back into his room. Will's behavior had brought his bristles up. Whiskey? He remembered when he and Joe had first seen Will Burke. Drunker'n two hundred dollars, he was, and fair cocky with grog, like a wolf with the hackles up.

Sarah was dusting the hearth when Jake entered his room.

"Is Mr. Burke leaving?" she asked.

"And good riddance," said Jake. He sat down at the small desk Joe had built for him. He found parchment and took out his quill, dipped it in a small bottle of ink, and began writing.

"I thought he was your good friend," said Sarah innocently.

"Good friends don't keep secrets," he said. She was talking more than usual. She almost never asked questions.

"Maybe they do," she said. "Maybe they have to, sometimes."

Jake stopped writing, whirled around in his chair to

face her. "What the hell's that supposed to mean?" he asked. "Seems to me you've got curious ears all of a sudden."

"Nothing," she said quickly, and scurried from the room, her face dark as a thundercloud.

"Damn woman," muttered Jake. He wrote furiously on the parchment, then put the quill away, capped the ink bottle with its black cork. He leaned over and blew the ink dry, lifted the parchment. It crackled like a dry cornhusk in the silence of the room.

Sarah went to Burke as he was taking his horses out of the stalls, surprising him. She was so quiet, she scared him at first. He never heard her come up on him, and when she spoke, his spine shivered and his heart bounced in its cage.

"I wanted to say good-bye," she said, but there was more than that in her words. Will knew that. Much more.

"Yeah, I got to be leavin'."

"You're a strange man," she said softly. "I think about you being up there all alone and wonder at it."

"It gets lonesome," he said.

"It gets lonesome here, too."

"Not so much, I reckon."

"More than I can bear sometimes."

"Sarah, you oughtn't to be talkin' like this."

"No, I suppose not," she said wistfully.

He wanted to take her—then. Take her with him to the mountains. Just ride out and don't look back and take this woman up there to keep him company. But it wouldn't be right. And likely enough, he'd have a fight on his hands. Lose a good friend to boot.

"I got to be goin'," he said gruffly.

"Will we see you again in the spring?"

"I reckon. Or sooner."

For a moment, he thought she was going to ask him if

she could go with him. But she fell silent, and he felt her watching him as he saddled Rocky. When he turned around, she was gone. He saw little motes of dust dancing in the light of the doorway to show she had passed that way.

He didn't see her again that day, although he looked for her when he rode out of the fort, his mules and horses laden with the goods he had bought, their panniers swaying slightly from side to side. Jake waved good-bye, and Will felt his throat tighten when he waved back. The day was bright and the sky clear, but he felt like he was riding away under a dark cloud.

Burke worked. He worked harder than he ever had before. He tied buffalo robes, hairy side upstream, across the stretch of creek, tied wool saddle blankets every few feet downstream for a quarter of a mile. He cut logs for his shelter.

When he found his first gold, he got the fever again. In his greed, he began to dig away at the banks of the creek. He found gold nuggets and flakes stuck to the roottips of trees that had sent feeders to the waterway. He didn't bother to clean up and left sign carelessly that he was working that section of the stream.

When Will wasn't digging for gold, he was peeling logs, cutting down trees, building his cabin. He was like a wild man, but the gold was there, and he filled his pouches, buried them inside his growing shelter.

One day he dipped the fry pan into the sandy bottom and swirled the grains until the gold separated from the black sand. The dust was the color of goldenrod, so beautiful that Burke just stared at for several minutes, struck with the wonder of it. There was something so pure about the golden grains that he wanted to shout aloud.

He was like a man drunk, and he lost all track of time and place. He dug with his shovel, and when he found gold, he got down on his hands and knees and dug with his hands until his fingers were raw, the nails packed with dirt. At night, when he could no longer see to dig or pan the yellow metal, he shone candlelight on the larger nuggets and rubbed them reverently with his fingers as if each piece were alive or held a magic that flowed into him whenever he touched the precious golden pebbles. He did not eat as he should and grew thin and gaunt. He stayed up too late, drinking and raving aloud.

It was no longer a question of wealth but just the possession of the gold that drove him. The finding of it. The hunt for it. It was all part of the same web that his feet stuck to, that his arms became entangled in, that shawled him until he wore it like a garment, a deadly cloak that felt like iron but was only wispy silk spun by some spidery phantom in his delirium. And he was a man caught in the web, waiting for the venomous bite that surely must come.

At times, Will broke out of the madness and hunted for food, not gold. But he was impatient, and sloppy. One part of his mind told him that this was dangerous, that he was risking his life, but another part said that it didn't matter—he had the gold, and only the gold mattered. There were lucid intervals, however, when he thought of the Ute and the Arapaho and he became wary and secretive, sometimes listening for five or ten minutes to the wind, smelling danger but seeing nothing, hearing no twig snap, no branch break, only wind, just wind.

But he kept digging and destroying the contours of the stream until parts of it resembled a graveyard, a graveyard littered with open graves, the white tree roots the bones, the dead raped bones that Will Burke had unearthed with pick and shovel and ripped out of their moorings with gnarled stubby fingers caked with dirt.

One day he heard the honk of wild geese when he was shivering from cold, watching the sand swirl hypnotically in the fry pan. They were headed south, spread across the sky in gently undulating V's, and he felt again that unnameable longing in the breast of every homeless man who finds himself alone in the wilderness. For no reason, Will wept as he watched the high-flying geese, listened to their plaintive calls so far away, so lost, so full of homesickness. His hands were wrinkled, the skin loose and rumpled from being in the cold stream water.

He looked down into the pan, saw the first flecks of gold clinging to the black dolomite, and felt empty. The gold looked dull under the dull light of a gray sky, and angrily he shoved the pan back under the water and watched as the rushing stream waters washed the sand and its treasure back into the creekbed. He began laughing insanely, and tears flowed down his cheeks. His laugh blended with the haunting call of the wild geese. He threw his head back and yelled at them, yelled at them as if they were his children, running away from home.

That night, Will drank the last of his whiskey, drank until he was staggering drunk. In the grip of his demons, he ranted and raved, wept and cursed, shouted in the depths of his delirium.

"Burke, you're a miserable son of a sea cook an' a slattern mother," he bellowed, "'an here you are, cut off from all the ties that bind, and what're you doin' with yourself? You're grubbin' for the gold, and the madness is in ye. And you're crazy. You're crazy, Will Burke, because the mountain took you into her bosom, and what did you do? You raped her. And you've

forgotten the soft silk touch of the beaver fur and the
sleek grace of the mink, the high proud antlers of the
mule deer, the sweet buglin' call of the elk in the
meadow, and the curious whistles of the young bulls.
You've forgot to look at the trees and touch 'em. Now
you dig in the earth like a hard-rock miner and slash
the land just for somethin' that glitters in the sun and
brings you a few shillin's fer your poke. Ah, you've
fallen far, Will Burke, you've fallen far. But it's glorious
to feel rich for a time. To be on the mountain and feel
rich. Richer'n Croesus hisself, eh? Ah, what is it? What
is it that pulls me here, lures me, lures me? It's not a
woman, but it's like a woman. Like a woman in silence.
Like a woman who says nothin' when you kiss her mouth.
Even like a woman who says nothin' when you pay her
money. But it's deeper'n that. Richer. Aye, that it is.
And I have no words for it.

"I have the drink lets me say things, say things like
birds caught in my hand, birds in my grip. But I can't
sleep nights thinkin' of the gold horde. I wonder, is that
fit for a man? What will it buy? Where will I go? It's not
the finding, it's the seeking. It's the finding too. Auugh,
it's all tangled up in me mind. I don't know. I'm drunk
and I'm crazy and I'm dirty, and I'm just broken inside.
I don't know. I'm scared. And I never was scared
before. I'm scared someone will take the gold away
from me. I'm scared someone will find out what I'm
doin'. Goddamn, I'm scared."

Burke didn't awaken until the sun stood high in the
sky the next day. His head throbbed with a thousand
drums. His vision was blurred, and his mouth tasted as
if he'd been eating burnt cork. He eyed the empty
whiskey bottle and fought down the bile that rose in his
throat.

"Gawd!" he exclaimed, and staggered down to the
creek. The morning frost had burned off, but it was still

cold. Will splashed his face with the frigid waters of the stream, and gradually his head began to clear.

He was still squatting by the stream when Paco Serrano rode up, a rifle across his pommel. He rode a tall black horse with small hooves. He wore a light elk-hide jacket lined with sheepskin and a flat-crowned *sombrero*. He wore no pistol. His pants were wool, store-bought, and his boots black and shiny, with long heels.

Will saw there was fire in the man's eye. Will stood up, the front of his shirt sopping wet, his beard dripping, his hair in sodden ringlets.

"This is my land," said Paco. "You have no right to camp here. What are you doing?" Paco eyed the damaged banks, the torn-up roots, the holes on both sides of the creek.

"None of your damned business," said Burke, although he felt naked without a rifle in his hand.

"You must leave," said Paco. "And never come back."

"And who in hell are you?"

"I am Paco Serrano. I own this land. You are tearing it to pieces."

"This ain't your land, Serrano. It belongs to Jake Stonecipher, and I aim to buy it from him."

"I do not know this Stonecipher."

"He owns the fort down where the Fountain comes out of the mountains."

"Yes, I know of the fort. Who are you?"

"Will Burke. I made claim to this section fair and legal."

"You cannot do this. It is stupid."

"Watch who you're callin' stupid, mister. I ain't in no mood to argy about property. I paid earnest money on it, and I'm stayin'. If anybody's trespassin', it's you."

"I could shoot you where you stand," said Paco, but there was no conviction in his voice.

Burke watched the Mexican's hands and braced himself. If it came to a fight, he was ready to take the man on bare-handed. "You might get a shot off," said Will, "but before you get another ball down that bar'l, I'll be on you like ten kinds of grizzly b'ar."

Paco wisely let his rifle balance on the pommel. He looked again at the diggings, the small cabin Burke had built, the shovel, pick, and fry pan lying beside the creek. His eyes narrowed in controlled anger. But this man, he knew, would not budge. If he shot him, he had better aim true. He had seen such men before, in Taos and Santa Fe. They could fight with fists or with knives, and they had no qualms about gouging a man's eyes out or slicing off an enemy's *cojones*. No, this one was trouble, much bigger than he had looked when Paco had first seen him. They were no more than twenty yards apart, and it was probable that the man would charge the minute Paco lifted his rifle.

"We will talk about this again, perhaps," said Serrano. "You would be wise to leave now and never come back."

"I am fixin' to leave, Serrano, but I'll be back. And everything better be here just as I left it."

"We will see," said the Mexican. He clamped the big-rowled Spanish spurs into his horse's flanks.

Burke watched him ride off, Paco's back straight, sitting perfectly, part of the horse.

"A graceful pair," Burke said to himself, and spit into the stream. His mouth still tasted like rancid meat.

He packed up his gold and headed straight for Santa Fe. If there was going to be trouble with Serrano, he wanted to have that land in his name. Stonecipher might buckle to the man, might back out of the deal. He had enough gold now to buy the land. Paco would be back, he knew. Burke would be ready for him the next time.

Will did not go down the Fountain but rode through

the Wet Mountains, crossed the Sangre de Cristo Range through Music Pass, turned left at the sand dunes, then rode through Medano Pass, followed Sangre de Cristo Creek through still another pass, then headed south for San Luis. By the time he hit Raton Pass, it was snowing hard.

When he got to Santa Fe and cashed in his gold, Will Burke was a rich man.

≈ 17 ≈

Joe Perkins watched the *pueblo* grow in the delta formed by the Arkansas River and Fountain Creek as if he were seeing a boil grow on his neck. "Like a damned anthill over there," he said to Jake one day after returning from one of his frequent inspections. "They'll put us out of business when they're finished buildin'."

"They're good for business," said Jake. He and Joe sat in Jake's new office. Jake checked Joe's ledgers, made notations on a separate piece of paper for supplies they'd need before winter set in. "They're bringin' lots of folks into the country, and folks are good for business."

"Competition," said Joe with a disdainful snort. "Ever' damn one of them folks is a trader, seems like."

"Well, that's what we came here for." Jake smiled. Joe had grown some since they first came to the Arkansas. He was dry behind the ears, all out of freckles and a lot of the lazy lank out of his step. He had become a savvy manager, an eagle-eyed shopkeeper, a man who drove a hard bargain over every transaction. Sometimes Jake had to step in to soothe a customer's ruffled feelings, but that didn't take anything away from Joe. He was fiercely protective of Jake's interests and loyal as a bluetick hound.

"Why, have you seen 'em down at Huerfano Creek? Thicker'n fleas. And they's a settlement they call Greenhorn on that creek, where it meets the Graneros, just past the Muddy. And look up on the Fountain. Lordy, they's a passel up there, too."

"Joe," said Jake patiently, "that's what all this country is for. People. It'll grow, and we'll grow with it. One day we won't have to worry about the Ute anymore. Blanco and his kind will be pushed out. That's progress. Why, one day there'll be folks living all up and down the Arkansas, and in the mountains too. There'll be ranchers and farmers and merchants, doctors, lawyers, newspapers—everything."

"Well, it seems to me we was here first and we're bein' crowded out."

"No," said Jake. "It'll just get better for us. Look at how we're growin'. People know we're here. Why, who wants to go to Santa Fe from Bent's along that lonesome stretch to Trinidad? There's Apache, Comanche, road agents, you name it, if you go that way. We're at the crossroads, Joe. Travelers can come from any direction and find a good meal, a drink, goods. They don't even have to go to Taos and Santa Fe if they don't want to. Pretty soon, we'll have just as much, maybe even a bigger town."

"I don't know," said Perkins. "There ain't no fur business no more, and them few farms ain't gonna feed all these folks."

"They will, Joe. Someday, they will."

"If you say so." Joe finished his inventory, slid the paper across the table to Jake. He leaned back in his chair and put his hands behind his head, spreading his arms out like wings.

"Joe, you ought to be thinkin' about settin' up your own home. Finding yourself a good woman."

"I don't want no Mex woman."

"Why not? There are some real beauties in Santa Fe."

"I don't like that Mexican grub," Joe said. "Chili peppers burn my asshole." He bounced out of his chair and left the room.

Jake laughed and turned back to his ledgers.

But when he was through, he slipped from the fort and returned to that place of solace, the river. The river was private with him. Jake never tired of watching its many moods, its changes over the seasons. He read it as if it were his private diary, its flow a record of his feelings each day, his moods, his secret thoughts.

Its smells, the sound of its current when it ran full, made his senses keen. When it moved slowly, he felt content, at peace. He knew it would fill up again and bring messages down from the high country in its flotsam, the chill cakes of ice bobbing as they passed by, diminishing in size as they flowed eastward through the plain. Its colors fascinated him, always shifting, bearing mud and dirt snatched from other places, carrying silt along in its current, spewing off grains at every twist and bend of its serpentine course.

The river was alive, and it was different each day, each moment, virtually every second. It was wild and tame, turbulent and serene; clear and muddy, never the same, like him, rising and falling like the slow tides of a moon-pulled sea; ever restless, ever moving, roaring in the spring, strangely silent in winter when frost glazed its banks and otter dived to its depths like seals.

The river had no harness, yet it had boundaries and destinations. It teemed with life and surged with hidden riches never glimpsed by man. Jake felt at peace with this river. The river made him feel at home. It was the one thing he counted on to be there always, like the sky and the mountains. The river was eternal, and he was only its guardian for a time. The river made him think, and he spoke to it in his mind. And when he left its banks, his thoughts washed away and drifted downstream, forever lost in its sliding current, still secret, still private, still unspoken.

When the first snow flew, Jake made up a list of goods he needed and called Joe into his office. "Have a seat, Joe. I've got a list of supplies I'll need in the spring."

"Lots of time till then," said Perkins, attaching his lanky frame to a chair.

"I know. But, this will give you time to yourself. You've been gettin' plumb on my nerves of late. Maybe you'll find yourself a woman and bring her back here. That's why I'm giving you your choice. You can either get these goods in St. Louis or Santa Fe. Just don't buy nothin' from the Bents."

"Well, Santa Fe's closer. But I saw me a little gal in St. Louie last time I'uz there. Frenchie, cute as a red button."

"All right," said Jake. "But I'm going to send some help with you this time. Delgado and a couple of other Mexicans. They can ride and shoot. You'll be driving back three wagons, so that'll be mighty temptin' to bandits or Injuns." Jake handed Joe the list.

Joe whistled. "You're gettin' serious," he said.

"I've been checking the settlements, and these are goods I think will be in short supply come spring."

"Shit," said Joe, reading the list. "Plows, harness, nails, lumber, hoes, seed, rakes, horseshoes, powder, ball, percussin' caps, cornmeal, coffee, salt, pepper, malt, sugar, pigs. Pigs?"

"Yep, pigs. These people are butcherin' damned near every one they've got. Get some fat ones, get 'em cheap."

"Shit," said Joe, but on the first sunny day, he left for St. Louis with enough money to buy three wagons, all the goods on Jake's list, and still have himself a time in the city for two months or three. Jake was glad to see that Joe had taken their best and fastest horse.

With him rode José Delgado, Silvino Pérez, and Tomás Santiago. Luz cried when her husband rode away, and Jake tried to console her. "They'll be back in the spring," he said. "Don't worry."

"Ay, *indios, bandidos!*" she wailed, then ran to her room to sob in private over the loss of her husband for a winter.

Jake watched until the three men disappeared. He knew this trip might be more dangerous than the others. There were a lot of people coming up the Arkansas now, and there was a lot of talk about Indians raiding along the river. One party turned back to Bent's Fort because Blanco and his Ute killed two members and ran off three head of cattle and a wagon, which they looted. There were also rumors of bandits on the Santa Fe Trail and the cutoff between Bent's and Taos.

"They'll be okay," he said to himself, but there were dark shadows in his eyes and a long winter ahead to worry about Joe and the others.

Will Burke returned to Fort Stonecipher in November. He wore new clothes, had shaved his beard, and had a new Santa Fe saddle under him.

"You got new boots, too," said Jake when Burke rode through the gate. "Hell, I could see your glitter a mile off."

"Pretty fancy, eh?" Burke grinned proudly. He wore a bright red shirt of shiny silk, a new *sombrero* with a high crown, black pants embroidered with white flowery patterns, and high-topped Spanish boots, gleaming black under a patina of dust.

"You look like a cross between a Mexican general and a Portugee juggler," said Jake.

"Well, I come to do business, an' these clothes suit me just fine."

"Will, I was just makin' a joke."

"How 'bout buyin' us a drink and bringin' that map over to the cantina."

"You've got the rest of the money?"

"Bring the map whilst I put Rocky up in the stables and fork him some hay. I'm thirstier'n a whiskey drummer at a church social."

Jake entered the saloon a few moments later to find Burke at a table, a whiskey bottle and two glasses poured full. The bottle showed that this wasn't Will's first glass. Jake sat down, spread the map out on the table. He set down two sheets of parchment written in flowery lettering. There was enough light slanting through the doorway to read it.

Will traced a finger over a section of Adobe Creek as Jake sipped from his glass. "I walked it off," said Burke, "and it's right close to three acres there."

"That's all you want?"

"Yep." Will retrieved a leather sack from his possibles pouch. He plunked it on the table. "Twenty-five hunnert in gold. Already counted out." He shoved the sack toward Jake.

Jake didn't pick it up. Instead, he looked at the map, speared the section with his right index finger. "Is this where you found the raw gold?" he asked.

"I just want to build me a huntin' cabin there, trap it," said Will stubbornly.

"It's mighty small."

"Them three acres is all I need."

"I could maybe lease it to you, Will. For ten years, say."

"No, I want to buy it outright. That was the deal."

"Maybe I ought to go up there, look it over first," said Jake, playing Will like a fish on a line.

"Ain't no need. It's just dirt and that crick."

"You wouldn't lie to me, would you, Will?"

"I might," said Burke. "I made you an offer, Jake. Twenty-five hunnert in cash. Take it or leave it."

"All right," said Jake. "I've already drawn up the papers. Just sign it right here on both copies, and I'll sign 'em, and the property's yours. You keep a copy and I'll keep one."

Will smacked his lips as he made his mark. Jake signed the documents and gave one to Will, kept one for himself.

"Well, now," said Will, "it's all legal, eh?"

"Legal as anything," said Jake. "You know, don't you, that land sales on the Arkansas are private. I recorded mine with a lawyer in St. Louis, but there ain't no sure way to claim this land excep' by bein' here and defendin' it. When I drew up the papers, the lawyer told me that part of this territory was owned by the U.S. government and part by Mexico, and no one is sure of the exact bounderies."

"That's good enough for me," said Will. "You got another feller up there says he owns that land, and I reckon my claim is just good as his."

"Who's that?" asked Stonecipher.

"Paco Serrano. He's been livin' up there for some time. Raises cattle and horses. He tried to run me off."

"Well, it could be trouble one day," said Jake.

"Likely," said Will, and poured the glasses full once again.

* * *

Joe didn't know what to make of it. Silvino and Tomás were edgy. José was wary.

All day they'd seen Indians, the same ones, showing up every so often but staying well out of rifle shot.

"Ute?" Joe asked Silvino.

"Sí, Muache Ute. They are Blanco's braves."

"How do you know?"

"I have seen them in Taos at the August fair," said Silvino.

"I have seen them also," said Tomás.

"Keep them rifles handy," said Joe.

The Ute stayed with Joe and the three Mexicans until they were within five miles of Bent's Fort on the Arkansas. The four men stayed close to the river, and when they camped, two stayed awake, two slept. They rode in loose formation, each man able to fire in any direction should the Indians attack. But the Muaches stayed out of rifle range and did not press the travelers.

Before they left, the Ute whooped and rode their ponies closer than they had been. A dozen of them rode in a circle, whipping their ponies. They hid behind them in a dazzling display of horsemanship, then rode off, disappearing over the horizon.

At Bent's, Joe told Bent what had happened.

"Them Muaches have learnt a lot of bad habits from the Apache," said Bent. "I spec we'll hear more from 'em come spring. More people that goes west of this here fort, less they like it." Bent stood about five feet seven. He had coal-black hair, brown eyes, his skin dark as an Indian's, his cheekbones cut high as any Sioux's or Cheyenne's, his jaw jutting out like a chunk of granite. The pox scars in his cheeks gave him a hard look, but he was friendly, always had a smile for friends and strangers. His partner, Ceran St. Vrain, was in St. Louis, he told them, would be back any day. But Joe was interested only in talking about the Ute.

"I think they were just playin' with us," said Joe.

"Injuns' play is gettin' ready for the real thing. Better you make the long ride through Santy Fee goin' back. They already spilt blood on them plains twixt here and Stonecipher's."

"Oh?" asked Joe. "When was that?"

"Last week. Pilgrims come through with two wagons, headin' for the *pueblo*. Ten mile out, them Muaches come down on 'em like hornets. Two white men made it back here—two boys, more like. We got us a war party together and went out there. Ute kilt 'em all, skelped 'em, rode off with most of their goods."

"Shit," said Joe.

"Shit is right," said William Bent.

Blanco, chief of the Muache Ute, sat his pony stoically as the animal slaked its thirst in the river. He turned at the sound of hoofbeats, saw his braves coming fast across the prairie, whipping their ponies to see which was the fastest. Blanco's pony lifted its head, whickered as it turned to see the galloping ponies. In the lead was Proud Hawk, following closely on his heels, his younger brother, Iron Wheel. The other braves slowed when they realized they could not beat Proud Hawk to the river.

Blanco tugged on the reins, turned his pony to meet the riders. He was a short, squat man, with a round puffy face, very little neck. Yet he was powerful, with sloping shoulders, muscles bunched up under his warshirt, thick strong hands. His nose was bulbous, the nostrils flared. He had thin lips, berry-stained teeth, a husky jaw that jutted formidably over his wide chest.

Proud Hawk skidded his pinto to a stop. Iron Wheel

jolted to a halt, and his pony reared when the brave yanked on the bridle.

Blanco waited for the other braves to ride up before he spoke. "What have your eyes seen?" he asked Proud Hawk.

"The white-eyes. He was one of two who killed our brother, Blind Worm."

"And the other?"

"He was not with him. Three of the men who went to the big clay house were the brown-skinned ones."

Blanco grunted. His small eyes glinted behind fatty folds of flesh. "This one we tracked—he will return."

"Yes. He goes to buy goods for the trader at the place where the river comes out of the mountains. He goes to the city of the French on the Father of Rivers."

"You speak true," said Blanco. He knew the comings and goings of the whitefaces. He knew of the *pueblos* they were building on the river they called the Arkansas, knew of the trading there. That was land claimed by the enemy, the Arapaho, but Blanco considered it Ute land. His land.

"He will come back," said Iron Wheel. "With wagons, many goods."

Blanco nodded. He caressed the rifle across his pommel, slid spit in and out of his teeth with his tongue. "When the snow is gone, before the flowers bloom, that is when this whiteface will return."

"I think this is so," said Proud Hawk.

"We will come back, too," said Blanco. "Hooo. We will take what they bring, and we will take the hair from their heads. We will find the other man, too, who killed my son."

The braves grunted.

"We go," said Blanco, "to the river of the moonshells where we will hunt from our winter camp."

With a chorus of high-pitched shrieks, the braves

brandished their weapons and turned their ponies north-
ward to the Platte. Blanco rode in front, his chest
swelling with the prairie air. Soon they met the main
band of braves, who waited for them far from the river
that flowed past the big adobe fort on the river.

One day, Blanco vowed, he would draw blood from
all who passed to the mountains along the river. Let
them build their *pueblos* where the boiling creek spilled
into the Apishapa—what the white men called the
Arkansas.

≈ 18 ≈

Consuelo Serrano patted the withers of her horse, Chato, a blunt-nosed six-year-old sorrel gelding with a blaze face, four white stockings, flax mane and tail. The horse stood fifteen hands high, stepped briskly through the tangled brush, the downed timber, the dead thickets of berry patches. She rode the animal like a champion, her long dark hair neatly coiled into a bun so that it would not catch on branches, her back straight, her lithe lean body in perfect harmony with the horse's movements.

Paco, a hundred yards away in the shadowy timber, watched her as she worked the cattle out of the brush, the horse working its way through the tangle to head off the wary brindled longhorn that was the leader of the bunch. He admired the clean graceful lines of his wife's body, each supple movement as she leaned in rhythm with the horse's quick shifts from left to right.

"Hooeeeya!" yelled Consuelo as the brindled bull tried to break from the small herd. She touched long spindly rowels to Chato's flanks, and the horse bounded forward to cut off the bull. The bull turned back in and angled to the left, the herd following, raking horns against the tall pine, clipping off chunks of bark. *"Andale,*

andale!" she called, and the horse backed off, crowded the last cow, pressing it onward.

Paco rode in from an angle, chuting the cattle downslope, out of the timber. A bell clanked on one of the small heifers as it gangled after the herd, hoofs snappping branches, legs knifing the brush.

"Good, good," he said to Consuelo, and she looked over at him, smiled wide. She grew more beautiful by the day, and he was glad that she had taken so to the mountains, to the life he had chosen for them. She had become a crack shot, could work cattle as well as any *vaquero*, did not mind the long hard rides at roundup, the drive down to the flat where the cattle would winter and stay reasonably plump on the prairie grasses. Yet he could not help wondering if this was one of her brave smiles or if it was genuine.

"That is the last of them," she yelled.

"Yes, yes," said Paco, and he hauled in on the reins, forcing his mount to a brisk walk. Consuelo slowed her horse now that the cattle were headed to the gather where the other *vaqueros* held the herd on a course down the canyon toward Apache Creek.

There, along the creek and to the place where it emptied into the Huerfano River, they had built winter cabins for the *vaqueros*, line shacks where they could hole up and keep an eye on the herd. There were always a few that must be given up to marauding Apache and Ute, an occasional Arapaho, but Paco had managed to build a herd that any man would be proud of, and he hoped someday to improve the breed. Already these cattle had shorter horns than their Mexican ancestors, but they were still too long for the timber. Last spring they had found a cow caught in the brush, her horns hopelessly caught in the tangles of a briar patch.

"Chato," Consuelo said as one of the cows started to

turn back. The horse lowered its head and pranced ahead. The cow turned around, and Consuelo laughed.

Paco knew she was excited. He had told her that after they finished the cattle drive, they would ride to the new *pueblo* on the Arkansas, visit Jake's Trading Post, which people were now calling Fort Stonecipher. Perhaps if she was with people for a little time, she would not mind coming back into the mountains this winter. They had heard from the *vaqueros* and others that the settlements were growing and there were fine goods to buy or trade for.

Paco had another reason for visiting the fort. There was the matter of Will Burke's living on Paco's property and digging in the stream. He had learned in Taos, when they last visited Consuelo's family, that the trapper had sold much gold in Santa Fe. Paco was certain that Burke had found the gold on Serrano land. He had been too busy to go back to the place where Burke had built the cabin, but he wanted to talk with Stonecipher, get the matter of the land settled.

"Soon, soon," said Paco, knowing that his wife, despite her eagerness to please him, despite her having come to love the land, missed the company of other people, the gaiety of browsing through the wares at Taos and Santa Fe at the August Fair. At least he thought that this might be the reason for the shadows of discontent he sensed in her at times when they were alone or when he came upon her unaware to find her in a somber mood, the darkness of brooding on her face like a cloud shadow across an otherwise sun-drenched meadow.

"And just in time," she said, tossing her head back, giving him a look of quiet admonishment.

But were the shadows there? In her eyes? He wondered.

Consuelo had wanted to drive the cattle down out of

the mountains sooner, before the first snow, but Paco had wanted to wait. He did not share her desire to leave the mountain. He had a certain foreboding about riding down to the flat. In his home, he felt safe, and he knew there was good reason for wanting to linger in the safety of the mountains. There was always talk of bandits along the heavily traveled roads and trails, and marauding Indians, Apache, Pawnee, Ute, even the Arapaho, and the wide-ranging Comanche and Shoshone cousins of the Ute. He had no wish to endanger Consuelo's life or his own.

But the first snow had come, and he knew they had to get the cattle down before the next one. Now that first snow was gone, thawed in the sun, but there was always the possibility of a big snow at that time of year, a snow that could lock them in, block all the passes, hold them in winter's gelid grip long enough to kill cattle and horses.

Other *vaqueros*, making the gather at lower elevations, drove cattle into Paco's bunch. The riders spread out along the herd, kept them moving downslope. The herd grew larger and larger until there were almost a hundred head streaming through the last canyon.

Consuelo dropped back to ride with Paco. She beamed at him as she trotted up and forced Chato into a gait that matched his horse's.

"Will Felipe be there?" she asked, a hint of anxiety in her voice, just the least shred of a panic that he sensed in her at times.

"He will be waiting," said Paco. "Do not worry, my precious one." Felipe Arias had driven the wagon down another route to meet them on the flat at the nearest line shack. The wagon carried their fine clothes, toiletries, food, water. They would change clothes in the little cabin before riding to Fort Stonecipher.

"I have made the sweat." She laughed, and he detected a sigh of relief in her voice.

"It is like perfume," said Paco.

She blew him a kiss.

Sweet, sweet, he thought. And he caressed his cheek with his hand to show her that he had received the kiss and cherished it on his skin. "Maybe we will take a long time changing our clothes," he said.

"Perhaps that is so, Paco," she said softly.

He wondered if coming down out of the mountains had not brightened her, lifted her spirits. "Witch," he teased.

"Devil."

She leered at him wickedly, and Paco felt a tug in his loins. Consuelo seemed to grow more beautiful each day. She had not taken on fat like her sisters or her mother but was lean and youthful. The mountain life agreed with her, despite the loneliness. But they were happy, he told himself. One day they would have children, and she would be even happier. They had talked about it some of late, but Paco wanted to wait a year or two more, until he had built more rooms onto the house and felt more prosperous. And Consuelo did not seem anxious to start a family just yet, unlike her sisters, who had dropped children ten months after saying their wedding vows.

The *vaqueros* on the plain waved their hats. The main herd was already gathered and tallied. Now, as the last of the cattle trotted down, the men made their marks. Paco swelled with pride as he saw the milling cattle, mentally counting them in his mind. In the spring there would be many calves, and he would have a fine year at the market.

Consuelo stood in the stirrups, saw the wagon waiting for them at the line shack. "I will meet you there," she said, nodding in the direction of the cabin.

"Yes. I will give orders to the men and be there very soon." She seemed so anxious to leave, he thought. Could she not wait, and joke with the *vaqueros*?

Consuelo rode off, putting Chato into a gentle gait. She waved at the men she passed, and they waved at her adoringly. She is like a queen to them, Paco thought. So beautiful, so pretty. He watched her ride away, and his pride swelled up in him. Yet he knew there was a sadness in her. There had been this little wall between them for some time. Not very big at first, but getting higher and higher with each year. The twinkle in her eye getting smaller and smaller each time they wintered in the house in the mountains. And this past year he had begun to notice the shadows in her eyes, the dark looks that she tried to smile away whenever he would come upon her unexpectedly, startle her. Whenever he asked her if there was anything wrong, she would shake her head, muster up that pretty smile, and say some little pleasantry so that he would not chase after her thoughts with his words. But the shadows would not go away fast enough for him to miss them, and the brave smiles did not fool him. He wished that he knew what would make her happy, happy all the time, as he was happy.

Women, Paco thought—he would never understand them. And this one, this Consuelita, she was the most baffling of all.

"Ah, Jorge!" he called, and rode to meet his foreman, check the tally sheets, give his farewells to his men.

"Did your woman leave you, *Patrón*?" joked Chavez.

"She did not want to see your ugly face, Jorge."

"I do not understand this," said Chavez. "Next to you, I am very handsome."

"You should see your face from this side," said Paco.

The men laughed, Jorge loudest of all. They were good men, and Paco paid them well for their loyalty.

Each year he gave them each a beef for their families, and they could pick their own out of the herd. They almost always took the culls.

"How many do we have?" Paco asked.

"Oh, many, many, *Patrón*," said Jorge. He handed Paco the tally sheets. "I can only make the marks. I cannot sum them up."

"There is nothing to that, Jorge," said Paco.

"Oh, and why is that?"

"You just count the legs and divide by four."

"Ah, yes. It is easy that way."

Paco toted up the marks, wrote down the figure. There were 478 cattle, including yearlings, bulls, cows, with no distinction in which was which. Later, he knew, Jorge would break down the herd for a better picture of what they might drive to market in the spring.

"Where do you go now, *Patrón*?" asked Jorge, when they were finished.

"My wife and I will go the river, stay at the fort for a few days. Then we will go to the mountains."

"Ah, you will not go to Santa Fe?"

"Not until the Nativity, perhaps."

"Do not worry. We have good men and good rifles," said Jorge.

"I will not worry, Jorge."

The men said good-bye to Paco, and he rode off to join Consuelo, feeling a little guilty. There was still much to do with the herd, but he wanted to make Consuelo happy. Perhaps they would have some fine cloth at the trading post, some beads and threads, pretty little baubles that would bring the bright twinkle back into her eyes.

Felipe Arias dozed in the back of the wagon. He stirred when Paco rode up to the line shack.

"Do not get up," said Paco. "Sleep. We will be a while changing our clothes."

"*Sí, Patrón*," said the sleep-sodden man, and closed his eyes, pulled the hat brim down over his face. He wore the big *sombrero*, the white clothes of the *peón*. He handled many of the household chores in the mountain house—a widower with a dozen children scattered over most of Chihuahua. It was said that he had killed his wife and fled to New Mexico because she would not stop having babies. He had worked with Paco's father and the sheep, but they did not want him anymore because he was always sleeping, so Paco brought him to the mountains.

Paco opened the door to the cabin, closed it softly. He slipped the latch and turned, adjusting his eyes to the dim light. The burlap curtains were pulled, and he had trouble seeing. "Consuelo?"

"I am here, my husband," she said.

He looked down. She lay on the bed, a lacy undergarment draping her naked body.

"*Ay de mi!*" he exclaimed in a rush of breath.

"Did you latch the door?"

"Yes."

"Then what are you waiting for?"

"For nothing," he said, and began stripping his clothes. He stumbled over a trunk as he made his way to the bed, and his toe pulsed with a throbbing pain that he ignored.

Consuelo tossed the flimsy garment aside, opened her arms. Paco swam into them, naked as she, and they embraced for a long moment, nestling their bodies against each other until they fit like spoons in a chest.

"I have been waiting for you," she whispered.

"I curse the moments I dawdled in getting here."

"Love me, Paco. Love me." There was that sadness in her voice that tugged at his heart.

"Yes, yes, Consuelo. I want you."

"I want you too, Paco." She clutched at him desperately

and lent her lips to him, pushed her face toward his. He kissed her and felt her sag in his arms, felt her crumple in silent willing surrender. He kissed her and felt her body jolt as if he had touched hot iron to her flesh. Her fingertips burrowed into his back, the nails stinging like thorns, digging in, digging in as she squirmed against him, against the hard bone of his manhood, as if trying to meld her flesh into his until they were one, one person, one soul.

He burned for her, burned with a smoldering fire that blotted out all reason. So passionate, he thought, so wild in his embrace, so eager, so—so desperate. And that was it, he knew. That desperation in her at these times when they made love. As if she were drowning and only he could bring her back to life, make her breathe again.

He tried to see her eyes, but they were closed. She seemed gripped by her own private demon, lost in him, lost to his touch, the pressure of his body against hers. She moaned, and her eyelashes fluttered. He broke the kiss and straddled her, and she pulled him to her. He sank into her, sank like a high wave into the sea, and there was the warmth and the sweetness of her, and the mystery, the eternal mystery that he could never fathom, never divine with his senses. She was the woman of dreams, the Eve of an ancient garden, the Sphinx brooding silently over the centuries—powerful, magnetic, hauntingly beautiful.

The seconds slid into minutes, minutes into hours, the hours danced away in timeless flight, and there was no time for them, no earthly time, just a floating timelessness where nothing mattered but that one explosive moment in eternity, that one rapturous second when time stood still and they touched the elusive magical presence of God, touched the god-spirit for just that one split second and felt the power and magnitude of the universe flood through them like a washing tide, numbing their senses, tingling their veins, blotting out all human reason.

After the dancing—the soaring, the high flight to the furthest reaches of the mind, to a place beyond imagination, beyond anything real or tangible.

And this time, thought Paco, this time was the sweetest and most mysterious of all. He cried out when he spun over the pinnacle of reason into the mindless ether of ecstasy. Consuelo cried out too, her fingernails digging into his back, and he knew it was sweet for her too, but he could not delve into her thoughts, could not measure the depth or breadth of her joy. She was at that moment both savage and insane, both child and woman, that was the mystery too, and he wished he could be inside her and feel what she felt.

He crumpled atop her, sated and weak, like a man washed ashore by the tide, a helpless creature floundering on an unknown shore.

She released her grip on him, and Paco rolled to her side, lay on his back, eyes closed, trying to recapture the one moment of splendor. But as always, it eluded him. It was gone, gone forever, and there was no recapturing it. It was gone and broken, shattered into a billion pieces, scattered back in the corners of that dark realm of the gods where man seldom ventured.

"It was good, my Paco," she breathed. "Very very good."

"Yes," he said, and felt her hand touch his flat belly. "It was very sweet." He closed his eyes and wondered if she would want him again. He reached out for her, groped the empty air.

The bed creaked, and he felt it give up some of its weight. He opened his eyes and saw her standing naked at the sideboard, pouring water from the pitcher into the bowl. A moment later, she squatted on the floor and made her ablutions with a hank of cloth, dipping it into the large bowl.

Paco breathed heavily and turned away. "I will get dressed," he said to himself.

Consuelo didn't answer. She stood up, opened a window, tossed out the water. Sunlight streamed through the opening, stunning Paco with its piercing glare. He blinked and threw up an arm to ward off the light.

But it was too late. He had already been blinded.

≈ 19 ≈

The madness, if that's what it was, seeped into Will
Burke again. He kept thinking about the gold lying up
there in the earth, along that stretch of Adobe Creek,
and he could not bear to spend the winter away from it.
Even though he knew that once he went back to his
cabin, he would be locked in by winter's snows and
unable to work his claim, he knew he must go back or
he would drink himself to death in Stonecipher's
fort.

But there was another reason he wanted to return to
the mountains, and this was harder to admit to himself.
Yet the reason was almost as strong as the lure of gold,
the thought equally maddening. Burke had fallen in
love with Sarah Reynolds. At least he believed he was
in love with her. He wanted her. Wanted her sometimes
so bad, he wanted to shout it at the top of his lungs.
But it was a love that was dying on the vine. A love that
lay in his heart unused, untested, unfulfilled.

Just yesterday he had seen Sarah come to the river
with two wooden buckets yoked over her shoulders,
alone. He wished her the top of the morning, and she
smiled at him. As she filled the buckets, he screwed up
the nerve to ask her something he'd wanted to for a
long while. He knew that she no longer shared Jake's

bed but slept in another room, alone. Granted, it was a room adjoining Jake's, but that was only a convenience, perhaps a pretense on Jake's part.

He had seen how Jake looked at her, his eyes dead as stone, empty of all feeling. That pained Burke, pained him because he saw the hurt in Sarah's eyes when Jake looked at her. Fleeting things that in his maddened state he recorded faithfully, as a drowning man will clutch at straws floating on deadly waters. "Would you come away with me if I asked you, Sarah?" he had said.

"Mr. Burke. Shame on you."

"I mean it, ma'am. I'd give you a home."

"Shush now, Mr. Burke," she had said. "I belong to Jake Stonecipher. You know that. Until he releases me, gives me my freedom, I will not dishonor him by listening to such talk. Good day."

She had lugged the water buckets back to the fort, leaving Burke standing there with cornmeal mush all over his face. He still felt the slap of her words as he made up his mind to leave the fort, return to the mountains. There was just too much torment here, from two directions. Maybe, he thought, I should just take her. Just grab her up and ride off with her, and to the devil with Jake Stonecipher.

But Burke knew he couldn't do that. Sarah would hate him for it. Jake would too. And a man couldn't have the woman he loved and his best friend in the world hating him, now could he?

Will packed up the next morning, donned his buckskins, tied his winter coat in the back of the saddle.

Sarah was nowhere to be seen when he said good-bye to Jake. "You're welcome to stay the winter," said Jake cordially.

"I know. I got to be by myself. The whiskey you make is too good."

Jake looked at the leaden sky. "Weather comin' in," he said.

"Yep. I figure to get up home before the next snow."

"That may be tonight."

"I'll chance it. Say good-bye to Sarah for me, will you, Jake?"

"She and Luz went over to the *pueblo* this mornin'. Luz's sister's moved up there from Taos, a pack of relatives she hasn't seen in a while."

"Too many folks crowdin' this old river."

"The more the merrier," said Jake, and Will knew he could never bring himself to ask his friend to give up Sarah. Not now. Not yet.

"Well, I took a likin' to Sarah," Will said lamely, ragging the bone in his teeth, reluctant to leave without leaving some message behind, dumb as it might be.

"Strange woman," said Jake. "Cold. Losin' the babe took all the spunk out of her, I reckon."

And Will knew it was hopeless. There was nothing so blind as a man who wouldn't see. Burke would bet gold against silver that it was the other way around. Losing the baby had taken all the starch out of Jake, or at least dowsed the fires in him that had burned for Sarah Reynolds.

"You watch out for them Ute, Jake," Will said, and mounted Rocky. "Winter nor snow don't slow 'em down none."

"I expect they'll leave us alone, so many folks movin' in upriver here."

"Don't count on it," said Will, and he dug heels into Rocky's flanks, took up the slack on the lead rope pulling his two Mexican mules. He rode through the open gate of the fort and did not look back. By the time he reached the Fountain, he had to put on his buffalo coat. The wind that blew down the canyon was from the

North, and it carried an ominous chill in its teeth, a gelid lash in the blustery whip of its tail.

Before the day was out, the second snow of the season had begun to fall. It was a thick, sticking snow, and Burke wondered if his madness might not cost him his life. It had certainly cost him his reason.

Luz and Sarah returned to Fort Stonecipher just as the first few flakes of snow began to fly out of the mountains like white feathers before the wind. They were laughing and giggling as they drove the small wagon through the gate. Snowflakes glistened on their shawls, melted on their noses.

Jake waved them in, stepped outside to look up into the mountains. The tops were shrouded in a ghostly mist. Only the foothills stood out, and they were fading as the snow thickened. He was about to close the gate when he saw another wagon coming in from the South, heading for the river ford. He squinted to make out who the people were, but they were too far away. Three of them, from the looks of it, and the driver was whipping the horse into a gallop.

Sarah stepped down from the wagon.

"I'll help you put the horse away, Luz," she said.

"I will do it, Sarah."

"I am excited."

"*Bueno, bueno.* It is good to see you happy."

It was true. There was a glow on Sarah's face. The wind had pinched color into her cheeks, but it was more than that, Luz knew. There was in Sarah's eyes a light that could shine only if there was a new man in her life.

"I—I'll go now," Sarah said.

"*Vaya,*" said Luz, with a guttural ripple of laughter. Sarah shook out her hair, loosened the sheepskin jacket she wore, and left the stables, light-footed as a deer. She went first to the cantina, peered inside. Two men looked up from a table, but the others were empty.

She nodded to the two Mexicans. "Have you seen Mister Burke?" she asked.

They shook their heads.

Sarah ran to Burke's quarters, but there was no answer to her knock. She looked everywhere, but there was no sign of the trapper. Finally she returned to the stables. Luz was currying the horse that had pulled the wagon. "I can't find Mr. Burke anywhere," said Sarah.

"*Se fue,*" said Luz.

"Gone?"

"His horse and his mules are not here."

"Oh, he can't have gone. It's starting to snow."

"Maybe he will be back," said Luz, but there wasn't the slightest trace of conviction in her voice.

"He can't leave," said Sarah. "Not now."

Luz turned the horse into a stall, closed the door. "You must not let Señor Jake see you like this, Sarah," she said.

"I don't care what Jake thinks anymore. He doesn't care about me."

"True, but . . ."

"I know," said Sarah. "I just thought . . . have a fandango . . ."

Luz clucked with her tongue. "It will still be much fun," she said. "Perhaps the *baile* will make Jake notice you. Go and tell him. I know he will be pleased."

"Yes, yes," said Sarah.

Luz had not seen Sarah this happy in a long time. While they had been visiting the *pueblo*, Luz's cousin asked if there was a place to dance. Luz told him about the big room Jake was building for just such events. It was not completed yet, but the rough flooring was down, and there was a roof over it and walls to keep out the wind and cold. José Peña, Luz's cousin, was a fine fiddler, and her brother Manuel played the guitar. Together they had planned a *baile*, and Sarah had offered to ask Jake if they could have one tomorrow.

"Go and tell Jake," said Luz now. "I am sure he will be happy at this news."

"Oh, I wish Mr. Burke were here," said Sarah.

"You must make the best of things," Luz told her.

Sarah kicked at a clump of straw as she left the stable.

Jake watched the wagon sway and rock as the driver negotiated the ford. As the wagon lurched up onto the bank, he heard footsteps behind him. Turning, he saw Sarah.

"Jake . . ." she said.

"Not now, Sarah. We've got visitors."

She stood beside him, saw the wagon coming toward the fort.

"Who are they?"

"I don't know. Strangers."

The two people in the back of the wagon did not wave. The snow was swirling faster now and starting to dust the earth with a patina of white flakes.

"Jake, where's Mr. Burke?" Sarah asked.

"He's gone," said Jake.

"Where?"

"Back into the mountains. Why?"

"I, uh, Luz was looking for him."

"What does she want?" asked Jake.

"There is to be a dance, if you approve. A fandango. Luz's cousins and brothers and sisters in the *pueblo* want to play for us."

"Why, that would be just fine," said Jake, looking out at the slow-moving wagon.

"When will Mr. Burke be back?" she asked.

Jake looked at her sharply. "In the spring, I suppose. Will comes and goes when he pleases. You know that. Why should Luz care about Burke?"

"I—I suppose that someone might be interested in dancing with him," she said.

"Burke probably don't dance," said Jake. "He just drinks."

Sarah backed away from Jake, stung by his comment. "That's cruel and unfair," she said.

"You stickin' up for Will Burke now?"

Confused, Sarah struggled to control her emotions. "Perhaps someone should," she said, and whirled away, the anger boiling up in her, washing through her senses like an angry fire.

Sarah raced across the *placita*, continued on past the blacksmith shop to the stables and beyond to the stock-yard at the back, an open area where the snow was thickening on the ground. Sheep blatted in the pens, and the hogs paced back and forth behind cottonwood rails. The cows stood at the feeder, chewing on hay. It was the only place Sarah could think of where she could be alone. She opened the back gate, let herself outside the fort. There no one could see her. She could look up at the mist-shrouded foothills, think of Will Burke somewhere beyond, heading for his lonely cabin.

She felt a surge of loneliness. A winter sadness crept into her consciousness as she saw the prairie whiten, the snow-dappled foothills fill with shadows, stippled only by the brush and trees that had not yet been shawled in ermine. She tried not to cry for herself. Burke would not like her to do that. Jake, in his blind smugness, would only smirk and reassign her to that corner of his mind where she was still Leaf Shadow, a dirty Shoshone squaw brought down out of the Wind River hunting grounds where she had been a slave.

Sarah tried to remember her family. Her mother, Marguerite Reynolds; her father, George; her sister, Annette; her brothers, Jim and Dean. They were only dim memories now, specters that she could scarcely recall, yet she remembered little things about them. Her mother quietly crocheting a quilt, sewing, bending over a pot hanging in the hearth. Her father, sitting on the wagon seat, so far away from her yet closer than he had ever been back on their farm in Pennsylvania—a silent brooding man with a pipe who seldom spoke. And freckle-faced Jim, tagging after his older brother, Dean, both of them teasing her, pulling her pigtails, chasing her with mud pies across a long-ago field of wheat stubble. But their faces were dim, all dim, and gone from her mind except in sudden flashes of light, in dreams, in the faces of others, Indian, white, and Mexican. Pieces of them only, fragments that she could never assemble into wholeness.

And she was changed too, she knew. Changed beyond recognition. She had no home, no family, no one to care for or to care for her. She was no longer a girl, yet she did not feel like a woman either. She felt empty inside now that the baby had emptied out her womb and her heart. Perhaps if the child had lived, she would be married and happy. Perhaps.

She had wanted Jake. Had loved him, she thought. When the baby was born dead, he had turned against her. He had killed whatever love she felt for him. And she had thought she could never love again. Until Burke. Burke stirred the dead ashes, kindled the tiny flame that was still flickering in her heart. But she had turned her back on him, afraid. Afraid of Jake, afraid of herself. Afraid of another disappointment perhaps.

She looked long into the clouds lowering on the foothills and wished she had the courage to take a horse and run after Burke, find him, and offer herself to him, as wife, cook, helper, or slave. But she did not know the way, and perhaps Burke had changed his mind about her. Perhaps he had been only teasing her.

No, she couldn't believe that. Burke was not that way. He drank because he was lonely, like her. He was a loner because he felt he was an outcast. Like her. Something in him had reached out to her, and she had spurned him. Now whatever he had opened up in her ached, and would always ache until he took her in his arms and kissed her and held her tight against him.

Sarah sobbed and doubled over with a nameless grief, an overwhelming sadness that dusted her like the snow and made her cold inside and afraid, more afraid than she had ever been.

"Sarah!" Luz hissed from the back gate.

Sarah turned around and dabbed clumsy chill fingers at her eyes, swiping at the tears that streamed her cheeks. "Oh, Luz, leave me alone."

"You should not be out here like this. You will catch the cold and be sick. Come, come. There is a beautiful lady come to the fort with her husband. They look like *ricos*, and Jake is acting like a stupid."

"What are you saying?" asked Sarah.

"We have guests, and I think Jake has the eye for this beautiful Mexican woman. I can tell. A woman can tell."

"Oh, Luz, that's nonsense. Jake just cares about himself and his little kingdom."

"No, no, this one is different. Come see, come see!"

Sarah shook herself, pawed at her face. Her eyes would be red and puffy, she thought, but it didn't matter. No one cared how she looked. Only Burke, perhaps, and he was gone.

She walked back to the gate, which Luz held open for her. She entered the stockyard, and Luz closed and locked the gate.

A sudden gust of wind blew snow down the back of her neck. She shivered and followed Luz into the fort to see this lady who had come out of nowhere and caught Jake's eye.

≈ 20 ≈

Jake waved the wagon into the fort, closed the gates. The wagon groaned as it came to a stop. The man in the back jumped down, helped the lady, who was delicate and graceful. Jake could not see her face because she wore a hooded jacket.

"Welcome," said Jake. "Your driver can take the wagon back to the stables after he unloads your belongin's."

"Thank you, señor. I am Paco Serrano, and this is my wife, Consuelo."

Consuelo pushed her hood back, and Jake's mouth dropped open. He stared at her dark eyes, her oval face, the smooth olive skin, her sleek dark hair; he drank in her beauty. Her radiant smile froze him in his tracks.

Luz came up then, spoke to them in Spanish. A million questions in the space of a few seconds, Jake thought, but he didn't care. He could not take his eyes off Consuelo Serrano.

"Jake, they are cold and hungry," said Luz quietly.

"Oh, yes. Would you like a drink, Serrano? I have heard of you."

"And I have heard of you, if you are Jake Stonecipher."

"I am. A drink, some food? Would your wife . . . ?"

"The same," said Paco. "We have just come a long way, and we are a little cold."

"Luz, will you fix some food? Where is Sarah? I'll take the Serranos to the cantina for a drink."

"She is in her room, I think. I will get Sarah. *Momentito,*" she said to Consuelo.

When Luz was gone, Jake spoke again. "I'm right glad you came, ma'am."

"Thank you, señor," she said.

Jake's heart pumped hard in his chest. Her voice was low and soft, and thrummed in his ears like a plaintive chord struck on a guitar. "We'll put you up in our best room," Jake said to Paco. "You goin' to stay awhile?"

"Perhaps," said Paco. "We have heard much about your fort and the new *pueblo.*"

"Good, good," said Jake, and led them to the cantina.

Miguel Espinoza was tending bar. One of the newcomers to the *pueblo,* he cleaned the stables, tended to the stock during the day. In the evenings, he served patrons in the cantina. Sometimes he brought his guitar and would sing when there were few patrons.

Jake waved the Serranos to a table, pulled a chair out for Consuelo, who smiled graciously. "What would you like?" Jake asked. "We've got good whiskey, beer, *mezcal,* tequila."

"Tequila," said Paco. "Consuelo?"

"Do you have wine?" she asked.

"We got some Taos *aguardiente,*" he said. "Miguel can water it down some."

"I will have the brandy and some water," she said, slipping out of her hooded coat. It was warm in the room, although there was no fire. She shook out her hair as Jake gazed rapturously at her. She wore a red and yellow calico dress, and there was a green velvet ribbon in her black hair.

"Miguel," said Jake, "tequila, *aguardiente*, water, and a whiskey for me."

"You're most kind," said Consuelo, and she batted her lashes at Jake. He felt the fire of her, the undercurrent of sensuality in her voice, the wild bold look in her eyes searching him, raking him with a frank stare.

"Think nothin' of it," he said, trying to break the rapture he felt in Consuelo's presence.

Paco cleared his throat.

"So, what brings you folks to Fort Stonecipher?" asked Jake when Miguel had served the drinks. Even Jake had been calling his trading post a fort so long that it was now a habit.

"Do you know a man named Will Burke?" asked Paco.

"I know him," said Jake.

"He is a trespasser on my property," said Paco.

"Paco, please," said Consuelo. "Not now. We are Señor Stonecipher's guests."

"Call me Jake. It's all right. We can talk about Burke and that land up there you claim."

"Burke, he says that you sold him that land."

"I did," said Stonecipher.

"But it is not yours to sell. I have the cattle, and that is the prime grassland. I do not want him there."

"Paco, this is not the time," said Consuelo in a vain effort to dissuade her husband from irritating their host.

Paco ignored her.

"Well, I laid claim to that property, Serrano," said Jake, a hard look settling in his eyes. "And I sold Burke three acres. Surely, that ain't much."

"The land was not yours to sell, señor."

"I assure you, Serrano, the land was mine to sell. I got the documents to prove it."

"So have I," said Serrano, patting his coat.

"Could we not talk about this a little later?" asked Consuelo.

This time, Jake turned his gaze to her. Paco Serrano was getting under his skin like an itch, and he didn't like it. "I think we should," said Jake. "I will show you my papers, and you show me yours."

"That is good," said Paco. He sipped the tequila. Consuelo mixed water with her brandy. Jake watched her every move, drank a healthy draft of the whisky in his glass. It burned all the way down. He looked at Miguel behind the bar. Miguel shrugged.

"You have built a nice fort," said Consuelo. "There are many people here now."

For the next several moments, the three chatted idly and safely about the changes along the upper Arkansas.

They were interrupted when Sarah entered the cantina. "You wanted to see me?" she asked Jake.

"Oh, yeah. Help Luz fix some supper for us, will you?"

Sarah looked long and hard at Consuelo Serrano, then at her husband. The Mexican woman returned her stare, and Paco seemed to look right through her.

"I will," said Sarah, and turned on her heel. She stamped out of the cantina into the snow-flocked *placita*.

"She appears angry," said Paco. "Is she your wife?"

"No, she ain't," said Jake gruffly. "Just a woman who works for me."

Consuelo said nothing, but she looked at Jake with renewed interest. And when he looked at her again, her eyelashes fluttered like miniature Spanish fans.

Burke fought against the blindness, the wind, the blowing snow that billowed down the river canyon with jarring force. The buckskin, Rocky, struggled against the hard wind, strained with every step along the trail. The mules pulled hard on the lead rope, trying to stop, turn their rumps to the withering wind. There was not a dozen feet of visibility now, and the landmarks blotted out; only the river, dark and surging, whitecapped, boiling, told Burke where he was, and the climbing hard now, the cold gnashing its teeth on his face, burrowing into his coat, numbing his fingers.

"Jasus!" he cursed, and wondered what kind of fool he was to ride into the mountains, into the teeth of such a storm. For it was far worse up in the hills, that storm, raging with albino demons, screeching like a banshee down the canyon, swirling clouds of white dust in front of him like flour in a twister.

"Got to find shelter," he growled, just to hear his voice, just to see if he could still speak. But he knew what he said was true. He had not come to the first creek yet, and the sky was darkening with each moment. There wasn't a chance that he could reach his cabin in the dark.

Will tried in vain to see just where he was. The river on his right, a white wall on his left. He was as blind as if he had no eyes. Almost.

He shuddered with the chill. It would be dangerous to leave the trail unless he knew he would find shelter. But he began to drift to his left, holding his bearings, steeling himself to remember to keep the river at his back. Rocky stumbled just off the trail and Burke wondered if he had made the right decision.

Once off the trail, the trees held the wind back, and Burke found he could see farther ahead. The snow was drifting quickly, however, and Rocky floundered more than once. He had to wait for the mules to walk around obstacles. The day darkened, and the snowfall thickened before he found a place out of the wind, a clear spot among a stand of spruce and juniper. There the ground was dusted, but the snow wasn't deep. There was some protection from the brutal lash of wind. Here he would build his overnight shelter.

Burke tethered the mules, roped Rocky to the base of a juniper with plenty of room to move. He unloaded the packs, stored them under a spruce. There was not much light left as he began to hack the lower branches of a spruce for a windbreak. He piled the branches up under a spruce where he would lay his bedroll. Satisfied, he found a clean patch for a fire. He cut spruce boughs and placed them over the bare spot so that the snow wouldn't cover it. He roamed within a few yards of the temporary shelter, gathering squaw wood from the pines for kindling. He found a downed pine and chopped firewood from its dead trunk. On his third trip to camp, he began to shiver. By the fourth trip, his teeth were chattering.

It took him a good hour to carry the firewood. By then, he had beaten a path to his shelter. The snow continued to fall, flocking the spruces until their branches sagged under the weight. He thought then that he was not far from the creek, but he dared not try to find it. By the time he had finished carrying firewood, it was pitch-dark. He grained the horse and mules but took no food for himself. Instead, he crawled into his blankets, pulled a heavy buffalo robe over him, and doubled up to regain the heat he had lost. He was so cold, he didn't even take off his moccasins.

He knew it was dangerous to get so cold, but he knew he would need a fire in the morning, and he didn't want to have to dig through four feet of snow to find wood. Satisfied, he closed his eyes, felt the warmth of his blankets and the robe seep into his chilled bones. Will slept after a time, snug and warm in his blankets, the silence of the snowfall soothing as soft rain on a grass roof.

*   *   *

The horse's scream awakened him. Then the mules brayed in terror, and Will fought his way up from the dream, struggled through layers of darkness to find his senses. He heard then the snarl of a puma, the thumps of hooves striking wood and flesh. The racket made his flesh crawl. Rocky screamed again, and Will scrambled to throw off his blankets, kicking and lashing out with his arms to hurl the weight from his body. It was so dark he could see nothing, but he drew his knife and approached the noise, crouching. The snow had deepened, and the footing was slick, treacherous. Dark shapes appeared in the white veil of falling snow. But he could not make out which was horse, mule, or cougar.

One of the mules was down. Something dark clung to its neck. When Will drew near, straining to see in the darkness, the cat snarled at him. Will yelled and charged toward the panther.

Then before he knew what had happened, the dark shape detached itself from the mule's neck, hurtled through the air toward him. He felt the heat of its foul breath on his face, winced as talons sank through his buckskins, raked his shoulders. The cat brought up its rear feet and tried to disembowel him as he fell. Burke hit the ground hard. Shock jarred his spine, shook his brain. Sparks danced like fireflies in his blind eyes.

He rolled, struggling frantically to get away from the slashing claws of the cat. The cougar snarled in his ear, rolled with him, holding on to Will's shoulders with a searing grip. The cat tried to bite Burke's head, but he shook free of its jaws.

The cougar's hot stinking breath suffocated him as he tried to break free. The cat's body seemed to writhe just out of reach of the knife, snapping back and forth as it tried once again to disembowel the trapper. Rocks rattled and sticks crackled as man and cougar fought each other, rolled back and forth across snowy ground.

Will bent his knees, got his feet back under him, and lurched upward. The cat screeched as it fell on its back. Will pounced on the animal, slashing blindly in the dark, smashing his knife into its side, ripping, tearing.

He smelled the stench of the cat's bowels, felt it bunch up and bring those terrible hind feet up once again to tear him apart. He rolled again and found the cat's throat with his left hand.

He squeezed the animal's windpipe and drove the knife into its back, drove it deep. He felt the blade slide across bone, cut through cartilage and flesh.

He stabbed again and again until his arm ached.

Will's breath burned in his lungs. He rolled in the snow but felt no cold. He hammered at the cat's head with the knife, kept gripping its throat.

The puma seemed unwilling to die. Blood dripped from its head and down to its neck. Will felt his grip on its neck loosening. The cat released its claws from Will's shoulders as the trapper's hand slipped from the animal's neck.

Burke lashed out with the knife, drove the knife deep under the cat's left armpit. He twisted the knife as it sank through the rib cage. The cougar lunged, jerking the knife from Will's grip, then collapsed. In the dark, Will could hear the cougar's terrible breathing, its long sobbing gasps for air, the rasps in its throat.

Exhausted, he sat there, his hands slick with blood, his buckskins covered with mud and snow, listening to the dying cougar. The downed mule bleated softly in its agony. The horse kept trying to break its tether, bolt away. The other mule was strangely silent.

Finally there were no more sounds from the cat. Will, his chest heaving, his breath no longer burning his lungs, crawled over to the dead animal. He felt its back, moved a hand to its armpit. He felt the blood-wet handle of his knife, eased it free. The cat was stone dead, lying still as a rolled-up rug in the snow.

Burke's shoulders burned with a needling fire where the cat's claws had dug into his flesh. He felt himself all over, discovered no broken bones. Slowly he got to his feet, swayed there, light-headed and giddy as the snow fell in a steady curtain. He staggered over to the downed mule. The mule quivered when he touched its rump, and he knew he would have to kill it when it turned light. He had no feeling in his hands; they felt as if the muscles had been ripped out and replaced by wet pudding. He could not get a firm grip on his knife. His breathing made a sound like a blacksmith's bellows, and he heard the rub of the ropes on the trees as horse and mule paced and jumped to escape the smell of the dead cougar.

Somehow, Will made it to his shelter, crawled back under the blankets, the buffalo robe. He could still smell the cat's breath on his face, feel its claws knifing into his shoulders, its feet digging at his belly. His horse whickered loudly and snorted. The still-standing mule brayed in reply. Burke began to shake as feeling returned to his hands. He laid the bloody knife beside his head and closed his eyes. When the shaking stopped, he fell asleep.

When he woke in the morning, Will discovered that his leggings were in shreds and there were deep gouges in his legs. His shoulders felt like raw meat churned up in a grinder. It was still snowing. He crawled out of his bedroll, shook off six inches of fresh snow, and grabbed his rifle.

He limped over to the downed mule. It was shivering in the cold, and blood seeped from gashes in its back and stomach. Will saw teethmarks in its exposed spine and knew that its spinal cord had been severed by the cougar's teeth. He looked into the sad brown eyes and cocked the hammer on his rifle. He poured fresh fine powder into the pan, blew on it, and closed the frizzen.

He took aim at the mule's brain and squeezed the trigger. Blowback stung his face as the rifle bucked against his shoulder. He saw the mule twitch before the white smoke blotted out those haunting eyes.

The horse and remaining mule jerked when the shot went off and strained against their ropes.

With trembling cold fingers, Will reloaded his rifle and walked over to the dead cougar. He kicked the snow from its hulk, turned it over. He knelt down by its head, lifted it. He pried open the jaws, looked at the cat's teeth. They were blunted, old, and some were missing. The cat's whiskers were gray and frozen, and there were gray hairs above its eyes. Its coat was moth-eaten, frazzled, blotched now with dried and frozen blood.

"Hardly enough of ye left to skin," he muttered, and dropped the head back in the snow.

The snow had drifted deep beyond the glade where he had made his camp, and it was still falling. Burke knew that he would have to tend to his wounds or he was in danger of gangrene setting in.

He built a fire, striking sparks off the steel with his flint, blowing on the thin tendrils of the squaw wood until it caught. Slowly he built up the fire. When it was blazing on its own, he grained the horse and mule, washed his wounds with snow.

Then he washed his knife, stuck it in the fire. Gritting his teeth, he put the hot blade to his shoulder wounds first, seared them shut. Then he tended to the clawed gouges on his legs. He screamed with the pain of the hot blade, and tears coursed down his ruddy cheeks.

Finally, after he had rested, he made coffee. He threw all of it back up.

It was late in the afternoon, after he had skinned the cat and removed its claws, that he could take coffee and get food in his stomach. When he was through, he saddled Rocky and packed the mule. He cached the rest of his goods under the spruce where he had made his shelter.

He had to get away from that place, that place of death. When Will mounted Rocky, he felt the strength drain from him. It was still daylight, but he knew he could not go far. He was still sick from his wounds, his stomach tipsy as a cork bobbing in brine. It was all he could do to keep the food and coffee down. But he had to get away, find another place to hole up until his body healed and the snow stopped.

He slumped in the saddle, let his horse find its way. Rocky lurched through the snow, heading for high ground, heading, Burke hoped, for his cabin by the creek. The wind had died down, but the snow still fell relentlessly. Burke knew he was in for a long hard winter.

As he dozed in the saddle, he wondered again why he had come back to the mountains at such a time. He could be back at the fort, drinking with Jake, looking at Sarah. No, that would have been hell too. This was the way, the only way, he could get over her. Live or die, the mountains were his home. One day, he knew, they would be his grave.

≈ 21 ≈

People from the *pueblo* began streaming into the fort early in the afternoon of the night they were to enjoy the fandango at Fort Stonecipher. The Mexican women came, smoking their *cigarillos*, the men laughing and talking, strutting in their cleanest clothes. The Americans came too, from far and wide, notified by runners from the fort and the *pueblo* bringing their playing cards and rum, pieces of gold and silver minted by various countries. The Americans wore buckskins and buffalo coats, carried as always their rifles and knives and 'hawks.

Jake was surprised at the throngs who braved the wintry weather, and when the fort was full, the visitors pulled their wagons in a circle outside and made shelters for themselves, hanging buffalo robes and blankets from the side panels, weighting them down with stones gathered from the river's banks.

The cantina filled up, and the men played euchre and poker, drank Taos whiskey and the beverage dubbed Jake's Folly, somewhat weaker and not so poisonous as the Taos variety of distilled spirits. The women set up tables inside the fort where they displayed their candy, cakes, wine, and cloth goods they had made.

"Where do all the people come from?" marveled Consuelo.

"More'n I ever seen all at once out here," said Jake, beaming.

Paco Serrano was amazed too. "There are so many," he said over and over as the people streamed in, all welcomed by Luz and Sarah, who also kept the cookfires burning, helped direct the visitors to rooms and the cantina. The fort filled with the rich scents of meat and beans cooking in a dozen stalls. The tangy aroma of corn tortillas and roast chicken, venison, and elk wafted through the rooms and out into the *placita*. As the day wore on, bleak and overcast, the snow stopped after leaving the prairie ermined with a more than foot-deep blanket.

"This is what I always dreamed of," said Jake, his eyes glittering.

"You are so young to have such big dreams," said Consuelo, a frank look of admiration on her face.

Jake smiled.

"I too have had the dreams," said Paco. "Do you not remember, Consuelo?" Serrano had not missed the American trader's attention to his wife since they had arrived at the fort. At first he was flattered, but the faintest annoyance had begun to creep under his skin as he noticed that Consuelo seemed to enjoy Jake's company. He had wanted to leave the fort as soon as it had stopped snowing, but Consuelo would not hear of it. She wished to dance, and he had agreed to stay until after the fandango. In fact, he looked forward to some enjoyment, and it would be pleasurable to do the *baile* with his wife once again. Perhaps that would keep her satisfied when they returned to the mountains.

Jake shook hands with the American visitors who had settled in the valley of the upper Arkansas. There were Dick Wooten and Alexander Barclay, Dick Owens and

John Burroughs, the latter two crippled after an en-
counter with a grizzly that had attacked them not far
from the *pueblo*.

As Dick Wooten had told it to Jake, Owens and
Burroughs were hunting, and a giant silver-tip grizzly
rose up out of the brush and charged them. Both men
fired their rifles, but they were so rattled, they missed.
With hair standing on end, they both scrambled for the
nearest tree, a squat juniper. Owens climbed to the top
of the tree, Burroughs right behind him. Burroughs
had put one foot on a lower branch and started to haul
himself skyward when the grizzly grabbed him by the
foot and dragged him down. Burroughs lay there playing
dead while the bear mauled him with raking paws,
snarling and whistling like a prairie dog. The bear,
thinking him dead, went after Owens. Owens kicked
and yelled, slashed at the grizzly with his knife.
Burroughs, badly wounded, crawled to his rifle, and
reloaded it with shaking hands as the bear clawed
Owens half to death. Burroughs brought the rifle to his
shoulder and shot the bear dead, but they both would
limp for the rest of their lives.

There were Calvin Briggs, Marcelino Baca, and Bill
Williams, all trappers, all with hair-raising tales of
encounters with grizzlies. Thomas Farnham, who fished
the river almost every day for catfish and speckled trout
was there too. Charles Autobees rode in from his ranch,
bringing his family, and Jake found a room for them
inside the fort. The mountain men brought beaver pelts
for the card games.

"This ain't goin' to be no one-night fandango, Jake,"
said Bill Williams. "The best 'uns last for three, four
days."

"We'll run it till it drops," said Jake, beaming. He
had made friends on the Arkansas. He wished Joe
Perkins could have been there to enjoy the frolic.

Jake learned some of the names of the new settlements—
Bussard's Roost, Mormontown, Metcalf's and Black-
hawk's—and still the people came, creating a small city
outside the fort, cramming it to the walls inside.

Trappers from the Bayou Salade, staying in the *pueblo*
over the winter, rode in, old friends of Jake's. Jim
Karns, a burly bearded Missourian, brought his Crow
wife, Red Wing, followed by Drew Ballentine, "White
Buffalo," with hair over his shoulders but a bright bald
spot where the Cheyenne and Lakota liked to cut out
an enemy's scalplock. Jake said hello to Bob "Bloody
Hand" Andersen, one of the same wild bunch, and J.
R. Asterwold; big Mike Finnegan, called "Bigun" for
good reason; Jaques "Three Eyes" Arnot; "Pappy" Roth;
"Stick" Wyatt; Wayne "Hawk" Blevins; and "Six Thumbs"
Johnston. They pitched their lean-tos in back of the
fort, bought three jugs of Jake's whiskey, and plopped
down in a row along the side of the dance floor to drink
and watch the festivities.

Some of the women carried small babies, and there
were gray-haired grandmothers who streamed into the
dance hall, puffing on pipes or chewing toothlessly on
candy. At nine in the evening, the musicians strolled in,
took their places at one end of the room. Sarah and Luz
had put benches along one wall, draped them with
thick buffalo robes to make couches. Many of the
women sat there, the men on the other side of the
room. Some of the women rolled *cigarillos* and chatted
merrily in Spanish, eyeing the odd assortment of men
across the wooden floor. Many of them wore white
camisas, blouses that revealed comely shoulders, and
brightly colored *enaguas*, the short full skirts that twirled
when they danced and revealed their legs and ankles.
The Mexican girls were freshly powdered and wore
strong perfume. Their wrists glittered with gold and

silver ornaments, their ears dangled with large round rings, and one or two wore cloth flowers in their hair.

When the musicians struck up the melody for the first dance, a row of men stepped onto the dance floor and began clapping to the music. The ladies rose from their seats and waited to be chosen. The men took their partners and danced in wide circles, their feet making the boards hum with the intricate steps of the fandango.

Jake stood on the sidelines, watching in fascination.

Sarah and Luz watched from the other side of the room. "I wish José was here," Luz said sadly.

"I'm sorry. You miss him, don't you."

"Much. I miss him much."

"Will you dance?"

"No," said Luz. "Not without my man."

Some of the trappers rose and joined in, dancing with each other, laughing, doing odd steps that were part war dance, part Irish jig. Many of the other dancers laughed.

One of the Mexican musicians began to sing, and some of the Mexican women murmured the words as they glided gracefully around the floor. It was then that Sarah noticed Jake watching Paco and Consuelo, who danced at the far end of the room. Paco was very good, and Consuelo followed his every step with grace and ease.

Jake's eyes glistened in the glow of lamps. He licked his lips. Sarah turned away, a fluttering in her stomach like a sudden swarm of bees. Luz noticed Sarah's movement, then looked across at Jake, whose eyes were fixed on Consuelo. Only on Consuelo now.

After several fast dances, including *el jarabe*, where the men threw their big *sombreros* on the floor and danced their partners around them in wild abandon, the band played a slow waltz. Paco held Consuelo close, but she was not looking at him.

Sarah caught the look between Jake and Consuelo. So did Luz, who said nothing. "He is going to dance with her," muttered Sarah.

"What?" asked Luz.

"Jake. He's going to dance with that Mexican woman after this one."

"How do you know?"

"Look at them," said Sarah bitterly.

When the music ended and the men and women separated, Jake stepped onto the dance floor. Paco Serrano went to the table where the drinks were being served and held up his cup. He did not notice that Jake was looking at Consuelo and she at him.

"It is as you say, Sarah," said Luz.

Jake nodded to the musicians, and they struck up a chord. Before Paco could finish his drink, the dance began. He wiped his mouth, turned, and strode toward his wife. He did not notice the American trader stalking the same prize from another side.

Jake chose Consuelo as his partner, brushing her husband aside as he took her in his arms. Sarah watched as Jake swirled around the dance floor, slightly out of step, Consuelo following him as if he had been doing the fandango all his life. The orchestra played "La Cuna," the cradle, for the sixth time, for their repertoire was limited. The small band of musicians played loudly with triangles, mandolins, guitars, violins, *tombes* (the small Indian drums), and a cornet, brassy and sweet.

The two dancers, Jake and Consuelo, seemed oblivious to the others on the dance floor, locked into the music, the look in Consuelo's eyes as intent as Jake's. Sarah felt a squeezing of her heart as she watched the pair sweep past her. She had never received such a look from Jake. She felt cheated. Although Jake was not a very good dancer, it did not seem to matter to Consuelo.

She followed his every movement, so that they appeared
as one person. When he stumbled, she laughed, and he
laughed with her. And again something wrenched Sarah's
heart. She felt tears well up in her eyes. Paco looked
over at her, and she turned away. There was a hard look
on the Mexican's face as he watched his wife dance with
Jake Stonecipher.

When the *baile* was over, Jake and Consuelo were
still holding onto each other, swaying gently even though
the orchestra was silent. They looked into each other's
eyes for a long moment. Finally, Consuelo laughed and
started toward her husband. Jake followed after her like
a puppy. Sarah saw Paco take his wife's arm and lead
her onto the dance floor as the orchestra stuck up the
strains of "El Italino," a lively tune with a strong beat.

Sarah walked over to Jake. "Are you going to ask me
to dance?" she asked him.

"Well, I don't know. I didn't know you knew how to
dance."

"Maybe I can. Maybe I can dance as well as Consuelo
Serrano."

"I guess I can dance with you," Jake said, a sullen
tone in his voice.

Jake put his hand on Sarah's waist, held her other
hand up high, and they twirled onto the floor. She
looked up into Jake's face, but he was looking at Consuelo,
who spun expertly in her husband's loose embrace
several feet away.

Again Sarah felt the sting of tears in her eyes. "I
didn't know you were the kind of man who chased after
other men's wives," Sarah said.

"What?" asked Jake.

"I'm talking about Consuelo Serrano."

"Hell, I just danced with her. I'm not chasin' after
anything."

"You never looked at me that way, Jake," said Sarah.

His jaw hardened. "Well, maybe I didn't," he said.

"What's wrong? Don't I please you anymore?"

"Not rightly," he said.

"Have I done something to displease you?" she asked.

"Maybe. I don't want to talk about it," said Jake.

"It's my past, isn't it. You can't get it out of your mind that I was a captive of the Shoshone."

"That's some of it," he said tightly.

"Do you remember what I told you, what they did to me?" she asked.

"I don't want to hear no more about it."

"Well, maybe you ought to hear it again," she said. "I was twelve years old. They took me into one of their lodges. And the braves, old and young, they kept coming, one after the other. And I screamed and screamed, but they wouldn't stop."

"Shut up, Sarah. I don't want to hear this again. Not here. Not now."

"They raped me," she said. "Remember? They raped me over and over until I was bleeding and sore, sick inside. And I hated myself for it. I thought it was my fault."

Jake choked and spluttered. "I—I . . ."

"I didn't tell you all of it before, Jake. I was too ashamed. But you can't stop thinking about it. Every time you look at me, I can see that you want to know all of it. Well, you're going to hear it. They didn't stop. They did it to me in the mouth, they did it to me in my backside. Sometimes two at a time, sometimes three, I just can't remember. I thought I was in hell."

"Damnit, Sarah, I don't want to hear this."

"It happened to me," she said. "And I blame myself. But I thought it would be different with you. I thought you would respect me and come to love me as I love you."

"Sarah, I can't—can't talk about this."

Suddenly he pushed her away. She reached out for him, but he stalked off the dance floor and out of the room. Sarah stood there for a moment, then broke down, the tears coming unbidden—hot, fast, stinging. And she collapsed there on the dance floor.

Luz saw the stricken woman and rushed to her. She lifted her from the floor and led her away from the gawking dancers and spectators. "Don't cry, don't cry," said Luz, over and over.

Sarah couldn't answer. She could only sob and feel her heart squeezed so hard it hurt.

"Do you love that man?" asked Luz.

"I don't know," said Sarah.

"I will take you to your room."

"Yes, yes. I don't know, Luz. I don't know if I love Jake anymore or not."

The two women walked through the shadowy fort to the cold *placita*, swept free of snow, patches still clinging to the support posts. In Sarah's room, Luz lit a lamp.

"I just don't know anymore," sobbed Sarah. "I thought I loved Jake."

"Perhaps it is another that you love," said Luz.

"Oh, Luz, I just don't know. I don't know if anybody could ever love me. Not after what I have done."

"What have you done, my child?"

"The Shoshone," said Sarah.

"That was not your fault."

"Jake thinks it is."

"What about Will Burke?" asked Luz. "Would he feel the same as Jake?"

"I don't know. Would he?"

"I do not think he would," said the Mexican woman. "I think he is a better man than Jake Stonecipher."

"*Oh?*" Sarah unrolled her buffalo-robe bed and stood there like a woman in deep shock.

"Jake Stonecipher is a man who thinks only of himself," said Luz angrily, "and only of the goods he sells. I think something has happened to him. I think he has turned cold as stone."

"I can't talk about him," said Sarah. "I can't talk about Mr. Burke, either. Leave me alone."

"It pains me to see you weep so," said Luz. "And over a man who does not see you. There will be much trouble, I think. Over Consuelo Serrano. Much trouble."

"Please leave me, Luz. Please." Sarah sank down on the buffalo robe, looked at Luz, and began dabbing at her eyes. "If Mr. Burke ever comes back here, I'm going to ask him if he still wants me."

"What? Did he ask you to go away with him?"

"Maybe."

"Do you want to now?"

"Yes, I want to now. I want him to put his arms around me and hold me. And I don't ever want to remember the Shoshone again and what they did to me."

"Well, that is a good sign," said Luz. "Maybe Will Burke will ask you to go away with him. And if you go away with him, maybe it will be that way. I will leave you now, Sarah, and we will see what happens between Jake Stonecipher and this Mexican woman who is married."

Luz left the room and closed the door softly. Sarah threw herself full length on the buffalo robe, drew her legs up toward her chest, and curled into a ball.

Then she began to weep again as the lamplight played on her shining hair, made the shadows move like strange figures dancing to the muffled faraway music.

≈ 22 ≈

The Muache Ute rode through the snowfall like ghost shadows. Their packhorses were heavily laden with the meat of elk and deer, their hunting mounts skittery in the pale light of afternoon with the death-smell in their quivering nostrils. Their shoeless hooves made little sound in the deep snow as they picked their way through the drifts along the traces of a trail made hours before by a lone horse and a packmule.

The Ute, formless creatures in buffalo coats and leggings, had come across the trail by accident. They had lingered long in the mountains hunting game, and they longed for the warmth of the lodges along the river of the moonshell, what the white-eyes called the Platte, where Blanco waited. But the trail was too odd not to follow. One of the braves, Antler, had blown away the snow from one of the deep tracks and had seen the marks of iron. A white-eyes had made this trail earlier that morning, and no one had wanted to follow in the direction he was going, but they were curious about where he had been. They knew of the white settlements on the Arkansas and the Fountain, of course, but they were surprised that a white-eyes would come into the mountains when the Old Man of Winter was blowing snow onto the earth.

When they came upon the camp of the white-eyes, Antler rode up carefully, the smell of dead animals strong in his nostrils. His horse sidled sideways, eyes flared in fear, nose twitching. The other braves waited, speaking no words, watching. There were two mounds, and all could see the cut branches of the spruce, the place where a white man had been during the night.

Antler dismounted and brushed snow away from the small carcass. He drew back in wonder, made sign with his hands. The other braves dismounted and came over as Antler was dragging the carcass out of its frozen position. Others went to the mule and scraped snow from its dead hide.

"This one," said Antler. "He has strong medicine."

He stood up, looked at the others.

Buffalo Head nodded. Makes Rope nodded too. And so did the others—Many Elk, Two Bones, and Walking Crow.

"This white-eyes took away the spirits of our brothers in the season of the fort by the river," said Antler.

The others grunted. They remembered finding the bones of their brothers, the tracks to the cabin. They remembered with sadness.

"Walking Crow," said Antler, "make us fire."

"What will we do?" asked Makes Rope.

"We will eat the meat of this puma," said Antler. "It will make us strong like the white-eyes who sent its spirit to the sky."

"Yes, yes," said the others, and they gathered squaw wood for Walking Crow, and some helped Antler cut up the meat of the cougar. Antler cut out the heart and the liver and made offerings to the Spirit Ones, said the prayers and scattered sunflower pollen on the snow.

The Ute ate the cooked flesh of the puma and

squatted silently in the circle among the trees as the snow fell among them.

"Why did the white-eyes not take the mule meat with him?" asked Buffalo Head.

"I do not know," said Antler.

"It is his medicine," said Walking Crow. "He took the hide of the puma. He took the claws."

"The puma was very old," said Antler. "It killed the mule and the white-eyes killed the puma."

"The white-eyes killed with the knife," said Walking Crow. "He took the claws. Maybe the white-eyes can change like Coyote."

"That is very strange," said Buffalo Head. "Maybe that is how he killed our brothers. Maybe he was the wolf, the puma, the running deer."

The others huddled in their coats and chewed on the puma meat. They did not sit close to the cooking fire, nor did they look into its blinding flames. They listened to the soft sigh of the wind and heard the tink of snow on pine branches. Beyond, they heard the trickle music of the creek, the little sobbing songs of water brushing against the banks.

"Only one with strong medicine would come to the tall land in winter," said Antler.

"Maybe the puma was a spirit when it came upon the mule," said Walking Crow. "Maybe the puma was a brother come to take life from the white-eyes."

"Do not speak of such things," said Antler.

"You are right," said Walking Crow. "We must speak to Blanco. He will know what this means."

"The meat is tough and does not taste good," said Makes Rope. "I do not like it."

"If we eat what this white-eyes has killed, we will have some of his medicine," said Antler.

"That is good," said Buffalo Head, and ground his teeth down on the tough meat.

The hunters did not talk anymore, but they listened and touched their bows and their rifles now and then, ran greasy fingers over their tomahawks and the butts of their knives. They heard all the sounds beneath the sounds and the sounds inside the sounds and wondered about the white man who had killed the cougar with a knife and had taken its hide for his medicine talk when he was in his lodge. They knew they had found a strange thing, and they wondered why they had been drawn to this place of death and emptiness where the snows did not fall so thick and the dead mule had a bullet hole in its skull and claw- and teethmarks on its hide.

"We will tell Blanco what we have seen," said Antler when they were finished eating. "We will ask him what we must do about this white-eyes."

"All of them," said Buffalo Head solemnly. "All of the white-eyes."

"Yes, yes," grunted the others.

The Ute dressed out the mule and quartered its meat, packed it on their horses. They could not understand why the white-eyes would leave such good meat. They took the puma meat too because they wanted Blanco to eat of the good medicine they had found in the snow that sun.

The Ute mounted up again and continued on their way to the river of the moonshell where Blanco waited in winter camp. They did not pass by the settlements but stayed to the old game trails that threaded the foothills until they rode out onto the plain and the darkness swallowed them up.

Paco began to get drunk at the whiskey table. His knees became wobbly, and he could no longer dance well. Jake, who did not drink much, danced with Consuelo. He had already forgotten about Sarah and her anger. Whenever he looked into Consuelo's eyes, his heart sank, and he felt his innards tremble nervously. He felt giddy with the music, her beauty, and his tangled feelings for her.

"I—I want to talk to you," he said as they whirled around the dance floor.

"So, talk to me," she said coyly.

"No, not here. Somewhere else. Somewhere private."

"Oh, I do not think that would be wise. Why do you want to talk to me?"

"There's something I want to tell you," said Jake. "But not here."

"My husband will get angry."

"Your husband is drunk," he said bluntly.

Consuelo looked over at her husband, who was having a drink with some other men. A shadow passed across her eyes. "I—I will meet you," she said. "But only for a moment. Where?"

"My room."

"Oh no."

"It will be safe," said Jake.

"It would be very bad if Paco found us there."

"I want you there," he said. "When the dance is over, I will go first and wait for you."

"I have some fear," she said.

"I know. Just meet me there. Please."

She looked up at his face, her eyes boring into his. He smiled. She smiled back. "Only for a moment," she breathed.

"Yes, Consuelo, just for a few minutes," Jake said.

When the dance ended, Jake walked with Consuelo to the side and left her there. Paco was not even looking in Jake's direction when the American left.

Luz, who stood at a little table offering *empañadas* and *dulces* to some children from the *pueblo*, watched with dark eyes as Jake left. She made a sound with her tongue like bones clicking together and shook her head. She saw Consuelo leave a few moments later.

"*No más, no más,*" she said to a little boy who had taken more than his share. And then the music started up again, and her cousin Manuel came over to her, asking her to dance. She took his hand, and he swirled her away. She wished that her husband were here.

Jake went to his room, lit a lamp, turned it down low, and stood there, waiting, his heart pumping hard in his chest. After a few moments, he heard footsteps. Then Consuelo was there. He closed the door, slipped the latch.

"No, do not lock it," she said.

"I want this private," said Jake softly.

"I—I . . ."

Jake took her in his arms, kissed her.

Consuelo responded, pressing herself against him as he embraced her. She was willing. But she pushed him away. "No, we mustn't do this," she said. "Quick, what is it that you wished to tell me?"

"Do you want me, Consuelo?"

"I—I don't know. This is all very strange to me. I—I'm confused."

"Well, you're some woman," he said. "And I want you to live with me. I want you to share my home."

"I—I'm married. I cannot. I cannot." But there was no force to her words, no conviction.

"Consuelo, I don't know how we're gonna do it, and I know it might not be right. But you want me, and I want you. Someday, when Paco is gone, I'm gonna come up there and bring you back here with me."

"No, you must not," she said.

"But, I will, Consuelo. You know I will."

"I can't even think of such a thing," said Consuelo. She drew away from him. She went to the door and fumbled with the latch, opened it.

"I want you, Consuelo."

She stepped out, slammed the door.

In the next room, Sarah sat up, startled. She could not help but overhear Jake and Consuelo in the next room. She heard Consuelo leave, walk across the *placita*. Sarah rose and went into the next room. She didn't bother to knock.

"What do you want, Sarah?" asked Jake.

"Well, you're certainly making a mess of things."

"What were you doin'? Eavesdroppin'?"

"No, I didn't want to hear it. I'm sorry I did hear it. Paco will kill you, Jake."

"No. I've already learned all about Mr. Paco Serrano. He's a coward. He don't know how to take care of a woman."

"And you do?"

"This one I do," he said.

"No, you just want something you can't have. You want Consuelo because she belongs to someone else."

"That's not true."

"No? Well, I was a gift to you, and you threw me out."

"It's not the same," Jake said.

"No, it's not the same," she said bitterly. "I gave myself to you, and it wasn't enough for you. You're greedy, Jake Stonecipher. Greedy for everything. But you don't know how to live. You don't know how to love. You don't know how to give."

"Just shut up," he said. Shadows blackened in the hard line of his jaw; lamplight flickered on his cheekbone, a raw orange smear that made his eye glare ominously.

"I'll shut up, Jake. But I'm very disappointed in you. I'm more disappointed in myself."

"You—you goddamned slut," he said.

His words slapped her across the face, stung her

heart. But there were no more tears inside her. She had cried for Jake Stonecipher. She had cried all she was going to cry. It was over. Now she had nothing to hope for but the spring. The spring when Will Burke would return to the fort. And if he did not ask her to go away with him, she would ask him to take her with him. Wherever he went.

"Good-bye, Jake," she said.

"You mean 'good night,' don't you?"

"Good night, too. But I mean good-bye. Don't ever touch me again."

"I won't," he said.

Sarah left the door open and stalked out, went back to her room. She could hear the faint strains of the music, the snatches of laughter, and she felt happy at last. She felt free. She felt somehow absolved of all her sins.

≈ 23 ≈

Paco Serrano cursed at the driver, cursed the mud and the mules. The river raged back at him, muddy and boiling with the snowmelt. Consuelo sat beside him, huddled in a buffalo robe, more miserable than she had ever been in her life. She looked back at the fort, its whitewashed walls shining in the sun, and wished she had had the courage to stay there with Jake Stonecipher. But she had not seen him that morning, and now her heart ached and her head still spun from leaving so quickly.

"Chingón, más prisa, más prisa!" Paco swore at the driver.

"No puedo," said the man.

The river raged at the wagon wheels, pulled at the mules savagely. Several days had passed since the fandango, and it had lasted for three drunken days. Since then, the snow had stopped, and the sun had come out and turned much of the land to mud.

"Paco," said Consuelo, "why did we leave so quickly? I did not buy a single thing."

"That *gringo*, he threw me out," said Paco.

"Who?" she asked innocently. She knew that Paco had gone to see Stonecipher about the land grants early that morning. She also knew that he had the big head from the whiskey. He had been drunk for three days and had tried to make love to her each night. But he had no ability, and she had let him sleep, snoring beside her while she thought of Jake Stonecipher and what he had said to her.

"That Jake Stonecipher. He told me to leave. He said that Burke owned some of the land that is mine."

"And does he?"

"I do not think so."

"You should have stood up to Stonecipher."

"He said he would shoot me if I ever came to the fort again."

"Are you afraid of him?"

"No," said Paco. "He is nothing. I will drive this Burke from my land. You will see."

Consuelo had never seen Paco so angry before. Nor had she ever seen him as drunk as he had been at the fandango. She fought with her confused feelings. Jake's promise to come one day and take her away from Paco made her shudder with a secret thrill. "Where are we going?" she asked. "To Taos?"

"No. I have had enough of people. We are going home."

"But, Paco, you promised."

"Do not say anything anymore," he snapped. "We are going home."

Consuelo felt the anger rise in her. She knew what it would be like up there, just she and Paco. They would be prisoners together.

The wagon cleared the river and bounced onto dry land. Consuelo looked back and saw Jake standing at the gate. He waved, but she dared not wave back.

She turned her head suddenly, knowing that she would probably never see him again. Paco would never come back to Fort Stonecipher, and she did not believe Jake would be so bold as to take her away as he had said he would. No, it was only a brief dream, a fantasy that had come and gone like the spring flowers that bloomed on the prairie. Jake had held out a rose to her, and now she was left with only thorns.

"*Andale, anda de prisa,*" growled Paco, and Consuelo huddled in her robe, pulled the hood of the capote over her head, shutting out all light, hiding the look of anguish on her face. "*Adiós,* Jake," she whispered to herself.

She huddled up in the wagon, closing in the ache that grew in her heart like a stone in a shoe.

In the spring, the land bloomed, began to emerge from winter brown into spring green. Joe Perkins rode out from St. Louis in early April with three sturdy Springfield wagons loaded with trade goods for Fort Stonecipher. José Delgado drove one wagon, Silvino Perez another, along with Tomás Santiago. Joe drove the third wagon so that his new wife, Charmaine, could be close. Joe was in love, "bustin' with it," as he said. Charmaine Girardeux was a distant cousin to the Chouteau family, she claimed, and he had finally wooed her and married her in a Catholic church after he was baptized in her religion.

Charmaine was petite, dark, with bright brown eyes, sharp features, a tiny little mouth and chin, good teeth, and bust enough to make Joe proud. He had met her at the Red Boar, become smitten enough with her to come back and ask her to be his wife. She was slightly older than he, and he knew she had not been pure. But she was sweet to him, and he bought her new clothes and shoes, and told her wonderful stories about the fort and all the people there, the riches to be made.

She held onto Joe's arm as they moved across the prairie and seemed to enjoy the adventure of the trip. At Bent's Fort William on the Arkansas, they stayed two days to give all the news of St. Louis and listen to all the news of the West. They set out from Fort William on a clear-skied April day, José in the lead wagon, the tang of winter still in the air. The river ran sluggish with mud and debris from the mountain meltoff, and they followed its serpentine course along the well-rutted trail.

Joe lagged behind, kissing and embracing Charmaine. She giggled with girlish laughter. They made camp that first night by the river, some ten miles west of the fort. Silvino tried to catch fish, but the water was too swift and murky. After supper, Charmaine sang a French children's song, Tomás told a funny story about a blind sheepherder, and José, as always, talked about his wife, Luz, and how much he missed her.

"We go too slow," said José before Joe joined Charmaine in their shelter under his wagon. She had hung the blankets from the sideboards each night during the journey to give them privacy.

"Can't go too damn fast, José. Shake the wagons apart."

"I am wishing to see my wife."

"We'll get there, don't you worry none."

"We can go a little faster, I think."

"Fine, you go right on. Don't you worry about us none."

"I am worried about Indians, Joe."

"Hell, you seen any?"

"No, but I remember what happened when we came this way before."

"Well, you keep them eyes peeled. You see any, you shoot 'em."

José said something in Spanish. Joe laughed and crawled under his wagon. After a while, the Mexicans heard giggling. José, Silvino, and Tomás talked for a time, and smoked, then put out the fire.

José had a hard time getting to sleep. He kept hearing the noises of lovemaking from under Perkins's wagon. He kept thinking of Luz and wondering if she missed him as much as he missed her.

The next day, José fretted because the lovebirds slept late and made noises of passion while he had the mules harnessed and worrying their bits in their mouths. Finally, when Joe was up, he told him he and the other drivers were going to leave.

"Just go on, José," said Perkins. "We'll catch up to you."

"We will not hurry at first," said Delgado.

Charmaine crawled from under the wagon, her clothes disheveled, her hair tangled. She straightened her blouse and winked at José. Embarrassed, the Mexican turned away and spoke to Pérez and Santiago in Spanish.

"Where are they going?" Charmaine asked.

"Goin' on ahead. Delgado's got him a burr in his crotch to get on back to the fort."

"What's this 'bird in the crotch'?"

Joe laughed and picked Charmaine up in his arms. He was still kissing her as the two wagons pulled away. An hour and a half later, he finally started off up the trail, Charmaine clinging to him like honeysuckle to a vine.

Charmaine ordered Joe to drive the horses off the trail so she could pick wildflowers. She made a pretty bouquet and presented it to him.

"I shoulda done that for you," he said.

"Oh, it gives me pleasure to make my man smile," she said in her faintly accented English. "They are very pretty, no?"

"Damned pretty," he said, and Charmaine pouted, as she always did when he swore. But she never chastised him about his language, and he liked that.

"Where are the other men?" she asked late that

afternoon after they had eaten a leisurely meal by the banks of the Arkansas.

"Oh, I reckon we'll come up on 'em directly," said Joe. "Can't be too far."

"It is so quiet out here. The sky is so big."

"Yeah. Reason I like it so much. Just wait'll you meet Jake. Why, he's the best man I ever knowed."

"I cannot wait to meet this man, *cherie*," she said. "You have talked about him so much."

By late afternoon, Joe began to wonder just how far ahead Delgado and the others were. He had stood on the wagon seat a time or two to see if they were ahead, but he had seen nothing. He began to get a prickly feeling inside that something might be wrong.

José saw the Indian first. He grabbed for his rifle and shouted over his shoulder at Silvino and Tomás. *"Indios! Indios!"*

Silvino, who was driving, threw the bullwhip tail at the mules, and Santiago started shooting. The Indian was far away and just rode in circles as if laughing at them. The mules jumped against the traces, and the wagon lumbered to close the distance between them and Delgado.

"Ayeeee!" screamed Santiago as a line of Indians on painted ponies appeared on the horizon.

"Mira!" shouted Pérez, nodding toward the river. Ute burst from the cover of cottonwoods, fanned out in attack formation, their feathers bristling from dark scalp locks, their faces smeared with hideous war paint.

Delgado swore softly as a dozen Muache Ute charged from the west in spearhead formation. "Blanco!" José muttered, because he knew that a chief in full head-dress, eagle feathers flapping in the wind, led the attack. Behind him, he heard the *pop-pop* of rifle shots, and the hackles rose on the back of his neck as he heard

the high-pitched yipping screams at the rear of his
wagon. He turned, saw a pack of Indians surround
Silvino and Tomas, little clouds of smoke hanging in the
air.

When he turned back, the charging Ute had fanned
out and were shooting rifles at him. He took quick aim,
fired, but knew he was off target. He fumbled with his
powder horn, but his hands shook from fear. Powder
spilled on his fingers and trickled down onto his
trousers.

The Ute swarmed over him like hornets. Delgado
heard the chilling *whick*-whisper of arrows flying through
the air, and when he looked up, he saw the faces of
Indians all around him. An arrow slammed into his
arm. He felt as if he had been hit with a sledgehammer.
The force of the shaft drove him back, and another
arrow whistled into his abdomen. He tried to stand up,
swing his rifle, but a Ute brave snatched it from his
hands, and he saw the blur of a tomahawk out of the
corner of his eye. Lights exploded in his brain.

Santiago reloaded his rifle as Silvino hauled in on the
reins, bringing the wagon to a jerky halt. Silvino fired
his rifle at one of the circling Ute and missed. The
yelling Indians rattled his senses. Tomás screamed as
three arrows porcupined his chest; he fell backward,
blood streaming around the shafts. Silvino jumped down
from the wagon, started to run toward the river. Five
Ute, led by Antler, caught up with him. Antler leapt
from his pony and wrestled the Mexican to the ground.
He slashed Silvino's legs with his knife, then let him
up. The Ute laughed as the wounded man struggled to
run. Two of them loosed arrows and watched as the
shafts punctured Silvino's buttocks, drove him face
forward into the ground.

Other Ute clambered over the wagon, began rifling
through the boxes and kegs.

Silvino screamed as Antler, Buffalo Head, and the others turned him over and began cutting off his genitals while four Ute pinned him to the ground. He was still screaming when Antler snatched his scalp from his skull.

Santiago looked up at the sky with glassy eyes. He felt the knife at his belly but, strangely, no pain. He looked into the painted face of a warrior and wondered where he was. He twitched a few times, and then the Ute threw his dead body from the wagon.

The Muache brought travois poles from the river, hitched them to riderless ponies. They sacked Delgado's wagon, stripped it of all usable goods, including gunpowder, flints, knives, axes, food, cloth, beads, and coffee.

Blanco himself took Delgado's scalp but did not kill him or disembowel him. José watched as the Ute looted the wagon, then rode off, whooping and calling to the other braves. A sickness rose up in him, and he vomited over the side of the wagon. Blood dripped down onto his face, clogged his eyes. He didn't care anymore. He wished the Indians had killed him. Pain lived in him like fire, and it burned his senses, burned in every pore, every muscle.

"Jesus, God!" whispered Joe Perkins when he saw Santiago's gutted carcass lying by the wagon. Goods lay strewn everywhere. The mules and horses were gone. The marks of travois poles told Joe how they'd taken the trade goods away. The wagon was virtually empty. The Indians had taken almost everything useful, destroyed the rest. Joe was sure that the raid had been planned for a long time. He remembered the Indians of the previous fall and wondered if they were the ones who had attacked the wagons. He felt empty, alone. He didn't know how he could explain all this to Jake. He cursed himself for lagging so far behind. Perhaps if he had been here...

"What has happened?" asked Charmaine.

"They kilt Tomás," said Joe.

"There is one over there," she said, pointing. Joe stopped the wagon, set the brake. His scalp crawling with spiders, he stepped down, carrying his rifle. He walked over to Silvino.

"*Ayudame*," whispered the Mexican. "Help me."

"Shit," said Joe. "Silvino, you're all cut up."

"*Agua.*"

Joe looked at the mutilation and gagged, fought to keep down the bile that surged up in his throat. A dizziness assailed him. "Silvino, I—I...there ain't nothin' I can do for you," said Perkins. "Santiago's dead."

"*Matame*," croaked Silvino. "Kill me."

Joe shook his head.

"Joe, don't leave me alone," called Charmaine. "I am frightened."

"I got to go, Silvino," said Joe awkwardly.

Silvino, with effort, extended his arm, held out his hand.

Joe stared at the man's bloody crotch and got sick again. He shook his head, walked away. "Ain't nothin' I can do, short of killin' him," he told Charmaine.

"Joe, we must leave. We must not stay here. They might come back."

"Where's Delgado?" he said aloud.

"Joe, please."

Silvino cried out. Joe quivered. He stood there, frozen, unable to move. "What can I do, Charmaine?" His voice quavered. "Tell me, Charmaine," he pleaded.

"You can do nothing," she said. "We must get help."

"They ain't no help out here. We can't just leave him."

Charmaine jumped down from the wagon. One of the

horses snorted and shook all over, rattling the traces. The sound startled Charmaine. She grabbed Joe, pulled him toward the wagon. "If we stay here," she said, "they will come back and kill us. Joe, please, come, come."

"*Matame!*" called Silvino. "Joe, don' leave me like this." The Mexican's voice carried on the dry still air, seemed to hang there like a single leaf rattling on a tree limb.

Joe looked at Charmaine, tears welling up in his eyes. She stared back at him, her eyes wide with fear.

"I—I can't just leave him," said Joe. He broke free of Charmaine's grip, turned to walk away.

"I will help you get him into the wagon," she said.

"Don't look at him, Charmaine. You get him by the shoulders. I'll take the legs."

Charmaine screamed when she saw what the Ute had done to Silvino. Joe slapped her out of it. They lifted Silvino and carried him back to the wagon. He held back his screams, but he was obviously in great pain. They loaded him into the back of the wagon, onto their pile of blankets.

"We got to get Santiago, too," said Joe.

Charmaine didn't answer. She followed Joe dumbly. They gasped for breath as they struggled with the dead weight of Tomás's body. They put a blanket over him. Silvino kept begging for water, but Joe ignored him. He looked once more at the ravaged wagon that the Mexicans had been driving. He helped Charmaine onto the seat of the Springfield, climbed up, and released the brake.

They found Delgado, still alive, his bloody head swarming with flies. Somehow they got him into the wagon too, and while Joe drove, Charmaine began to try to pull the arrows from José's tortured body. She winced every time he groaned.

An agonizing week later, Joe pulled up to the fort.

Joŝe was still alive. Silvino had died the night they found him. Joe had covered both bodies with heavy layers of salt and buried them under blankets. But he and Charmaine were both sick with the smell of decomposing flesh.

"What happened?" asked Jake when Joe brought the wagon through the gates.

"Injuns," said Joe. "Tomás and Silvino are dead. José's still alive, just barely."

Luz saw her husband and let out a piercing wail. She, two other women, and two men lifted Delgado from the wagon, carried him away.

"You fight 'em off?" asked Jake.

"I never even saw 'em," said Perkins. "Jesus, Jake, I wasn't even there until it was all done."

He would never forget the look in Jake's eyes as long as he lived.

≈ 24 ≈

Paco Serrano rode out in the thawing spring to help with the roundup without Consuelo.

"You do not wish to come?" he asked.

"No," she said.

"You have changed, Consuelo."

"No, Paco. It is you who have changed. I prefer to stay at home."

"Maybe it was bad to stay here this winter."

"No, it was good. There was time to think."

"I will be less on the roundup without you."

"You will do well without me, Paco."

He shrugged and rode away, taking his string of horses. When he left, the house was very quiet. The next day, Consuelo bathed, dressed in warm comfortable riding clothing, and saddled her horse. She rode to the creek where the American, Will Burke, had made his home. During the long winter, Burke was all Paco could talk about. He planned to confront the trapper after he returned from selling his cattle at the market. He seemed obsessed with the American.

She had found the place where Burke had built his cabin and had seen it from a distance one day when she had been out riding by herself. The creek was running full with the snowmelt when Consuelo rode up behind the cabin.

"Hello," she called.

A bearded man emerged from the cabin, walked toward her. He carried a rifle, walked with a slight limp. "Yeah?"

"Are you Will Burke?" she asked.

"I am."

"I am Consuelo Serrano."

"I know who you are, ma'am. I seen you a time or two."

"Me?"

"Yep. You rode up here oncet, and I seen you at your place, Paco's house."

"I am his wife."

"I reckoned that. What brings you by?"

"Are you going down to Fort Stonecipher?"

"Fixin' to leave now. Come on, we can talk whilst I finish a-packin'." He turned, limped away.

Consuelo followed him on her horse. She stopped in front of the small cabin. Burke was indeed preparing to leave. His mule was laden with panniers, and these were stacked high with furs. He threw a blanket over them and tied a diamond hitch as she dismounted.

Traps hung from the outside walls of the cabin. They seemed freshly oiled. Elk antlers lay strewn beyond the woodpile, and there were bones and animal skulls lying about. There was a stack of willow withes next to a pine tree. Smoke rose from the chimney, the door to his cabin open. Rocky stood saddled and hipshot, tied to a hitch post a few yards from the door.

"Why you askin' if I'm goin' down to the flat?"

"I have a message I would like you to give Jake Stonecipher. He is your friend?"

"We've shared a cup or two."

"That is good. Would you give him a message, then?"

"Might. You know Jake?"

"My husband and I visited the fort during the first snow last year."

"Oh? And what business did your husband have with Jake?"

"He does not want you on his land."

Will tied the last knot and went inside the cabin. He returned with a bedroll, heavy saddlebags. He threw these behind the cantle, tied them down with leather thongs, made sure the saddlebags were cinched tight.

"Is that what you want me to tell Jake?" he asked.

"No. Mr. Stonecipher already knows that. He told my husband that he owns this land and that he sold it to you."

" 'At's right."

"I hope there is no trouble."

"Likely there will be if Paco don't mind his own business. Now, what was it you wanted me to tell Jake?"

"Tell him that my husband has gone to round up cattle. I will be home alone."

Will pushed back his beaver hat, scratched the side of his head.

"That's all?"

"He will understand."

"You and Jake . . . ?"

"Thank you, Mr. Burke," she said, and climbed back in the saddle. She touched a finger to the brim of her hat and turned the horse without another word.

Will watched her go, a look of puzzlement in his eyes. After a few moments, he went back inside the cabin one more time. When he returned, he closed the door, latched it. Then he untied Rocky's reins, mounted him, and took up the mule's lead rope. He was still sore from the cougar attack, but around his neck he wore the blunt claws. It had been a winter's pastime, boring the holes and stringing them through with a rawhide thong.

"Well, damned old Jake," said Burke as he rode away from his home.

And, he wondered, where did that leave Sarah? God, he had thought about her all winter. During the long nights when his wounds festered and his fever raged, he imagined that she was there, ministering to him with tender hands, bathing him with cool water, soothing his troubled brow. In his delirium, he saw her beside him in his bed, and when he awoke, sweating and cold, he called her name, hoping she would hear him. He had been snowed-in for months, gnawing on thoughts of her, aching for her, and when he had gone trapping, his legs healed, his head no longer sore, he thought he heard her voice in every sound, on every whispering winter breeze.

He felt light-headed now, riding back down to the fort, wondering what he would find there. While Consuelo Serrano's message was somewhat cryptic, he thought he might know what it meant. And if Jake had his eye stuck on the Mexican's woman, then he must have given up Sarah for good.

Before he reached the Arkansas River, Will was whistling, in high spirits, and by the time he could hear the Fountain's spring roar, he was singing, and his throat was parched dry for a drink of hard whiskey.

Jake stood outside the fort, waving to Burke. Arapaho tepees bristled along the river, and there were more people moving between the fort and the *pueblo* than Will had ever seen before—all smiling, all nodding to him, although he knew not a one of them. There was something new about the fort too. There was an American flag flying from one of the bastions, rippling in the afternoon breeze, pretty as anything Will had ever seen. Will waved back.

When he rode up, Jake was grinning wide. "Ho, Will. You got some furs, I see. Only one mule?"

"Othern was kilt."

"Sorry to hear that. Thirsty?"

"You buyin'?"

"I'll make it up when we weigh you out."

Will laughed. Ten minutes later, he and Jake were sitting in the cantina, a bottle of Jake's whiskey between them. Will had not seen Sarah, or Joe Perkins. He had not told Jake the message yet either because he wanted to wait for just the right moment. Whiskey in his belly, all of his bearings pinned down.

"What's that around your neck, Will?"

Burke jangled his necklace, laughed. "That's all what's left of my mule," said the trapper.

"Painter?"

"Yep. Notice you got you a flag flyin'. Anything to it?"

"Lots of arguments 'bout who owns this part of the country. Thought I'd make it official." Jake grinned.

"Injuns figger anyplace they be belongs to 'em. I got the same idea."

"That's the way I look at it."

"How's Sarah?" asked Will.

Jake's face darkened. He took a sip of whiskey. "Don't see much of her. She comes and goes. Spends a lot of time in the *pueblo* with Luz Delgado. Luz is a widder woman now. Blanco's bunch, I think, killed two of my drivers on the trail, and José didn't live but about three weeks after Perkins brought him in full of arrow holes. Joe didn't have a scratch. He moved up to Hardscrabble last I heard. They practically got 'em a town there."

"Sorry to hear tell," said Burke. "You give Sarah up?"

"Sort of," said Jake sheepishly.

"I'll buy her from you, Jake."

"You? Sarah? Hell, Will, you can do better. The woman's barren as a dried gourd. I don't think she ever got the Injun out of her."

"What'll you take for her, Jake?"

Jake swallowed. He saw that Burke was serious. "Hell, I don't own her."

"Red Horn give her to you."

"Well, I don't want her no more. You want her, you take her. Damned woman."

Will said nothing. Jake had changed. There was a hard side to him that hadn't been there before. An indifference, a coldness.

"You have a good winter?" asked Jake, changing the subject.

"Good enough. Got me a visitor 'fore I left. Brung me a message for you."

"For me?"

"Paco's wife. Consuelo." He pronounced it "Consuely." "Said to tell you her husband was gone, rode off to spring roundup. Said you'd want to know."

Jake smiled slowly. Light beams danced in his eyes. "Well, I'll be damned."

"You dippin' into another man's poke, Jake?"

"That's none of your business, Will." Jake stood up. "You finish your drinkin', and I'll tote up your furs and pay you off."

"Hell, I can take 'em down to Taos," said Will. "You want to brush me off like a seed tick."

"Suit yourself," said Jake.

Will watched him leave. Yes, Jake Stonecipher had changed, all right. When a man gave up his friends, he was either crazy in love or just plain mean of heart.

Burke figured Jake was a little of both.

*   *   *

Will was waiting for Sarah when she came back to the fort that evening. He hadn't drunk much, and he'd taken a bath in the tub out back where a Mexican woman hauled water, heated it, and charged him twenty cents in silver. She kept Jake's water troughs filled, and he let her keep a big wooden tub near the back gate.

He saw Sarah and Luz riding toward the fort long before they saw him. He felt his pulse quicken. She wore a buckskin dress, and her hair was in braids. She looked, he thought, more Indian than white next to Luz, who dressed bright as a patchwork quilt. He waited until they drew near, then stepped out of the gateway. He waved.

Sarah seemed not to recognize him at first. But then she waved back. And smiled. Will felt a tug at his heart.

"Hello, Mr. Burke," she called.

"Howdy, Sarah," he croaked.

"You go on, Luz. I want to talk to Mr. Burke."

Luz rode on past. Sarah stopped her horse, looked down at Will.

"It's right good to see you, ma'am," he said.

"It's good to see you, Mr. Burke. Did you have a good winter?"

"Yes. I mean, no. Good trappin', bad thinkin'."

She laughed. He stood there awkwardly, at a loss for words. Sarah climbed down from her horse. She seemed glad to see him. Her face had a welcome shine to it, and her eyes sparkled. "Are you going to stay long?" she asked, handing him the reins.

"Depends," he said.

She started walking into the fort. He followed along, pulling the horse behind him. "Oh? On What?"

"Well, I been talkin' to Jake, and . . ."

"And?"

"Lord, Sarah, it ain't easy."

She stopped, turned to him. "What's not easy?" she asked, her voice soft and coyly lyrical.

"Talkin' to you, dammit!"

"I'm sorry," she said. "I don't know what it is you want to say to me."

"Well, I'm damned glad to see you, Sarah. Hell, you're about all I thought on—all damned winter."

"Do you always swear every other word, Mr. Burke?"

She turned and continued walking across the *placita*. Will looked at her proud back, the way she held her head high. He wanted her. Wanted her bad. Just seeing her had made his heart tumble like an apple in a millrace.

Luz had dismounted, was waiting for them. "I will take your horse, Sarah," she said. "I see that Burke wants to talk to you." There was a merry twinkle in her eyes.

"Thank you, Luz." Will handed the reins over to the Mexican woman. He watched her head toward the stables.

Sarah turned to him, smiled. "Did you want to talk to me?" she asked.

"Well, damn it, yes."

"There you go again."

"I know. I ain't in practice. Talkin', I mean. You 'member what I asked you last fall? When we was down by the river?"

"Why, no," she said airily, "I don't recall."

She said it so sweetly, he didn't take it as teasing at first. His heart seemed to fall through a trapdoor in his chest. "Well, I asked you to come away with me. Now, talkin' to Jake and all, and knowin' you and him, I mean, well, kind of like things change, and he don't ... I mean, what he said was or what I told him or asked him, and, well, it don't look it did, and what I been thinkin' and everything, and, well, I just sort of, I mean you and him, well ..."

"Whatever in the world are you trying to say, Mr.

Burke? Are you asking me to go away with you? To live with you? Do you plan to marry me? Or do you just want me to do your washing and mend your socks and sew your buckskins and cook your meals for you?"

He stared at her, dumbfounded.

"You and Jake talked," she said, "and Jake told you he didn't want me anymore and that you could have me. Isn't that it?"

"Why, yes, I mean, sort of. Well, I kind of asked . . ."

She touched a hand to Will's arm. "Mr. Burke, please don't let us go through all that again. Jake gave me to you, or you took me from him, and you want me to live with you."

"Well, I thought we might go down to Taos or Santa Fee and find a preacher, or . . ."

"I would like that, Mister Burke."

"I didn't—*buy* you nor nothin'," he stammered. "I mean, I wanted to, and I offered . . ."

"I'm glad that Jake didn't sell me," she said stiffly. "Now you come with me to my room, and we'll talk this out. I'll fix you supper. I have some wine and some whiskey that I keep. I'm glad you're back, Mr. Burke, and that your offer still stands."

"You are? You do? I mean . . ."

"I know what you mean, Mr. Burke. Come with me before you get your tongue tangled into a knot."

"Yes'm," he said sheepishly. He followed her across the *placita*, light-headed as a fool.

When they were inside her room, she closed the door. "Now," she said, "you may kiss me, Mr. Burke, and then I'll pour you a cup of whiskey."

"*Kiss* you?"

"Unless you'd rather shake hands on our agreement?"

"Hell no," he said. He took her in his arms, and she melted into a softness that surprised him—soft and warm. He kissed her and felt his blood rise in his brain, felt it hammer at his temples and throb in his heart. He held her close to him and marveled at her softness and her warmth. She was delicate and small and willing. And warm. And soft.

"Sarah," he husked, breaking the kiss for a moment.

"Yes?"

"Don't call me Mister Burke no more?"

"I won't," she said, and kissed him again.

Will was a long time getting to that drink of whiskey Sarah had offered him. For Sarah was warm and soft, and made him just as giddy as any hogshead of Taos Lightning.

≈ 25 ≈

Jake Stonecipher rode up into the mountains after Will and Sarah left for Taos to get married. He had a general idea where Paco had built his home. Will had drawn him a map, possibly as a show of gratitude for his giving up Sarah so easily. Jake was glad to be rid of her, but in her last moments at the fort, he had been civil, almost kind.

"You don't mind my going with Mr. Burke?" Sarah had asked him.

"No. Will's a good man. He'll take care of you."

"I'm sorry, Jake. Sorry that we had trouble between us."

"I'm sorry too, Sarah. I reckon I acted pretty mean to you."

"That doesn't matter. It's you I'll worry about."

"Me? Hell, I'll be just fine."

"You're going to take Consuelo away from Paco." It was a simple statement.

Jake lowered his head, nodded.

"Paco won't let her go," she said.

"He ain't there."

"Well, he'll come after her, then. One or the other of you will get killed."

"No, Sarah. Paco's got no backbone."

227

"Good-bye, Jake. I wish you well."

"You too, Sarah. Godspeed."

All he could think of was Consuelo as he rode toward the Wet Mountains. When he found the junction of the three creeks, Hardscrabble, Adobe, and Newlin, he knew he was not far. That afternoon, he found Serrano's house.

Consuelo saw him ride up. She stood on the porch, waiting for him. "You came, Jake," she said.

"You knew I would."

"Yes."

"Do you want to come with me?"

"I am ready," she said.

"I want you, Consuelo."

"Not here. Not in my husband's house."

"Where is your horse? I'll saddle him up."

"He is already saddled. I will not take but a few small things."

"Did you know I was coming today?" he asked.

"I saddled my horse every day, hoping you would come."

Jake liked that. They rode back down to the flat in two days, camping along the upper Arkansas where the three creeks were one and fed into the river. Consuelo picked wildflowers for her hair, and they made love in their lean-to almost all night. When they got to the fort, Jake gave her two new dresses and material to make more. For a week, they made love and seldom ventured from Jake's rooms. After that, Consuelo began to make her nest, decorating the adobe walls, adding little knickknacks, putting flowers in clay vases that she set at strategic places, moving the furniture around, making them a better bed. Jake went back to work and never gave Paco another thought.

When Paco returned to the mountains, he thought at first that something terrible had happened to Consuelo.

There was no note, no sign of where she might be. It was only when he noticed that her pretty dresses and shoes were gone, her vermilion, comb, hairbrush, and hand-mirror missing, her horse and saddle as well, that he realized she had left him. But he had to know for sure.

He rode to Will Burke's early the next morning after his return, two months after he had left for roundup. His stomach knotted when he saw Will's cabin, that he was building onto it. Burke had also ruined more of the creek, gouging out another section.

Burke was nowhere in sight as he rode up to the front of the cabin. "Burke?" he called.

The door opened. Will stepped outside. Behind him, Sarah appeared in the doorway.

"Is Stonecipher here?" asked Paco.

"No."

"But is that not his woman?"

"Not no more," said Burke. "He done kicked her out. She's my woman now."

Sarah's eyes flickered at the mention of Jake's name.

"Then he has another woman?" asked Paco.

"You might say that."

"Who is this woman?"

"Don't you know?" asked Sarah, stepping out of the doorway into the sunlight. "Jake stole your wife, Mr. Serrano. He threw me away like an old sock."

"No! I will kill him."

"Consuelo didn't look too unhappy about it," said Burke. He and Sarah had stopped by the fort after getting married in Taos. "Fact is, she looked downright happy two weeks ago."

"I will kill him," said Serrano, wheeling his horse, digging the Spanish rowels deep into its flanks.

Will and Sarah watched him ride away.

"I hope he does kill him," said Sarah under her breath.

"Likely, it'll be the other way around," said Will. "Paco will cool off, and then he'll brood for a time. You notice he headed back to his place, not to Jake's."

"I noticed," said Sarah. "When will it happen?"

"When Paco gets up his nerve," said Will.

Consuelo Stonecipher became the queen of the Arkansas Valley. People flocked to her fandangos. Men vied with one another to hunt with Jake, to become his friend. Jake became a noted marksman and hunter. He hunted deer for sport and meat and hide. If he wanted buffalo, he hunted Bayou Salade or the eastern plains. He hunted turkey in the fields at harvesttime, ducks and geese in the spring. Along the river bottoms, in the deep grass, he hunted grouse.

Consuelo loved to go fishing with him on the Arkansas River after the winter ice melted. They caught catfish and hickory shad, speckled brook trout in the clear cold waters of the Fountain.

When a year had passed without Paco coming after her, Consuelo began to think that he had wisely decided to give her up without a fight. She was only mildly disappointed. In the second year of her marriage to Jake, after a week of watching him play poker and euchre with the trappers and hunters, she held another of her famous fandangos.

That was the night, late in summer, when Paco rode in to kill Jake Stonecipher and take Consuelo back to his ranch. He had brooded about this injustice long enough, and the hate had built up in him so that he was able to summon the courage to face Jake.

The dance was in full swing when Paco rode up to the fort, tied his horse outside the gate. Jake was playing cards in the cantina, did not notice Paco as he strode across the *placita*, a brace of flintlock pistols in his sash.

When Paco walked into the dance hall, which by now had been covered over with a sod roof, the ladies remarked at his bearing, his dashing good looks. But he brushed past them and strode to Consuelo, who was holding court on a divan set along the main wall. Men and woman stood and sat around her as if she were royalty.

Paco thought she had never looked more beautiful. That only made him angrier at what Jake had done.

The people parted to let Paco through.

Consuelo looked up at him, startled. "Paco!" she said. "What are *you* doing here?"

"I have come to take you back home," he said.

"Don't be a fool. I am home. Go away."

"You are coming with me," he said tightly.

"No, Paco. I am staying."

"Why?" he asked. People began to whisper. One man left the room to tell Jake what was happening.

"I love him. It is too lonely in the mountains. Look. See how happy everyone is? That is why. There are many reasons."

"But we will have much wealth," he pleaded. "I have done well. I have built new buildings. My herd is very big now. You—you are living in sin." He almost choked on his words. His faced reddened, and his neck swelled against the collar of his shirt.

The women did not like Paco's accusations. They encircled Consuelo, trying to protect her.

"You had better go before Jake gets here," Consuelo said.

"I am not afraid of him," said Paco.

There was a commotion. The musicians had fallen silent, knowing that something was wrong. Jake pushed his way through the gathering crowd around Consuelo and Paco.

"So, here comes the thief now," said Paco in Spanish. *"Ladrón!"*

Jake stepped between Paco and Consuelo. He towered over Serrano. He seemed very calm.

"Go away, Paco," he said. "You are making my woman unhappy."

"She is my woman. You stole her from me."

"I took what was mine."

"No, you are a thief. I have come to take her back."

"Go on, Paco, before you get hurt," said Jake.

Paco stepped back, jerked his pistols from the sash, began to cock them. Jake took one step toward Paco, shot a hard right fist into Paco's jaw. The pistols fell to the floor, uncocked, knocking the flints cockeyed. Paco lashed out at Jake, stinging him with a left hand across the face.

The crowd fanned out as the fight broke out in earnest. Jake rammed a fist into Paco's belly, knocking the wind out of him. Paco backpedaled, then charged. He swung wildly, and Jake cracked his jaw with another well-aimed blow.

Paco turned and wrestled with Jake, his legs pumping like pistons. Jake went down. The two rolled, trying to strike each other with their fists.

Jake hammered a rolled-up hand into Paco's nose, and blood squirted out of Paco's nostrils. Jake scrambled to his feet.

Paco rose up, braced himself for Jake's charge. Jake waded into him, both arms flailing. He cracked open Paco's cheek with a left, knocked his head back with a sharp uppercut.

Paco went down in a heap, senseless and bloodied.

"Take him out of here," panted Jake.

Three Mexicans lifted Paco up like a sack of meal, dragged him across the dance floor. They escorted him from the *sala*, put Paco on his horse, and sent him away. Paco did not return that night.

But word of the fight spread, among the Mexicans, the people of the *pueblo*, through the settlements, to the Arapaho, and finally to Blanco and his Muache Ute.

For some time, Blanco had been angry over the numbers of settlers coming up the Arkansas River, settling along the creeks in the mountains and on the plain. He was a cagey man, and he did not want to start a fight he could not win. He was a patient man as well. But there was a streak of greed in the Ute that coupled with his hatred for the white men made him shrewd and dangerous. He saw the wealth that these strangers brought to the Arkansas Valley. He saw opportunity as well, but he knew he must find a way to take some of the wealth for himself and not be hunted down and killed.

One day he and his braves rode up to Paco Serrano's big log home on the Columbine Ranch. Paco had named his spread for the beautiful blue flowers that grew in profusion in the wide meadows in the shadows of the Wet Mountains.

"What do you want?" asked Paco when he saw the Ute on their ponies in a semicircle facing his porch. The Indians were not painted, but he was nervous. They were armed, and he was not.

"Make talk," said Blanco in broken Spanish.

"We will talk, then," said Paco. "You tell your brave ones to ride off, and we will talk."

Antler bristled. He, like the others, understood a smattering of both Spanish and English.

Blanco waved his men away. They melted into the

trees, but Paco could still see their rifles and bows, their feathers, among the trees.

"Good," said Paco.

Blanco dismounted, and he and Paco sat on the steps of the porch like neighbors.

"We will smoke," said Blanco. He set down his battered trade musket, its stock wrapped with leather and studded with ornamental brass tacks. He opened his beaded possibles pouch and produced a small clay pipe and a smaller pouch filled with rough-cut tobacco.

He filled the pipe, produced a small magnifying glass. He held the glass over the bowl, concentrated the sun's rays on the tobacco. Soon a thin tendril of smoke rose from the bowl. Blanco sucked air through the pipe. The tobacco caught, began to fume. When he had it going well, he passed the pipe to Paco.

Paco felt the strength of the man sitting next to him. He saw the hard corded muscles, the sun-bronzed skin. Blanco's moonface was lined with age, crow's-feet at the corners of his eyes, parentheses framing his sensuous mouth, lines across his forehead. He smelled of sweat and horse.

"I do not like the white man who took your woman," said Blanco, after they had smoked for a time. "He has a bad face. His heart is not good. He buys furs from the Arapaho with whiskey. He makes the fort on Ute land."

"I do not like him also," said Serrano.

"Blanco will kill him sometime. Blanco wants a place to hide his braves. He wants a place for other red men to come and be safe. We will rob the travelers and the traders. Ute, Apache, Navajo, all will ride and take horses and cattle. One day we will drive all the white-eyes away and take back our hunting grounds."

"I cannot do this," said Paco.

"Serrano, if you do not, we will kill you now. Look."

Blanco swept an arm in a wide arc. Paco saw that the Utes had surrounded them. They all had rifles or bows pointed at him.

"I would be a traitor to my own people, my own kind, Blanco. Do you understand?"

"There is talk from Santa Fe that the Mexicans want all the American white-eyes driven from the valley of the Arkansas River. There is talk of Mexican soldier men coming to fight the American white-eyes. The American white-eyes hate you as they hate us. You cannot get your woman. The big man, the one they call Jake, he beat your face, and he took away your courage like a sneak thief. He has killed some of my braves. He takes all that we have."

"You want me to harbor your braves so that they can steal from the settlers. Some of the people in the *pueblo* are Mexicans, countrymen."

"You will have your woman back in your lodge."

"No. I cannot do this, Blanco."

"You will not know we are here. We will hide like the small animals in the rocks. We need a place to bring our horses, to rest after we fight. Give us this much, and you may have this land as long as rivers run."

Paco buried his face in his hands. He knew Blanco would kill him and burn him out if he refused. Yet how could he live with himself if he did what the Ute wanted him to do?

Blanco nodded to Antler. Antler, who had made fire with straw and a magnifying glass, stood up from behind the woodpile. He touched a piece of kindling to the flames, made a firebrand.

"He will burn your lodge to ashes," said Blanco.

"No, don't," said Paco, rising from the step.

Blanco smiled and shook his head. Antler threw the torch to the ground. The Ute all laughed.

From that day on, Blanco used Paco's ranch as a hideout. He began to gather stragglers from other tribes, to enlist them in his cause. He started out attacking Kiowa and Arapaho, stealing from them, but gradually he began to strike at the travelers going to and from Bent's Fort William and Taos and Santa Fe.

Paco never saw the Indians come or leave. He knew only the stories his men told him, and he shuddered every time he heard Blanco's name.

≈ 26 ≈

Burke worked his way up Adobe Creek, figuring the gold had to come from a mother lode farther up. He disregarded boundaries as he sought more and more gold.

He had built an extra room on his cabin, and he treated Sarah with respect, gave her the love she never had. Sarah and Burke lived in the mountains almost like Indians, going down to the pueblo only when they had to restock their larder. They did not go to Fort Stonecipher but bought their goods in the growing settlement that everyone called Pueblo.

Sarah learned on one such visit that Paco had taken a woman into his home. She was a Ute woman, Luz Delgado told her, called River Willow. Luz said that Paco had brought her to the *pueblo* a few times and had taught her to speak Spanish and English. Paco called her Candelaria.

"She is not an out-of-door wife in a tent," Sarah told Will, "but a regular wife. They have a son."

"We got two boys ourself," boasted Will. Their sons were named Sean and Kelly, the latter sobriquet being Burke's mother's maiden name. Sean was six, Kelly five in that summer of 1846 when they visited the *pueblo*. Jake and Consuelo were also parents, with a son and a daughter, named John and Rosalie. John, whom everyone called Little Jake instead of Jack, was four, and Rosalie was two.

There was much talk about Mexico that summer. It was said that the Mexicans planned to reclaim their territory and oust all settlers from the Arkansas Valley. Jake and the others scoffed at such talk, but he kept guards posted and questioned travelers from Santa Fe and Taos when they passed through the settlements. Blanco's renegade band was still roaming the territory, striking at travelers and isolated settlers, despite pleas from Stonecipher to the U.S. government for protection.

Joe Perkins and his French wife, Charmaine, became parents of two daughters, Renee and Elaine, now three and one. Joe had opened a trading post at Greenhorn settlement and guided hunting parties to Bayou Salade and the Wet Mountains. He seldom saw Jake, but when they did meet, there was a coolness between them chillier than any northwest snow-blowing wind. Although Joe had made his peace with José Delgado's widow, Luz, Jake seemed to carry a grudge as a blind man carries a cane, partly out of necessity and partly out of pure meanness.

When Burke, Sarah, and the children had been back at their home for a month, Sarah took the children for a long ride one morning. When she returned that evening, she called Will away from the creek diggings before she had supper on the table.

"There are many Indians camped in the mountains," she told him. "They come and go. Too many."

"What are you pokin' at, woman?"

"You take a look, Burke. See for yourself. Over on Paco's spread. They didn't see us, but Sean and Kelly were frightened."

"You maybe had no business goin' onto Serrano's property."

"We wanted to stay in the valley and have a picnic, but there were two or three hundred head of elk there first."

"I'll take a look," said Burke. "You tell me where you saw 'em."

He too knew the stories. Blanco's marauding band always disappeared when anyone tried to track them. Most didn't bother, but sometimes one of the slaughtered victims left family who in the heat of anger sought revenge. Some gathered up posses and chased after the Indians only to come back without having seen a single Ute.

The next morning, Will set out early. He crossed the valley beyond where Adobe Creek rose and saw the huge elk herd grazing the lush grasses in the lee of the Wet Mountains; he stopped counting at three hundred. He rode up into the mountains, went quiet through the timber, heading for Serrano's place.

He found the Ute camp, saw the Indian tepees, the pole corrals, the horses. Like all Ute camps, it was well away from running water. He also saw Jicarilla Apache, Navajo, and more than two dozen Muache Ute.

He left his horse tied a mile from the camp, crawled closer. As he watched, Paco and two of his men ran in four head of cattle. Paco and Blanco spoke while the Indians killed the cattle. As the Indians began butchering them, Paco and his hands rode away, as if what they had done was an everyday occurrence.

"Mighty curious," Burke told Sarah that night.

"Maybe those are the Indians who are robbing people along the road to Taos," she said.

"I seen some of 'em down on the Rio Hondo last time I went to Taos," admitted Burke. "They run off when they seen me."

"I do not trust Paco Serrano."

"He's up to somethin', for sure."

"Be careful, Burke," said Sarah. "I feel bad about the Indians being so close. I worry about the children."

"Yeah," he said. "Me too."

Jake listened to Alexander Barclay's tale of woe. Barclay told him he had almost gone under trying to make a living off his farm up at Hardscrabble. The grass there was depleted, and he had moved down to Stonecipher's Fort in September, took up with Joseph Doyle, who had also fallen on hard times. Doyle suggested they talk to Jake, who knew the country better than anyone.

"There's a place you could raise cattle," Jake told them. "Two miles west of here, where the Arkansas bottom broadens out to about a half a mile wide. There's a fine stand of grass there and cottonwoods along the river you can use for lumber and firewood. Better hurry, though. The Arapaho are telling me it's going to be a hard winter."

Jake sold the two men what they needed, and they left Stonecipher's with a wagonload of building implements—adobe molds, axes, spades, stakes. Doyle and Barclay began building the Houses, as Alex Barclay called them.

The Houses made three sides of a hollow square, and the two men finished them in October. They consisted of a number of adobe and chinked-log rooms for dwellings, a log "lumber house," and adobe store and corral.

Jake felt satisfied that he had kept such men close to the settlements. Each American who stayed made his claim to the land more secure.

Consuelo gave birth to another daughter in October of that year, 1846. Jake was away trading with the Mormons who had settled in the valley at Mormon Town. When he returned, Consuelo had given him

Josefina, and Jake called her Jo. Consuelo accused him of sentimentality, saying that he had named her after his old friend Joe Perkins, but Jake denied it.

"Me and Joe ain't friends," he said gruffly, but Consuelo knew he pined for Joe Perkins. He just didn't know how to break down the wall that had grown up between them. Jake had become a taciturn solitary man, but she knew he loved her. It was just that he worried all the time—about business, the Indians, the Mexican government, the American government.

He had not been the same since the fur trade died out a half-dozen years before. He rode far and wide, making friends among new settlers, urging them to trade with him. The competition had stiffened since the *pueblo* had built up so much, and the other settlements in the mountains had grown and flourished. He still thought he had made the wisest choice, to build his fort by the Arkansas River. That was still the hub, he told her, and by God, someday he'd be bigger than the Bent brothers and St. Vrain.

Paco watched the Indians ride off to the south early that same month and breathed a sigh of relief. He knew he would not see them again until late spring, but he hoped they would never return. By late November, he wished he had gone down from the mountain himself, because the blizzard that blew in from the North was the worst he had ever seen. He knew before it was over that he would be snowbound and that he would lose stock, not only the horses and few cattle he kept at the ranch but those cattle that grazed the plains.

Jake saw the storm coming and ordered woodcutters into the mountains, but it was too late. They returned as high winds blew the snows down off the mountains, sent the temperature well below freezing.

The snow stayed on the ground, covering the grass. The Arkansas River froze over, and snow covered the ice. Paco's men watched as the cattle strayed, and they had to hunt them in subzero weather. Some of them sought shelter at Stonecipher's fort. Some told of their horses running off and trying to catch them up in blinding snow when their hands and feet were frozen.

Money was tight, but Jake found an opportunity to make money when the blizzard hit that November.

To the east, a twenty-eight-wagon train owned by Bullard, Hook & Co. carrying merchandise to Santa Fe, crossed the Arkansas River at Cimarron Crossing. The teamsters camped in the sand hills on the south side of the river. During the night, the blizzard blew down on them from the northwest so quickly and so violently that the oxen panicked. The stock broke through the guard, scattered, bellowing in the darkness. Three mules died in the sudden chill of winter, and the snowy plains swallowed up twenty oxen. The teamsters cached their goods, abandoned half their wagons, and made for Bent's Fort 150 miles west with the goods they could carry in the thirteen wagons pulled by the oxen they had left.

Joe Doyle was at Big Timber when Jim Bullard, the wagonmaster, rode in, he and his men exhausted. Doyle listened as Bullard told him what had happened.

"We'll pay any man who can bring us enough oxen to rescue my abandoned wagons," said Bullard.

"I'll do 'er," said Doyle. "Soon's this storm's over. I'll make the gather. I got some, and I knows others what can give us the yoke you need."

"You get me fifty yoke of oxen, you got a deal," said Bullard. "That'll give me some spares, maybe enough to get through. My oxen are pretty stove-in."

"I'll do my level best," said Doyle, excited at the prospect of making some cash money. As soon as the storm cleared, he rode back to the Houses, told Alex Barclay about Bullard's predicament.

"You go on to Stonecipher's, see what you can round up. Rent all the yokes and harness you'll need. Jake will give you credit, I reckon."

"How many yoke can we muster?" asked Doyle.

"Eight or ten, maybe. Countin' yours."

"I'll be ridin'," said Doyle. He set out in the bone-numbing cold for Greenhorn. He rounded up ten yoke from George Simpson, sent him to Stonecipher's to wait for him. He rode on to Hardscrabble, got eleven yoke from Kinkead and Burroughs. By the time Doyle got to Stonecipher's, everyone knew something about what had happened to the wagon train.

"I don't have enough harness for you, Joe," said Jake. "But you ride over to Mormon Town and see Bob Crow and Dimick Huntington. They'll rent you yoke and harness to take up the slack. Tell 'em I sent you."

"Thanks, Jake. I appreciate the credit."

Jake smiled indulgently. "I'll be surprised if you rescue Bullard's wagons before spring."

"We'll damn sure try," said Doyle.

Doyle and Barclay drove the oxen and hauled the equipment to Big Timber. There Alex borrowed still more oxen from Bill Guerrier, he and Doyle staying the night in Guerrier's lodge. Some of Bullard's men left for the crossing of the Arkansas with Barclay's oxen. Others moved the wagons from Big Timber to Bent's Fort, where they camped for the winter. By then, everyone knew that no one would get through to Santa Fe. Or anywhere else. Not until winter held its gelid breath long enough for the huge drifts to melt.

Jake waited out the hard winter, wondering when Doyle and Barclay would be back. He began to worry about his investment. They had cleaned him out of harness, yoke, shovels, and picks, and had made a big dent in food staples.

"Do not worry, my husband," Consuelo consoled him. "They will pay you."

"I don't know. I should have taken the job myself. Those two would have gone belly-up if not for me. If brains were powder, I don't think either one of 'em'd have enough to blow their noses."

At the end of February, some of Bullard's men got bored at Big Timber and rode to Stonecipher's for some serious drinking and cardplaying. Jake asked them how Barclay and Doyle were doing.

"Barclay's out huntin'," said Bill Letterman, a beefy drover from Cedar Creek, Missouri. "Doyle's havin' seven kinds of fits waitin' for Bullard to come back from Bent's. We was all goin' plumb crazy there in Big Timber. Ain't a damned thing to read, and all the card decks is wore down, faces blank as a baby's butt."

"You watch," Jake told Consuelo. "Those boys'll fiddle around and lose the contract."

"Give them a chance, Jake," she said soothingly, smiling at the daughter suckling at her breast.

"Fact is," said Jake, not listening to his wife, "I still own all that harness and the goods they got on credit. I may just have to go and do the job myself."

"Whatever you say," said Consuelo, rocking back and forth in her chair, fingers smoothing her baby's thin thatch of hair.

Barclay and Doyle showed up late in February, joined Bullard's men in a contest to see who could put away the most liquor. Alex got so drunk Joe had to cart him back to the Houses in a wagon. Barclay's bear-sized hangover turned into a severe illness. He raved in the throes of delirium for two days with a raging fever, spat up cupfuls of blood until Joe thought he might die.

In the spring, Doyle and Barclay went back to Bullard's camp at Big Timber, expecting to get the contract to haul his wagons out with the oxen they had borrowed.

Jake Stonecipher had beat them to it. Carrying papers authorizing him to use the borrowed oxen, he secured the contract, retrieved the lost wagons, and sent them on their way to Santa Fe. Doyle and Barclay watched Bullard's wagons move up the Timpas toward Raton Pass, swallowed their bitter disappointment. They returned to the Houses, gave back the oxen Jake had not used, and got roaring drunk at Stonecipher's.

Jake even bought them drinks to show his goodheartedness. "You got to be quick in this country," he told them.

≈ 27 ≈

Just before the blizzard hit, Will Burke boarded up his cabin at Sarah's urging, saddled their horses, loaded the mules with packs of clothing and food. The snows were already deep in the mountains, and Burke had been pacing the floor, frustrated at not being able to work the creek for gold.

"I will not spend a winter up here with a crazy man," Sarah told him. "We'll likely kill each other before spring."

"That bad, eh?"

"Do you want to leave two orphans to fend for themselves in the wilderness?"

"I reckon we could go down to Stonecipher's."

"No, Burke," she said. "Taos. The boys will have fun there. I won't feel trapped."

Burke set buffalo robes downstream, anchored them well. He did not want to miss the gold flakes washing down in the spring runoff in case he had trouble getting back into the mountains. He and Sarah, with Sean and Kelly, rode over snowy Raton Pass to Taos where he rented an adobe house until March. Then he rode to Santa Fe where he sold some of his gold.

When he returned, he left most of the money with Sarah. He paced the floor for three days until Sarah threw up her hands. "Burke, is it going to be like this all winter?"

"Sarah, them boys're plumb scratchin' my nerves to raw. My hands have got the fidgets, an' these walls are closin' in on me."

"Why don't you ride up to Turley's, Burke? Get it all out of your system. You've been licking your lips so hard, you're going to wear them out."

"Well, I wouldn't mind a taste with some of the settlement boys what come down for the winter."

"We'll be just fine, Burke. Just come back when you get tired of burning out your stomach."

Will laughed. "Woman, you know this old coon too well."

"The truth is, Burke, you're making me nervous too. The boys and I will be just fine."

"You're a mighty fine woman, Sarah."

"Oh, you. Just try not to get in any fights."

"Yes'm, I'll be back in a day er two."

Burke kissed his woman good-bye, hugged the boys, and rode out, headed for Simeon Turley's. Turley owned a mill and distillery on the Rio Hondo, a dozen miles north of Taos.

At Turley's, Burke ran into men he knew from the settlements on the Arkansas, William LeBlanc and Tom Autobees. He tasted the tang on the air, sniffed the aroma of sour corn mash, the heady scent of whiskey, the musty fragrance of cigar and pipe smoke. Simeon was busy filling kegs, loading a pair of wagons for a trip to Santa Fe. John Albert, one of his workers, told Burke he was a fool to leave his woman in Taos.

"Oh? How's that?" asked Burke, wetting his dry as he watched Turley and Albert heft the heavy whiskey barrels on the wagon.

"They's trouble a-brewin' 'mongst the Pueblo Injuns," said John. "Trouble twixt the Americans and the greasers."

"Mexicans?"

"Spaniards," grunted Turley. He had a bad leg, walked with a pronounced limp.

"What about Santy Fee?" asked Burke.

"Charlie Bent says they's gonna be a war for certain sure. He can't hardly handle it." Charles Bent was the governor now, and many New Mexicans resented him, Burke knew.

"Well, I'll stay the night," said Will, "go on back to Taos in the morning. Set me out a keg to take with me."

"Suit yourself, Will," said Turley. Will, Bill LeBlanc, and Tom Autobees proceeded to get drunk at the little tavern Turley had at the distillery.

John Albert and Charles Town started out in the wagons. Both appeared very nervous since they had to pass through Taos on their way to Santa Fe.

"You get in any trouble, get on back here," Turley told them.

Tom, Will, and Bill LeBlanc were still at it when Turley joined the group about ten o'clock that evening. He pulled up a chair, poured himself a cup of his own whiskey.

"Damn Injuns," said Autobees. "They get riled, them Mexicans might have a handful."

"This has been brewin' a long while," said Turley. "Charlie Bent's right in the middle of it. I told him it was a big mistake him bein' governor of a bunch of Injuns and Mexes."

"Charlie can take care of himself," said LeBlanc, his face waxen in the lamplight of the *taverna*.

The four men were still drinking, trying to solve the politcal problems of the region, when they heard a commotion outside the distillery. Hoofbeats thumped the ground, and they heard the breathy wheeze of a horse. It was well after midnight, but the men had eaten an hour or so before and were now drinking strong coffee.

"Simeon, Chrissake!" yelled Charlie Town as he burst through the door, his eyes fiery and wide as brass buttons.

"What're you doin' back here, Charlie?" asked Turley.

"Hell, they got the whiskey wagons, Simeon," Town shouted. "Me 'n John had to run for our damned lifes. I got me a horse and rode him into the ground gettin' back here. All hell's broke loose in Taos."

Burke steeled himself, a muscle in his jaw rippling under the skin.

"Calm down, Charlie," said Turley. "John all right?"

"I don't know. We split up. Hell, them damn Pueblo redskins kilt Charlie Bent and started butcherin' every damned American they could lay their hands on."

"Christ," said Autobees.

LeBlanc's face melted to a pallid mask.

Burke rose from the table, swayed unsteadily for a moment. He shook his shaggy head, braced himself.

"Better git," said Town. "I got to get me a fresh horse and ride to Santy Fee, see can we get some soldiers up to Taos."

"What's the all-fired hurry?" asked Turley. "They got what they wanted. Charlie Bent. It's over, ain't it?"

"Like hell. They's a mob a-headin' this way. That's why I'm a-goin' t'other. Just wanted to warn you first you'd better clear out. That mob'll be here come sunrise. They ain't more'n two hours behind me and all spread out. I got to ride twenty mile to get around 'em."

Burke thought of Sarah down in Taos, all alone. Something hard grabbed at his gut, and a jolt of anger surged through him. Before he could move, Town left the room. Moments later, they heard him swearing as he changed saddles.

"Better get your guns, check your loads," said Turley. "Looks like we're in for the deal."

Autobees and LeBlanc left. Will grabbed his rifle where it was leaning against the wall.

"Simeon," said Burke, "I got to go to Taos."

"Better stay, Will," said Turley. "We'll need your rifle."

"My woman's in Taos," said Burke.

"Well, you ain't, and that may be a blessing. You help us take care of that mob, and you can ride there without runnin' a damned gauntlet."

There were shouts outside as Tom and Bill waked men, told them to arm themselves.

Burke hesitated.

"I'd say we have an hour," said Turley, stepping outside. "Be light about then."

"I'll stay," said Burke, "but I wished to God I was in Taos."

"You'd probably be wolfmeat like Charlie Bent by now, Will."

Turley organized the defenders, saw to it that the men had plenty of ammunition, protection. He placed men behind the adobe walls that shielded the distillery. They stood on benches so that they could fire over the walls.

Before dawn, John Albert rode in, almost witless with fear. "Jesus God," he panted. "That mob ain't more'n ten minutes ahind me."

"Get a rifle and get up on that stack of barrels," ordered Turley. "Maybe we can talk them out of a fight."

Will stood atop a large crate, peering into the darkness. It was quiet except for a man coughing, another blowing his nose. Burke shivered in the predawn chill.

The defenders of Turley's mill and distillery heard the ragged prattle of voices long before they saw the angry mob of New Mexicans and Indians. As the sun smeared the eastern sky with a liverish pink and scalded the clouds with vermilion, a line of men on foot and a few on burros and horseback appeared over the horizon.

"Steady up," said Turley.

Five hundred yards from the buildings, protected by adobe walls and a large gate, the mob halted. Several men brandished weapons and shouted insults that carried to the men standing on the benches behind the walls.

A cluster of men broke free from the mob and started toward Turley's. Three were Indians; four, Mexicans. They carried a flag of truce.

"Hold your fire," yelled Turley, but he eased his rifle over the wall and kept a thumb on the hammer.

Several minutes later, the seven armed men halted at the gate. One of the Mexicans, a man named Carlos Arminta, yelled up at Simeon. "Turley," he said in English, "we are telling you something. Surrender. I promise safety for all the men inside the stockade."

"We ain't surrenderin'," said Turley flatly.

"You goddamn Turley," said Arminta.

The Indians brought their rifles up. Turley and the other men ducked behind the walls as three rifles barked.

The Mexicans fired, then ducked. They ran back as the mob surged forward. Bullets whined through the air, thunked into the adobe walls, shattered windows inside the stockade. Turley and the others returned fire, but they were at a disadvantage. There were too many in the mob, and they kept up a steady hail of lead balls.

Several men were killed inside the stockade. A couple of visitors tried to escape and were cut down by the Pueblo Indians, who were waiting.

"Turley, my barrel's so hot it's going to melt," said Burke. "They'll get us if we don't get help."

"I know, Will. We just have to hang on, try and get out of here come dark."

Somehow the defenders managed to hold off the mob during the day. But as night cloaked the land, the mob set fire to the mill, the fire throwing an eerie glow over the stockade. Sporadic rifle fire peppered the adobe walls, caromed off the flagpole like whining hornets.

The mob seemed fascinated by the fire. They shouted and cheered as they triggered off random shots at Turley's stronghold.

"Men," Turley told the handful of survivors, "get out any ways you can. They'll fire us next and cook us like sausages."

Turley, Bill LeBlanc, and Tom Autobees dug a hole through the back wall of the adobe fort. Burke and John Albert opened the back door leading to a fenced garden and made a run for it, firing into the advancing crowd of rebels. Another man, unknown in the darkness, ran with them. A shot boomed. The man screamed once and staggered under the impact of a storm of lead. Finally he fell and was quiet.

Turley, favoring his game leg, tried to run. But his limp held him back. Burke saw him throw up his hands and go down, his face lit for a moment by the flames from the mill.

Burke got separated from Albert, reached the log fence beyond the garden, and crawled beneath it. He became part of the earth and log rail, held his breath.

The mob, driven to a frenzy by the escaping men, screamed and fired more bullets into the stockade. Indians sent flaming arrows over the walls, and the fort caught fire.

Shadows raced past him, poured through the back

gate, trampling the dead plants in the garden in their mad rush to join in the killing.

Burke lay there, listening to the crowd as they finished off the men inside who had not escaped. When the fires died down and there was enough darkness for cover, he crept off into the piñon-dotted hills behind Turley's house. On foot, he headed for Raton Pass. He had his rifle, pistol, knife, possibles pouch, and enough powder and ball to last him a few days. He had no water or food. He was cold and hungry. The weather was freezing.

In the distance he heard the screams of men he had drunk with, laughed with, talked with, and the shouts of Indians and Mexicans on a rampage.

He looked back, once, and saw the pulsing embers of what had once been a mill and a distillery. He could imagine the horror as the rebels got into the whiskey, jubilant with victory. He wondered if Tom and Bill had gotten away. There was still some scattered firing, but he figured these were victory shots since all inside the stockade must now be dead.

There was no going to Taos now. Even if he got through, he wouldn't have a chance. The rebels were drunk on their victories. Nothing could stop them short of an army.

He prayed that Sarah and his sons were safe. But even as he nurtured the thought, he knew he was trying to grab the wind. It was almost certain they were dead, killed in the first rush of the mob to murder every American in sight.

Will didn't cry. The bitter cold snapped him from his grief, made him shiver as if he had been dowsed with icy water from a steam. He had to stay alive, and all he had for protection were the buckskins he wore. Already the chill and killing winter wind blew down from the pass so far away in the darkness, the pass he must cross if he was to live to fight another day.

He looked at the stars so distant and cold and took his bearings. His stomach murmured with the first soft growls of hunger. He shuddered and started toward the pass at a dead run, hoping he could stay alive long enough to find shelter. The snow underfoot was so cold, his toes lost all feeling. Then the shooting pains started in his feet, a warning of dangerous frostbite.

And the wind howled as it rushed down from the Sangre de Cristo Mountains, scathed the plain, searing Burke with its deathly breath, cutting into him with frosty knives, slicing the heat away piece by piece.

But Burke knew that if he stopped, if he did not go on, he would die. For that mob would swell and grow, and march over him to the Arkansas Valley and slay every man, woman, and child in its bloody path.

≈ 28 ≈

When the moon rose, Burke found the trail to Raton Pass. He knew he had to build a shelter and start a fire or he would perish in the cold. His feet and hands felt as if they were frozen solid. He wondered if he could cut piñon branches to keep out the wind, wondered if he could even hold flint and steel in his numb fingers.

He finally stopped, on a hill thick with juniper and piñon. Shivering, he began to cut limbs from the live trees. He stacked them in a circle around a single juniper. He wondered if he could find dead wood in the snow. There were no pines where he could gather squaw wood for tinder. When he had built his shelter high enough, he cut more branches to pull over him once he was inside and had a fire going.

In the darkness, he roamed the hill. He knew what he was looking for but doubted he could find it. The moon shed little light, and the trees were deceptive. He examined each promising one, keeping his bearings so that he could find his shelter again. His breath made a frosty cloud on the silver air.

Finally Will found the tree he was looking for. It stood alone on a high tor, surrounded by lesser trees, a large juniper. Even in the darkness, it looked as if it had been struck by lightning. Its limbs were blasted to splinters, it branches drooping, shattered, tangled.

A bull elk had rubbed the tree with his massive rack, shredding off the velvet, rubbing the antlers until they gleamed black from the tree's sap. The bull had also established this spot as his own, warning younger bulls of his power and strength, notifying the cows in season that he was here.

Will touched one of the splayed branches, felt its dryness, its age. The rub was old, the wood dry. He took out his knife with senseless fingers, hacked the dead branches from the tree. He saved splinters, every small scrap of wood that might catch fire when he struck his flint on steel, fumbled them into his possibles pouch.

Burke cut a large branch from the tree, his hands hurting so bad, he dropped the knife several times. Tears welled up in his eyes. He used this branch as a small travois, stacked the dead wood on it, and hauled it toward his shelter, the needles gliding across the snow in a loud whisper. When he found his way back, he threw all the dead wood inside. Then he put the larger branches over the top until he had a dome-shaped shelter. He crawled in, pulled the branches up against the dome after him.

He sat there, blowing on his hands to warm thcm. He crossed his arms and put his hands beneath his armpits. As some heat entered his flesh, the pain became excruciating. Finally, knowing he could wait no longer, Will dug out the splinters from his pouch, groped for the little German silver box that contained his flint, steel, and burnt cloth.

Carefully, he built a small tepee with the splinters, set dead juniper needles at the base. He used every twig he had, made sure he had small pieces of wood to place on the cone if he got the fire started.

He lay flat on his stomach, stuffed a small piece of dry burnt cloth next to the fine tinder. His numb fingers grasped the flint in his right hand. In his left, he held the steel, impervious to its cold. He scratched the flint across the ragged chunk of steel. A few feeble sparks flew off the steel, but the cloth didn't catch. He blew on his fingers again, but his own breath was so cold, he felt no heat.

Burke cleared his mind of the pain, concentrated on striking sparks with the chunk of flint. The cold burrowed into him, and he knew that if he didn't get warm soon, he would just curl up and die.

"Light, damn you," he mumbled.

He struck the steel again. Sparks flew into the cloth, the tinder. He cupped his frozen hands around the tiny embers, blew softly on the sparks. The embers pulsed and glowed. He kept blowing until a small flame quivered out of the cloth, licked at the shavings.

"Not too hard," he said. "Easy now, Burke."

He felt himself drifting away from lucidity. He knew he was becoming addled from the cold. He continued to nurture the feeble flame. Then the slivers of dry wood caught, and a tongue of fire burst from the shavings, lashed at the larger pieces of wood.

Will sat up, extended his hands over the small fire. Pain coursed through every fiber of his flesh. Tears leaked from his eyes. He rubbed his hands together, trying to restore the circulation. The flame wavered but continued to burn, eating at the fresh dry wood.

"Jasus," he moaned as his fingers warmed. He stared at the flames, mesmerized by their life-giving beauty. He gently placed a larger piece of wood on the pyramid, collapsing it. But the fire held, and he added more wood. The juniper boughs kept most of the wind away, but he still felt cold inside, and his feet were lifeless appendages. He stripped off his moccasins and stuck his bare feet close to the fire. Again the pain, the excruciating pain. He rubbed his feet, added more wood to the fire. He drew his feet back, then put them close again when the heat-pain left them.

"There now," he said. "You're warmin', Burke, you're warmin' fine."

He huddled next to the fire, fed it until his senses returned. He was sleepy but knew he dared not sleep. The fire would go out, and he would never awaken. He sat there, rocking gently back and forth, turning in every direction to let the heat soak into him.

He kept the fire within bounds, warmed himself slowly. It would do no good to burn up all the wood and have to go out in the cold again, search for the elk-shattered tree. If he tended the fire right, it would last until morning. He fought off the sleepiness, caught himself nodding several times.

He put his moccasins on and stood up, walked around the fire. He could smell the sap from the live boughs as the flames dried them. It would not do to catch his shelter afire. The wind still prowled the knoll, and he felt its icy sigh when it gusted through the boughs of his shelter. He stamped his feet, rubbed his hands, walked around and around to stay awake. He talked himself through the night, half mad, groggy from lack of sleep. The fire grew smaller toward morning as his wood supply dwindled.

"Just a little while more," he begged, and laughed at himself for speaking aloud. "Burn slow, little fire, but stay warm."

He saw that his wood would not last and began stripping the roof of his shelter. The smoke nearly drove him out into the open, but he learned how to sneak the tips of the branches in, let them dry until they crackled and caught. The warmth kept him alive; feeding the fire kept him alert and busy. All of it seemed unreal to him, almost dreamlike, and by morning he was babbling to himself. Worse, he had formed an attachment to his temporary home. The sun came up, and the wind died down, but Burke was reluctant to leave the shelter.

He kept feeding the fire, and the smoke choked him. The sun rose still higher, and there was so little shelter left that he finally realized he must go. He shivered as he let the fire die out, shook off the urge to go back to the dead juniper and get more fresh wood.

"Time to go, Burke," he muttered, and took his bearings from the sun. He staggered from the depleted shelter and headed north, wondering if he should go to Bent's or Stonecipher's. But he knew he'd never make it to Bent's. If he could make it to Greenhorn settlement, he might have a chance. There he could warn the settlers, rest up, and continue on to Stonecipher's, try and get some help.

The snow deepened the closer he got to Raton Pass. Burke thought he could make three or four miles an hour, but he had to find game trails, places where the winds had swept the ground bare of snow, and sometimes had to wander far off course. Still, he made the pass, finding shelter at night, building better fires so that he could sleep, banking them with heavier logs. Hunger pangs ragged his gut until it seemed in a continual snarling rage. He felt at times that his belly had grown teeth and was eating him alive.

He lost all track of time, and sometimes he stumbled along in a daze, not caring where he was or where he was going. He made it through the pass, but he was wet and cold, his buckskins freezing to his body, his moccasins beginning to wear through.

On the flat, he found a herd of elk feeding in a pocket of the foothills where they could reach the grass. He shot two and made camp, built a fire. It took him half a day to skin both of them out. He ate the heart and liver of a cow raw and cooked a haunch. He cleaned the flesh off the hides, scraping them with his knife, then cut holes in them for ponchos. He cooked as much meat as he could carry with him and left the carcasses behind.

But the meat had given him sorely needed strength. He forged ahead over bleak snow-flocked trails, the double ponchos, the hair side in, kept him reasonably warm. Only his feet and hands and face suffered from the exposure. His face felt as raw as the flesh rotting on the elk hides.

One day, long after he had come down over Raton Pass, perhaps a week, perhaps two, he saw a man on horseback riding out on the plain. Will had left Spanish Peaks behind him two or three days before and had followed Cucheras Creek northeasterly until he found a well-traveled trail that led toward Greenhorn.

Burke, an odd and frightening sight in the elkskin ponchos, waved and hollered at the man. The rider stood up in his stirrups for a better look, then, terrified, wheeled his horse to the northwest and rode off at a gallop.

Will felt a surge of despair as he watched the man ride away, disappear in the distance. His feet felt like blocks of wood, his teeth were chattering, and he had only a few scraps of cooked elkmeat left, turning rancid.

"Don't know if I can make it any further," he whispered, his voice scratchy in his throat.

Still, he staggered on, slinging his rifle across his shoulders, hanging his tired arms from them as he slogged through the snow.

More riders appeared a few hours later. Will no longer had the strength to wave. "Go to hell," he growled. "Go to bloody hell, ye heartless bastids." The riders disappeared, and Burke thought he might have imagined them.

Half an hour later, he saw the tops of cabins and adobes. "Greenhorn," he breathed.

The settlement shimmered like a mirage in the sun. A cry of exultation rose up in Burke's throat, and he started to run. But the effort churned his senses to mush, and his brain filled with smoke. Light-headed, he fought to breathe in gulps of elusive air. He stumbled over a snow-covered prickly pear, lost his balance, and fell to the ground.

He skidded on the snow. The fall knocked the wind out of him. He struggled to rise, and his head spun with a sudden dizziness.

He looked toward Greenhorn, but from the ground he could no longer see the buildings. For a moment he thought he had imagined it. Then he saw the dark shape of a man on the horizon, walking toward him.

Will squinched his eyes shut and opened them again. The man was still coming toward him. Burke tried to get to his feet, but he could not make his legs work. He pulled himself up by his arms but couldn't get his legs under him to stand.

The man drew still closer, walking faster now, but shadowy in the glare of the sun.

Burke lifted his hand to wave but fell back, gripped with a blinding nausea.

As the man drew closer, Burke saw that he was large and dark-skinned, the biggest man he had ever seen. Although the man was wearing white man's clothes, Will saw his face plain.

The man approaching Burke was an Indian, a giant savage with broad shoulders and powerful arms.

Burke's strength ebbed from his arms, and he collapsed on the ground, certain that he was mad or on the verge of death.

≈ 29 ≈

The big Delaware loomed over Will Burke, shadowed him with his giant frame. Burke heard the man breathing, lifted his head, opened his eyes. Will recognized the man. They called the Delaware Big Nigger.

"Burke? That you?"

"It's rightly me, Big Nigger," said Burke.

"Haw. They say you ghost. They say you Injun feller. Heap scared, every damn man."

"That Greenhorn over yonder?"

"Greenhorn, you betchum."

Burke tried again to get to his feet. He grunted with the useless effort. Big Nigger bent over, picked him up. Burke felt his senses reel. He held on to his rifle, but he knew that if the big man hadn't found him, he probably wouldn't have made it the last few hundred yards to the settlement.

Big Nigger carried Burke inside a stockade. Someone gave Will a drink of whiskey, and a woman poured hot broth into him.

"How come you're afoot?" asked one of the settlers.

Burke told him the story of the attack on Turley's, how he had made his escape. "You better get some runners out. Them rebels will come over that pass one fine day and start shootin' everything that moves. They already tasted blood, and I speck they'll be after more."

"What about you?" asked the settler, a man they called Hank.

"I got to get rested up and go to Stonecipher's, warn him. Can I buy a horse or a mule?"

"You can. But you're in no shape to ride."

"I know," said Burke, and he drank more whiskey until the lassitude of the very weary engulfed him. He remembered someone putting him in a bed, and then it was dark and he was finally warm.

Burke rode into Stonecipher's four days later. He told Jake what had happened at Taos and at Turley's. Jake sent runners to all the settlements along the Arkansas. The *pueblo* bristled with intense excitement as the men prepared for war. Jake took charge of all the preparations, elated at the challenge.

There were two Mexicans staying at Jake's fort, Pablo Jerez and Hector Elizando. Jake ordered them put under guard, locked in an empty magazine room.

He sent Joe Perkins to Bent's Fort with a message that Ceran St. Vrain should get together an army and come help them fight.

"Be Injuns and Mexicans?" asked Joe.

"I think we'll probably have to fight the Spaniards before this is over," said Burke.

"Let 'em come," he told Burke. "We're generally gettin' ready to receive the Spaniards, Mexican, Pueblo Injuns—whatever comes down that trail a-lookin' for trouble."

"I keep thinkin' of Sarah and the boys," said Burke. "Wonderin' if I hadn't ought to go a-lookin' for 'em."

"Will, only a crazy man would go back there by hisself," said Jake. "You just wait, and we'll go there with you, whip whatever stands in our way."

Still, Burke was uneasy. He felt restless, and the worry over Sarah, Sean, and Kelly gave him fits that first night.

In the morning, Burke and Stonecipher discovered that Jerez had escaped from the fort during the night. The guard, Jack Wilson, had fallen asleep. "Well, that shows me something," said Jake. "We won't have many Mexican friends when this pot boils over."

"Hell, I'd have run off too," said Burke. "You got them boys convicted and hung without even puttin' 'em on trial."

"From now on, Will, I don't trust nobody," said Jake. Burke saw Consuelo's eyebrows arch, but she said nothing.

Three days later, Elizando escaped, taking three of Jake's best mules.

"That does it," said Jake. "Will, I'm gettin' some men together to track that scoundrel. You fit enough to ride?"

"Beats a-settin' around here waitin' for somebody to drop a hammer," said Burke.

Jake and Will, taking ten men from Pueblo, tracked Hector Elizando. The trail led them into the mountains, over ground familiar to Burke. "Looks to me like he's headed for Serrano's," said Burke.

"The sonofabitch," said Jake, and steam jetted from his nostrils and mouth. It was not so cold in the timber, and most of the early snow had melted away. The mule tracks were easy to follow.

"Just ahead," said Will as they drew near Serrano's house.

Jake motioned to the other riders to fan out. He and Will rode on ahead.

The house was still. Smoke streamed from the chimney, turned invisible against the snowpeaked mountains in the distance.

"At least the Ute ain't here," whispered Burke.

"What?"

"Paco's been lettin' Blanco and his Ute summer up here. Gives 'em beeves and lets 'em pitch their lodges downcreek."

"Why didn't you tell me this before, Will?"

"Hell, Jake, it'd be like tellin' you a dog had fleas. Ute have summered in these mountains since long before our time. I figured Paco wanted to keep his hair, same as me."

"That bastard," said Jake, the anger in him burning his face.

Jake motioned to the others, sweeping his arms to indicate that he wanted them to surround the house. The men moved through the trees like dark ghosts. After a few minutes, it grew quiet again.

"Paco!" Jake called. "You come out."

There was no answer.

"Serrano, you come out that door now!" he yelled again.

Still there was no answer.

Jake brought his rifle to his shoulder, steadied it against a pine tree. He fired a round at the front door, the ball raising dust and splinters from the wood. He reloaded his rifle. The door opened, and a hand holding a poker appeared, a white handkerchief dangling from the end of the poker.

"Come on out, Paco!" yelled Burke.

Paco stepped outside. He tossed the poker back inside the house.

"I'm ordering you to surrender, Paco," said Jake, "along with Hector Elizando and any other Mexicans or Indians you got hidin' in the house."

"Why?" asked Paco as Jake leveled his rifle at Serrano, his thumb twitching nervously on the lock. "I have done nothing to you."

"You're a Spaniard, and we're at war," said Jake.

"I am not at war," said Paco.

"No, and you ain't goin' to be," said Jake firmly. "Now, you call Hector out here, or I'm going to tell my men to start dropping hammers."

One of the posse members rode up to Jake. "Some of the others say hang 'em now," said Bill Dailey, a blacksmith, one of the men from Pueblo. His voice carried to the porch where Paco stood.

"There'll be no hangin'," said Jake. "You hear me, Serrano? Quicker you move, the quicker this'll all be over."

"What do you want with me?"

"I just want you where I can keep an eye on you. We don't need nobody comin' in our back door."

"All right," said Paco. He turned back to the house, called to Hector in Spanish. A few seconds later, Elizando appeared in the doorway.

"Anybody else in there?" asked Burke.

Paco shook his head.

"We better check," said Jake. He whistled for the others, who rode up.

"I wish to talk you, Jake," said Serrano.

"Step off the porch, the both of you," said Stonecipher. "Just come on out here in the open. Keep your hands where we can see 'em plain."

Jake and Hector walked down the steps, stood in the opening.

"Bill, you catch up my mules. The rest of you, search the house real good. Better put a man out back until you're through."

Dailey nodded. Saddles creaked as men dismounted, tied their reins to the hitchrails out front. They streamed into the house. One man walked around back, rifle at the ready.

"Jake," said Paco, "I will go with you if you will not put me in irons."

"You will be treated fairly," said Jake.

"Best ask him about his Ute wife," said Burke.

"You tellin' me Paco's got him a squaw?"

"That's what Sarah told me."

Jake scowled. "Paco, where's your woman?"

Paco's face drained of color. "She has gone," he said.

"Ute is she?"

Paco nodded.

"Looks to me like you are just pretty damned thick with them Injuns," Jake told him.

"You stole my wife, Jake. I was given a woman. She has borne me a son."

The men in the posse came back out of the house.

"Nobody in there," said Dailey to Jake.

"Let's get the mules and head back," said Stonecipher. He whistled. The man behind the house walked back out. The men did not mount their horses but stood looking at the two prisoners.

"Mount up," said Jake.

"We figger these two Mexes need a good drubbing," said one tall lanky man they called Fat Pat, skinny as a heron's leg. "They got us away from a warm fire and a hot cup. Least we can do."

"Pat, you just back off there," said Jake.

"You wouldn't shoot me, would you, Stonecipher?" Pat grinned.

"I might."

Pat stepped out of the clot of men, struck Paco with his fist. Paco went down. The others broke into a run and swarmed over Elizando and Paco. They pounded their fists into the two Mexicans. Burke and Stonecipher slid from their saddles and waded into the group, pushing them away with the butts of their rifles.

The fight broke up. Burke lifted Paco up. He was bleeding from a cut lip, his face looking bee-stung from all the lumps on it. Hector, dazed, stared at Jake woozily, his nose spewing blood down his chin and onto his shirt.

"Get 'em some coats," said Jake to Bill Dailey. "Where in hell are them goddamned mules?"

A man came around the side of the house, leading Jake's stolen mules.

"Now let's get the hell out of here. You've had your fun, boys."

Burke held his rifle ready, braced for any further trouble. Grumbling, the men went to their horses, mounted up. Bill Dailey went into the house, returned a few moments later with two coats. He threw them to Hector and Paco.

The Mexicans donned their coats.

"Take 'em to the stables, Will," said Jake. "Get 'em mounted. Take Bill Dailey with you. I don't trust them others."

Burke nodded.

Fifteen minutes later, the men rode out, the posse bracing Hector and Paco, Burke in the lead. Jake rode behind, alert for any sign that the posse meant further harm to his prisoners.

Jake rubbed the cold from his gloved fingers, looked at Paco's back up ahead. Maybe, he thought, he should have let the men beat Paco to death. Once the people in Pueblo learned that he had been harboring Blanco and his band, they might want to hang him from the nearest cottonwood tree. He wondered what Consuelo would think when she saw her former husband. One thing he did know. If he had let the men kill Paco, she would have left him, gone back to her people in Taos. She had told him as much one night when he said that Paco might join the rebels to save his own skin.

"Paco just wants to be left alone," she said. "He is as much a part of this land as you."

Jake had been worrying over that bone ever since. He and Consuelo had not spoken of it, but she was a Mexican. Would her people kill her for taking up with an American? Would she join the rebels if they overran the fort? Hard questions.

And Jake had no answers.

The Ute woman Paco called Candelaria, arose from her hiding place in the corncrib out back of the house. She had heard the men ride away, taking with them her husband and the Mexican Elizando. She clucked to her son, Ernesto, held him close to her breasts.

She went to the stables, saddled a fleet pony given her by Blanco himself. She took food for a week, wrapped herself and Ernesto in warm buffalo robes, and haltered another horse, attached a lead rope to the rope loop at the muzzle.

Before the white-eyes had left the high meadow, she and Ernesto were riding to Blanco's camp down on the plains. There was big trouble, she knew. For now, she was no longer Candelaria but River Willow once again. She spoke to the small boy, called him by his Ute name, Little Owl. He had the round moonface of her people, his father's dark brown eyes that seemed too large for his face.

As she rode, River Willow knew that she would see Paco Serrano again, when Blanco returned to the mountains. But she did not know if she would ever be Paco's woman again. For Blanco had told her that if there was ever any trouble between the Mexicans and the *gringos*, he would attack the settlements and drive both peoples from Ute lands.

This had been Blanco's promise. River Willow knew that Blanco was a very wise and brave man. If he said that he would kill all the white-eyes, then that is what he would do.

Even Paco Serrano.

≈ 30 ≈

Rumors flew through Pueblo and Stonecipher's like autumn leaves in the wind. Messages came from Bent's Fort and Santa Fe. Paco and Hector sat in the powder magazine room under heavy guard. Jake forbade Consuelo to visit him or talk to him. Colonel Sterling Price, at Santa Fe, expecting a shortage of food because of the Indian uprising, sent Lieutenants Luddington and Willis, guarded by sixty Mormons, to Bent's Fort with wagons and teams. The soldiers drew four months' provisions.

Word came to Stonecipher's fort that Colonel Price had routed the Taos rebels.

"I want to ride down there, Jake, and see if Sarah and the boys are still alive," said Burke when the news came in.

"I got word that Ceran St. Vrain might be puttin' together some men. Best you ride over to Bent's first and see what's up."

"Makes sense," said Burke. Joe Perkins had been to Bent's twice, and the long winter had dragged on through a nervous Christmas and a new year, 1847, with conflicting reports from every direction.

Two men rode in from Bent's Fort, said that Ceran St. Vrain had organized a volunteer company and had asked that any who wanted to fight join him in Santa Fe.

A few days later, word came from Taos that the rebels were still fighting. A day later, a rider came into the fort, his horse lathered, his side aching, to tell Jake that there were five hundred Spaniards camped on the St. Charles River. Jake sent Joe Perkins to Barclay's Houses with a message to gather up their families and as much of their possessions as they could cram into wagons and move into the fort.

Will Burke, Bill Dailey, and Joe Perkins rode out for Santa Fe to join up with St. Vrain's forces.

Ceran St. Vrain welcomed the new men and rode for Taos. He attacked the town that spring of 1847.

The fighting was fierce, the Indians determined to defend themselves. Will Burke was in the thick of it. He saw Big Nigger fighting with the Taos Indians. The Delaware called out the names of the mountain men he knew, then shot them dead when they came running toward him. Will tried his best to kill Big Nigger, but as St. Vrain's volunteers swept through the town, the Delaware escaped.

Burke found Sarah in the smoking aftermath of the battle in bullet-riddled Taos. She and the boys emerged from an adobe house after the town was secured, the victors drinking in the cantinas, the wagons carting off the dead.

"Burke," she said. "I am happy you are alive."

"You too." He hugged the boys, kissed his wife. "Why didn't them Injuns kill you?" he asked, but knew the answer even as he spoke.

Sarah had become an Indian again. Her long hair was plaited, and she wore a buckskin dress. Sean and Kelly too looked like young Pueblo bucks with their breech-clouts and moccasins.

"I will make myself pretty for you again," she said.

She began combing out her braids as Will tumbled with the boys on the ground, the three of them laughing with the joy of it.

Leaders of the insurrection were tried at Taos in April of that year. Archibald Charles Metcalf had been appointed sheriff on March 1. He was charged with the duties of hanging those sentenced to death. He did so with obvious relish. Burke, Sarah, and the boys rode to Stonecipher's with the news of the battle, the trials, and the hangings.

There Jake held a trial of his own. Paco Serrano was found to have no connection with the massacre at Taos, freed, and sent back home. Hector Elizando was found guilty of stealing mules, ordered to pay two dollars. He worked for Barclay and paid the fine, spent the extra money on Taos Lightning. He got drunk and stole one of Jake's horses, rode away. Like Big Nigger, he was never seen again on the upper Arkansas.

Paco returned home to find Blanco and his warriors waiting for him. River Willow and his son, Ernesto, were there too.

"There is much war to the south," said Blanco. "In the places called Texas and Mexico. The *gringo* white-eyes are fighting the Mexican white-eyes, and there is much killing."

"I know," said Paco.

"There are many soldiers on the plains. They shoot the Indians. Blanco will paint his face for war."

"You cannot win," said Paco. "They are too many. They are prepared for war with the Indians."

"Let them kill each other," said Blanco. "Do not tell the white-eyes that Blanco will make war too."

"Why is my woman with your braves?"

"She rides with Blanco. But if you want her, she will

stay in your lodge. Do you want the Mexican woman back in your lodge?"

Paco drew a breath. He looked off beyond the chief and his men. "I do not know, Blanco."

"Maybe we will give her back to you. Then you will have two women."

Blanco spoke to River Willow. She nodded, walked toward Paco, carrying Ernesto. She kept her eyes lowered.

"Go into the house, Candelaria," said Paco softly.

Blanco watched, his face a stony mask, as the woman he called River Willow took the boy inside the house.

"You will not tell the white-eyes," said Blanco, and stalked away. It was not a question.

Paco walked to the porch, watched as the Ute, Apache and Kiowa melted into the forest, rode to their camp. On his land.

He swallowed bitterly. He had not promised Blanco anything, but he was torn between his hatred for Jake Stonecipher and his hatred for the renegade band of Indians. His sense of justice was too strong just to let the Indians massacre people he knew. At the first opportunity, he vowed inwardly, he would ride over to Burke's and tell him of Blanco's plans.

But the next day the Indians were gone.

Paco decided that he'd better not tell Burke anything. He would not put it past Jake Stonecipher to accuse him of helping Blanco.

During the long summer, Paco's riders told him of the Ute depredations. Blanco's braves raided farms, stole corn, horses, cattle. Their numbers grew. Finally Paco rode to Burke's place and told him what Blanco had said.

"You should never have let them camp on your land," said Will.

"They would have killed me, burned down my house," said Paco.

"And now they're killin' settlers all along the road to Santa Fee and between Pueblo and Bent's," said Burke.

"I am sorry," said Paco, and rode sadly away.

Burke rode down to the fort, taking Sarah and the boys with him. He told Jake what Paco had told him.

"Blanco has left the bigger settlements alone," said Jake. "But we got worse problems."

"I think Blanco will get strong enough to attack even you, Jake," said Burke.

"We just heard that Phil Kearny has marched into Santa Fe with seventeen hundred men. The Americans around here are ready to kill Mexicans. It wouldn't take much."

"You worried?"

"I'm worried about Consuelo. She might not be safe if there's an American uprising."

"Well, you come get me if you need help. Me'n Sarah and the boys are goin' back up in the mountains."

"Still after the gold, Will?"

"None of your damned business, Jake."

It was September, and the aspen leaves had turned golden in the foothills. Burke ignored the changing season and dug for gold in Adobe Creek.

One day Sarah came up behind him, put her hand on his shoulder.

"Eh? Oh, it's you." Burke stood up. There was dirt embedded in his fingernails. His face was smudged with grime, his buckskins muddy.

"Look at you, Burke," said Sarah. "Look at this creek."

"Hell, I'm gettin' the gold, Sarah. For you and the boys."

"You have taken a place of beauty, made it into a mud bath. All for gold. The gold you'll spend, but what about this place? Can you replace the columbines, the wild mountain flowers you destroyed?"

"They'll grow back," he muttered.

"Burke, don't you have enough by now? Can't you just stop and enjoy what's left of our lives?"

He looked at her. She looked like a queen in her white elkskin dress, her figure slim and sleek, her face clean, her hair soft on her shoulders.

"I don't know," he said.

"It's time to go down to Jake's," she said.

"You want to go there?"

"I don't want to go to Taos."

"Maybe you're right. Be winter soon. Just let me . . ."

"No, Burke," she said. "Now. Tomorrow." There was the firmness of a woman's resolve in her voice.

Burke sighed and threw down his shovel. "We'll go tomorrow," he said, and watched her walk away. A lump formed in his throat, and he felt the sting of tears in his eyes. He loved the woman, and yet when he was digging for gold, he had eyes for nothing else.

"I'll make it up to you," he said, but Sarah had gone out of earshot.

The Burkes moved into the fort by the end of September. Will left a few days later to hunt the bugling elk in the Wet Mountains.

Blanco struck the settlements in Huerfano, Greenhorn, and Hardscrabble, sweeping through them in three days. Those who had escaped the slaughter came to Stonecipher's bedraggled, tired, terrified. Blanco struck Fort Stonecipher last, at the dawning of an October morn. The fighting was fierce.

White smoke floated over the adobe fort and hovered over the waters of the Fountain and the Arkansas. A band of Jicarilla Apache broke into the fort, shot up several men, killed and scalped others. They dragged Consuelo off with them.

Jake tried to stop them. He went down, struck by a glancing lead ball that knocked him unconscious as it streaked across his temple, leaving a bloody furrow through his sideburns. Another man, shot stone dead, fell over him, probably saving Jake's life.

Burke rode out of the mountains at the height of the fighting, both mules packed with fresh elkmeat and hides. A group of men from Pueblo had flanked Blanco, were shooting with deadly accuracy.

"Split 'em up!" yelled Burke, and shot a Kiowa who was riding toward the fort.

Burke and a dozen others fought their way to the fort. The Indians fled, taking women prisoners with them. Will saw Consuelo as she looked back over her shoulder, her face streaked with tears.

Will found Jake under the dead man, revived him.

Jake had a thundering headache. "I want to get after them Injuns," said Stonecipher. "They took Consuelo, Luz, God knows who else."

"I know," said Will, grateful that Sarah was still alive and had not been captured. She and the boys had hid in the stables with some other women. Several men died defending them from the Indians trying to break in through the back gate.

Jake, groggy and in pain, stood up, hunted for his rifle. He filled his pouch with powder and ball while Burke tried to enlist men to go with them.

"No one'll go with us, Jake," said Burke. "You lost a lot of shooters here."

"I know. But hell, I got to find Consuelo."

"I have a pretty good idea where we can find her," said Will.

"Where?"

"At Serrano's. That's where they'll go to hole up, lick their wounds."

"Let's get to it, then," said Stonecipher.

The two men rode out from the smoking fort alone. They rode into the mountains, hard on the heels of Blanco's Muache Ute and the savages from other tribes who followed his warpath.

There was a chill in the air, a dullness to the sky, a feeling that death was only a breath away, whispering in their ears, killing the things that grew on the earth. The aspen leaves had gone brown, and the winds had stripped them from the trees. There was a sadness to the land, yet the river ran, and the mountains stood lofty and solid, immutable and mysterious, brute monuments that marked the graves of men and seasons, impervious to all change.

≈ 31 ≈

Jake and Will followed the tacks of Blanco's band into the mountains.

"Not goin' straight for Serrano's," said Will pensively. "You know where they're headed?"

"We'll know in another coupla hours," said Burke, a grim cast to his face.

Two hours later, they smelled the acrid tang of woodsmoke. A few minutes later, they rode up to the smoking ruins of Will's cabin. He walked through it. Everything was gone, everything ashes. "Now they'll head for Serrano's," said Burke.

"I'm damned sorry, Will. Good thing Sarah and the boys weren't here."

Will saw a gaping hole in the earth under the place where he and Sarah had had their buffalo-robe bed.

"They got the gold I left up here," he said.

Jake said nothing.

They left. There was plenty of Indian sign along the way to Paco's.

Blanco rode up to Serrano's. He didn't have to call Paco out.

"I give you back your woman," said Blanco. "If you do not want her, I will kill her."

"I will take her, Blanco."

Consuelo looked at Paco, her eyes brimming with hatred. "Do you know how many men died so that you could have me back? I think they killed Jake."

"I did not mean for this to happen."

"You are filth, Paco," said Consuelo.

Blanco shoved her toward her former husband and laughed harshly. Then the Ute ordered his men to follow him. "We will camp far from this place on the creek you call Graneros," said Blanco. "We have killed many white-eyes. We have much grain and whiskey and cattle."

Paco watched them go. He helped Consuelo into the house. Candelaria bristled at the Mexican woman. Consuelo sat on the divan, hung her head, covered her face with her hands.

"Let her sleep in the stables," said Candelaria to Paco.

He looked at her, torn between this Ute woman and the woman he had loved since he was a young man. The truth was, he realized, he had made peace with himself over the loss of Consuelo and had come to love Candelaria and their son, Ernesto.

"No," he said. "This was once her lodge. She will live under my roof, or you can go back to your people."

Candelaria glared at her husband. She spat at Consuelo and left the room. Ernesto called to his mother from the kitchen in the back of the house.

"I'm sorry, Consuelo," Paco said.

"Go with the devil," she replied in Spanish.

Jake and Will rode up to Serrano's.

"They been here," said Burke. "Gone now."

"Let's find Paco," said Jake.

The two men approached the house warily.

"Paco Serrano!" called Jake.

The door opened. Paco walked out on the porch. He was unarmed.

"Do you have Consuelo?" Jake asked bluntly.

"She is here. She is safe."

"Give her back, or I'll kill you where you stand, Serrano."

"She is yours, Jake. If you'll wait until I saddle up, I'll ride with you and Burke. You are hunting Blanco too, are you not?"

"We are," said Burke.

"Then I will take you to where they are," said Paco.

"We'll wait," said Jake.

Consuelo walked outside. Jake dismounted, took the steps two at a time as Paco went inside. Jake embraced his wife. She sobbed against his shoulder.

"Wait here until we return," he said. "Blanco's got Luz and some other women."

"I know," said Consuelo. "I thought you were dead." She touched the side of his head where the ball had gouged his flesh.

Jake winced. "I'll live, I reckon. Wait for me."

"Yes, yes," she said.

The three men rode northwesterly, following the pony tracks along the foothills.

"They'll camp up above the creek," said Will, "up on Greenhorn Mountain somewhere."

The Indians had not gone that far. Burke spotted their camp above Fisher's Hole, close enough to the place where the St. Charles River rose so that they could carry water to their camp. The Indians were drunk. They seemed to be gloating over their victories.

"What now, Will?" asked Jake.

"We'll ride right in on 'em. Nothin' a Ute understands more'n a man who ain't afraid of 'em."

"I do not think . . ." Paco started to say.

"We'll do what Burke says," said Jake.

Blanco's face twisted in surprise as the three white men rode into his camp. Some of the Apache rose up and grabbed their rifles. "*Matalos!*" they shouted. "Kill them!"

Blanco lifted his arm, held the Apache in check. He looked around, wondering if these three white-eyes had brought an army with them. They seemed unafraid.

"Where are the others hiding?" he asked Paco in Spanish.

"Don't say nothin', Paco," said Burke. To Blanco he said, "Blanco, I want you to give up all your prisoners, or I'll put a ball right between your eyes."

"You are brave, but you will die if you shoot me. Your women will die. They will sleep forever with no stomachs."

"I ain't gonna wait, Blanco. You get them women and kids out here pronto."

Jake held his right hand up as if ready to give a signal. Blanco looked at Stonecipher. This was a man the Apache said they had killed. He was still alive. He was very *fuerte*, this one.

It was a bluff, but it worked.

Blanco looked at Paco, a questioning look on his face.

"It is finished, Blanco," said Paco. "I will no longer hide you and your braves on my land."

"This is Ute land. Always. Ute land."

"No more. Many soldiers are coming from Bent's Fort and from Santa Fe. They will wipe you from the earth, leave your bones on the ground like the skulls of buffalo."

Jake and Will looked at Paco with newfound respect.

Blanco and his braves talked furiously for the next several moments. Jake sat his horse, his hand still in the air. It was beginning to quiver slightly.

Blanco barked some orders. Disgruntled braves brought the women and children to the center of camp. Others brought stolen horses for the hostages to ride.

"We will meet again, Chake," Blanco said to Stone-cipher. "I will come again to your big fort on the river."

Jake said nothing. He held his hand in the air like a bird frozen in flight.

When the women and children were mounted on their horses, the three men flanked them. They turned their horses and rode out of camp. None of them dared show any emotion until they were out of sight and earshot. It was like sitting on a powder keg with flames licking at the staves.

They arrived back at Serrano's late at night. Consuelo embraced Luz Delgado. The two of them helped the other women and children make up beds.

"Where is Candelaria?" Paco asked Consuelo.

"She took the boy and rode off," said Consuelo. "I tried to stop them, but she was too strong for me."

"Maybe it is just as well," said Paco. "I too will go until Blanco is captured or killed. This is not a safe place anymore."

"I am sorry, Paco," she said. "You are a good man."

Paco did not reply.

In the morning, he said good-bye to Consuelo. He rode away, headed for Santa Fe.

"He's got backbone," said Will.

"Yes," said Jake, putting an arm around Consuelo's waist. "I wronged him."

"Hush," said Consuelo. "What is done, is done."

"That's sayin' it," said Will as he left to saddle mounts for the women and children.

"What about you, Will?" Jake called after him.

Will stopped, turned around. "What?"

"What are you and Sarah going to do? You have no home up here. This is Ute land."

"Why, we'll build a bigger place, a better one. This land ain't nobody's less'n you fight for it. I aim to stay. What about you, Jake?"

Jake looked at Consuelo. She smiled up at him.

He thought of the river, the secrets it held in its murky depths, the flow of its waters. The river, like the mountains, would always be there. Men would come and go, but the river stayed.

"I think we'll all outlast Blanco," said Jake. "This is good land, all of it. I'm not goin' anywhere unless they carry me away in a pine box."

Will cranked his head in a nod of approval, then walked toward the stables.

"That's the kind of man this country needs," Jake said to Consuelo. "He don't buffalo none."

"What does this mean, this 'buffalo none'?"

"It means he's got iron in his backbone. It means Burke will do to ride the river with, stormy or calm."

"And, that is you too, my husband," she said softly. "You do not buffalo none neither."

Jake laughed and drew Consuelo into his arms, kissed her. She smelled of spruce and pine and river. The scent in her hair was the strong scent of the land and the mountains that fed the Arkansas River, gave it life for its long journey across the plains and down to the Father of Waters, the Mississippi, and mingled with those waters as they surged toward the Gulf of Mexico. And the clouds brought the waters back in rain and snow in an endless cycle, feeding and nurturing the land season upon season, for lifetimes and lifetimes. Forever.

≈ **AFTERWORD** ≈

It would be another six years before anyone in the Arkansas Valley heard from Blanco and his Muache Ute again. He would come back, as he had promised, and destroy the town of Pueblo. By then, America's conquest of New Mexico would be complete. But the destruction of the Arkansas Valley settlements would begin, and only Jake Stonecipher, Will Burke, Paco Serrano, Charles Autobees, William Bent in his stone fort at Big Timber, and a few others, would hold out.

The army ragged the Ute until they signed a treaty with General Garland. Gold seekers from Cherry Creek, disillusioned at the slim pickings, drifted down to spend their winters at the mouth of the Fountain, listening to Jake Stonecipher tell his stories of the shining times. The emigrants liked it so well there they stayed. They began to rebuild Pueblo, using some of the same adobe bricks that they found in the tall grasses that had grown over the graves of the original settlers.

Today, there is little trace of Hardscrabble, Greenhorn, or the other settlements and forts, but you can still see the wagon tracks cutting the prairie, marking the trail south to the Sangre de Cristo Pass and Taos. Paco married a girl from Santa Fe, Alicia Cornejo, and his descendants are still up there in the mountains where he lived out his days. They have spread to farms and ranches in sight of Spanish Peaks along the Cucharas and over to the Santa Isabel Wilderness. Burke's great-grandchildren live in Denver, the Stonecipher clan in Cheyenne, less than a hundred years later.

But they are all remembered, even though the course of the Arkansas had been altered by time and the weather, tampered with, the land pocked with modern buildings, houses, crisscrossed with railroad tracks and hidden under concrete and asphalt. They are remembered as the first to see the beauty of the upper Arkansas and to fight for land that they came to know and dearly love.

These were the first, and they left their heritage along the old buffalo trails and the streams they forded, in the seeds they planted in virgin soil.

They will be remembered. They are remembered.

If you enjoyed Jory Sherman's epic tale, THE ARKANSAS RIVER, be sure to look for the next installment of the RIVERS WEST saga at your local bookstore. Each new volume takes you on a voyage of exploration along one of the great rivers of North America with the courageous pioneers who challenged the unknown.

Turn the page for an exciting preview of the next book in Bantam's unique historical series

≈ RIVERS WEST: Book 7 ≈

THE AMERICAN RIVER
by Gary McCarthy

On sale in Spring 1992 wherever Bantam Books are sold.

Young Morgan Beck waited impatiently in the small rowboat on sheltered, pristine Monterey Bay. There were two ships anchored in the deep blue harbor besides their eighty-eight-ton brig, *Clementine*. One was a Mexican sloop with a hull heavily encrusted with barnacles, the other an American whaling vessel that reeked of blood and oil. The Mexican ship appeared abandoned except for a large dog, whose incessant barking carried loudly across the flat surface of the water.

Morgan frowned and shielded his gray eyes from the sunlight as he gazed across the glistening bay. From a distance of half a mile, he could plainly see the impressive customhouse, the presidio and its chapel, and many adobe homes with their colorful red tile roofs.

The beach itself was as white as the foam on the sea and the town was ringed by steep mountains covered with oak and Monterey pine. Clinging majestically to the rugged seaside cliffs were ancient, twisted cypress, and there were several small fishing boats in the water. His father, Eli, had told him that Monterey was handsome, but Morgan hadn't been prepared for the rugged beauty now before him.

A limp Mexican flag hung over the presidio and another over the governor's headquarters. Morgan doubted if Governor Juan Bautista Alvarado even remembered the fine horse and silver-inlaid saddle his father once had presented to him. The governor received such gifts as a matter of course, an expected cost of doing business in his California province.

Morgan's hands worked the oars, holding the boat very still as the sun warmed his broad back. He was nineteen years old, slightly over six feet tall, and fair of skin. Wisps of blond hair trailed out from under his seaman's cap and his hands were large and long-fingered. He listened to the strident cries of sea gulls quarreling over the *Clementine* even as Captain Sutter gave last-minute instructions to the crew and his Sandwich Island followers.

Tilting his face into the sun, Morgan shouted, "Captain Sutter, the tide is going out! We need to pull for shore right now!"

"Coming, coming!" Sutter called, a moment before appearing to climb down the *Clementine*'s stiff rope ladder.

"Hold her steady now," Sutter ordered, carefully placing his foot into the craft and almost losing his balance because he was clutching a leather case wrapped in oilskin.

Morgan waited until Sutter was seated and composed. "Ready, Captain?"

"Yes, yes," came the hasty reply. Then: "By the way, isn't this what Americans celebrate as Independence Day?"

"It is."

Sutter smiled and his blue eyes locked on the distant presidio and adobe mission. "Then I'd say that this coincidence bodes well for us. I trust that this will also prove to be *my* day of independence."

Morgan slipped the oars deep into the water. He leaned forward and pulled hard, liking the feel of his own power and the way the boat surged away from the brig. Facing the *Clementine*, he looked up as he heard the beautiful Manuiki call out to Captain Sutter, who, dressed in a fine Swiss military uniform, removed his campaign hat, twisted about, and waved with the innocent exuberance of a fresh-faced schoolboy.

Morgan had never met anyone even remotely like John Augustus Sutter. In personality, appearance, and taste, he was the exact opposite of his own father, Eli, a former mountain man now turned California trader. Eli was tough, cynical, and suspicious of all Mexicans except his Mexican wife, Estella, whom Morgan also adored.

Eli had not much warmed to Captain Sutter, who was, in the old trapper's opinion, just "too damn excitable and talkative."

Morgan smiled, remembering his father's assessment, because it was largely true. Sutter could talk for hours and hours. The amazing thing, though, was that people would listen and then most likely find themselves nodding in agreement. Morgan had offered to help for free in return for the captain's expected future business. Even Eli had fallen under Sutter's spell, something that

Morgan wouldn't have believed had he not seen it with his own eyes.

"You row strongly," observed the captain.

"Thank you."

"And I have it on good authority," Sutter said with a wink, "that you are an expert marksman, hunter, and trapper."

"There are better, even in Alta, California," Morgan said. "My father being the best of them all."

"I can believe that from the stories I heard him tell."

"He's lived more in one lifetime than most men would in ten. He broke the trail into Blackfoot country. He's fought and killed more Indians than we'll ever see, Mr. Sutter."

"Well, I don't know about that."

"It's true, sir. Pa was with Ashley and Jim Bridger the very first time they broke new trails through the Rocky Mountains."

"Is that right?" Sutter brushed the tips of his mustache with his thumb.

"That's right. It was in the summer of twenty-two. A couple of years later, Pa and Bridger were the very first white men ever to see the Great Salt Lake."

"Was that the same year he killed a grizzly with a knife and a Ute spear?"

Morgan frowned and kept his oars working. "I think so. He told you about that, huh?"

"He sure did. It's a shame to realize that a man of your father's talents is forced to eke out a living hauling hides and working for Mexicans who treat him second rate."

Morgan's face stiffened. "That'll change. He's feeling poorly right now, but he'll get stronger soon. He just needs a warmer climate."

"Like the one I'm going to tame." Sutter leaned forward intently. "You should talk to him for me. I could use him, too, Mr. Beck, providing he's going to be strong enough to work."

"He will be," Morgan clipped. "I can promise you that. Just give him a few months in warm weather and Pa will be a new man."

"Why is he so set against joining up with me?"

Morgan shifted his callused hands on the oars and glanced over his shoulder. He was still several hundred yards away from the beach.

"Mr. Beck, did you hear me?"

"Yes, sir, I did. And I don't rightly know why Pa is so against what you plan to do. He just . . . just gets set in his ways and I guess he didn't want to leave my stepmother."

"I understand." Sutter inhaled deeply and stretched his legs. "But I'll tell you something; he needs to change his mind about my inland colony. I can offer him—and you—more opportunity than you'll ever see in Yerba Buena. *I'll* be in charge, not the Mexicans."

"Yes, sir."

Sutter relaxed. "Anyway," he said, "I'm just glad to have you along with me right now. I could have used your father's influence with the governor, but I'm sure that you'll be very helpful with the introductions. I've got a feeling you're a young man with a very bright future."

Morgan felt his cheeks warm even as he realized that he was being flattered by a master. Annoyed at being such an easy target, he pulled even harder at the oars and felt their boat surge ahead.

One last time, Manuiki, the young Kanaka woman, called melodiously, "Bye, bye, Captain Sutter!"

Sutter studiously chose to ignore her but Morgan was enjoying the show too much to make a similar effort. Besides, Manuiki was too pretty for any man to ignore. Her long black hair shimmered lustrously and her bare arms and shoulders were the color of ripe wheat. Morgan could not help but grin at Sutter's obvious embarrassment because Manuiki's voice could be heard all the way into Monterey.

Morgan finally said, "She just wants you to call out a good-bye one last time, Captain. I don't think she'll be still until you reply."

"Oh, hell," Sutter grumbled, turning around and favoring Manuiki with an offhand wave in the hope of silencing her. "Good-bye!"

It worked. Manuiki, at last satisfied that she had not

been ignored, turned away and disappeared. Sutter expelled a deep breath and turned around before saying, "Mr. Beck, in what little time we have, tell me about Governor Alvarado."

Morgan did not alter his stroke. "I'm afraid that I don't know that much. My father has dealt with him much more than I."

"But your father is not a very communicative man and I must know whatever I can about the governor."

When Morgan frowned, Sutter grew impatient. "Begin by telling me his age."

"I would guess he is about your age—mid-thirties. Perhaps he is a little older."

"Temperament?"

"Serious and formal."

"Even imperious?"

"What it is," Morgan said, not sure that he knew exactly what "imperious" meant, "is that Governor Alvarado *expects* things."

"Then I take it you are not"—Sutter appeared to grope for the correct word—"not greatly warmed by him."

"No. Nor is my father. You see, Captain, as Americans, we have always had to court official favor in order to remain in California and conduct business."

"But I thought your stepmother was related to the Alvarado family."

"She is, distantly. But even so, it is not easy. My father can be a little outspoken and it grates hard on him to offer the governor a gift each time he arrives in Yerba Buena."

Sutter's eyebrows arched. "And that is how business is done in Alta, California, is it?"

"My father said it was no different when the Spaniards were in charge. Even the padres expected gifts."

"I am told Governor Alvarado was once a revolutionary, that he seized his office at the point of a gun."

"True. Less than three years ago, Alvarado and a small rebel band attacked the former governor's residence. I am told they fired only one cannon ball and were rewarded with victory."

Morgan shook his head in a gesture of contempt.

"Not a drop of blood was shed. The previous governor had no stomach for fighting."

"I wonder," Sutter mused aloud, "if Governor Alvarado, faced with a similar revolution, would give up just as readily."

"Whatever else may be said of Alvarado, he is not a coward. He would fight to the death rather than be humiliated."

"You think so?"

"I do and so does my father. One of the men who helped Alvarado was also a mountain man. He said Alvarado was prepared to die before a defeat."

Sutter leaned back, removed his campaign hat, and turned his face up to the sun, causing Morgan to think that he had never seen a man who looked more confident or calculating. Surprising, really, considering this visit was so vital to the captain's ambitious plans.

"If I am granted enough California land," the captain mused, his Swiss accent lending an air of culture to his voice, "I will build an empire—a Swiss colony which I will call New Helvetia. I will send away to Europe for good families and I will give them land and help them build houses, a church, and a school."

Sutter's head dipped, his chin resting on his chest. "You see, Mr. Beck, I come to build, not to plunder and run like a pirate or a common thief. And so, I wish very much to help the governor by taming the great inland valley called the Sacramento."

Morgan had heard all this before but still had his doubts. "Captain, it might not be possible, even with the best of intentions. You see, to the governor's way of thinking, and to all the other Mexican officials, we are foreigners, people never to be trusted, not even if we marry into their families."

Sutter chuckled. "My young friend, you are far too pessimistic. It is because you have lived in California as a second-class citizen—first to the Spaniards, then to these Mexicans. But nothing stays the same. And as for what difficulties I now face, there is something you must understand."

"I'm listening," Morgan said, irritated by the man's

condescending attitude, an attitude exactly like that of Governor Alvarado himself.

"You see," Sutter began, "when two men both stand to profit from an arrangement, then there is nothing to overcome except misunderstanding and suspicion. Agreed?"

Morgan kept rowing.

"And these letters of introduction—" Sutter said, tapping his leather case with a forefinger, "they should end all suspicion concerning my character. That means I must only dispel all possible sources of misunderstanding between Governor Alvarado and myself."

Morgan thought that the captain made it all sound too easy. He was sure that this entire affair was doomed from the start. Eli thought so, too.

"Mr. Beck," Sutter said, interrupting his thoughts, "you wear the look of a skeptic. Do you think I have come so far—all the way from Switzerland—to fail now?"

"I . . . I don't know. But even if you are successful in this appeal for land, it is doubtful that it would do you any good. As my father explained, it is very dangerous inland and filled with hostile Indians. No offense, Captain, but you are not a seasoned woodsman."

"No offense taken," Sutter replied. "But give me credit for examining the difficulties I face. After all, your father showed me that old Blackfoot arrow wound in his side. I have also noted the prominent terrible scar across the back of your right hand. Indians?"

"Yes," Morgan replied. "My father and I were jumped as we were trapping beaver along the shores of Suisun Bay. We are lucky to be alive. There have been others who have gone inland and never returned."

Sutter's eyebrows knitted. "I'm sure that is true," he conceded, "but I *know* Indians. I learned of them while trading in Santa Fe and I learned even more about them when I accompanied the Hudson's Bay Company trappers all the way west to Fort Vancouver. Furthermore, I observed Alaskan Indians in Sitka and found them no more intimidating than the Russians, who use them exactly as I intend to do—firmly but with kindness. And of course, there are my Kanakas. They are

Indians, too. And though they seem happy, I am told they can be very fierce in war—even the women."

Morgan suppressed a smile. He had noticed that Sutter got along very, very well with his hired Kanakas, especially with the lovely Manuiki, whose large brown eyes never seemed to stop laughing at them both.

Sutter unwrapped his leather case from its oilskin and studied a sheaf of papers. Morgan took the opportunity to study the man. Sutter was handsome and exuded immense and unwavering confidence. His hair was fashionably long and he wore sideburns and a mustache that lent him a military aspect exclusive of his uniform. It was said by some that the captain bore a remarkable resemblance to the South American liberator, Simón Bolívar, but Morgan had no way of knowing if this was true.

It was obvious that the captain was very intelligent and possessed a superior education. He spoke French, German, and English fluently and knew more than a few words of Russian and Spanish. Sutter had been an officer of the Swiss Guard in the French service, and that also seemed to impress people. Sutter had revealed himself to be an able student and admirer of Napoleon.

Sutter's head snapped up. "Mr. Beck, assuming I receive a big land grant rather than being forced to take it by force, you must help me satisfy the Mexican government's official demands, no matter how petty or troublesome they become. Do this and I promise I will see that you are generously rewarded."

"With money?"

Sutter chuckled but shook his head. "No, with something far more valuable—land."

"Free land is worth nothing except to the Indians. I'll take the money."

"Don't make foolish statements like that. Always remember that good land, the kind I intend to settle, is worth far more than gold. A man can lose his soul to money, but the land will always give him sustenance. It asks but little and gives abundantly. All that it requires is honest effort, and once it is plowed, planted with seed, and tended with care, it will repay its keeper a thousandfold."

"But, Captain, I have no desire whatsoever to be a farmer."

Sutter's eyes flashed with annoyance. "Then what would you become?"

Morgan shrugged. "I don't know. I do a little hunting and some beaver trapping. I help my father in his shipping business and we build and sell boats like this one. I am happy."

"Happy?" Sutter clucked his tongue with pity. "Happiness is doing something with your life of lasting importance. It is finding a quest worthy of your abilities and pursuing it to its completion."

Sutter's voice thickened with passion. "You *must*, Mr. Beck, learn to strive for more than the simple day-to-day pleasures. You must believe that you have greatness in you and seek a noble destiny!"

Morgan tore his eyes from Sutter's excited expression and tried to concentrate on his rowing. The man's zeal made him uneasy because he had no real vision of which to boast. His pleasures were quite simple. He enjoyed pretty women and good books. He loved hunting and riding a good horse. The sound of the ocean was his music. In truth, Morgan had to admit his favorite pleasures seemed childish compared with Sutter's lofty dreams.

But no matter, he reasoned, because the captain was blind to reality; he was a hopeless fanatic. And, as Eli had prophesied, those who flew so high were bound to fall very, very low indeed. Eli, while offering his son's services, had privately believed that Governor Alvarado, a shrewd man, would see right through Sutter and toss him out on his high-and-mighty ear.

"Mr. Beck?"

Morgan glanced up from his shoes, where he had fixed his attention. He was surprised to see that the captain looked quite upset. "Sir?"

"I . . . I wish to apologize," he said with obvious difficulty. "I had no right to pontificate. You see, I occasionally fall victim to my own visions and dreams. Dreams that—within the next hour—might very well crash down around my feet, making me look a total fool."

This confession was so unexpected and uncharacteristic of Sutter that Morgan suddenly discovered that, like his father, he really wanted the Swiss to succeed. "I hope not, Captain. I mean that."

"Thank you!" Sutter brightened. "But I'll try to keep myself in check from now on. But . . ." Sutter groped for the right words. "But you must understand that dreams freely spoken with passion cause jealousy. Men with dreams almost always stand alone, subject to ridicule. I would advise you to remember that, even though I cannot."

"Yes, sir," Morgan said, feeling awkward. "Captain, we are nearing the surf. You'd better protect those papers and hang on tight."

A sadness, or perhaps a disappointment, passed quickly across Sutter's eyes. "Yes, Mr. Beck, of course."

Sutter quickly rewrapped his papers and case in the oilskin as the surf rumbled in their ears.

"Mr. Beck, I have no wish to insult you, but please don't allow this craft to capsize. It would not do to have Captain Sutter present himself dripping wet like a dog to the governor of California."

"No, sir," Morgan said, bringing the rowboat expertly through the gentle surf and beaching it on the sand.

Morgan jumped into the shallow water and hesitated, wondering why the captain did not do the same.

"My boots," Sutter explained without budging. "They are polished."

"Oh. I forgot."

Morgan pulled the little boat up higher and Sutter hopped onto the white beach where he revealed a trace of nervousness by smoothing his coat and picking at a speck of imaginary lint.

The captain's eyes lifted to the presidio and he said, "It would be far more impressive if we had arrived in a fine carriage. But there's no help for that, so come along. You can make the introductions and then leave the rest to me."

"Yes, Captain."

Without further hesitation, Sutter marched forward, arms swinging, head up, and back straight as a martinet. In contrast, Morgan plodded through the heavy sand feeling like a draft horse. His wet boots caked thickly with sand making them very heavy. And even though he was taller than the captain and had much longer legs, he had to work to keep up with Sutter. Why, he wondered, was this man in such an all-fired hurry to have Governor Alvarado humiliate him and then coldly dash his dreams?

Morgan wished he knew how to prepare Sutter for Alvarado's customarily abrasive manners. But sometimes, he supposed, a man had to learn the hard way.

"Come along, Mr. Beck, don't hang back! And let me remind you once again that we are men about to change the course of Western history!"

"Yes, Captain," Morgan called, hurrying after the man but not believing a word of it.

Two hours later, Morgan stretched his long legs across the brown tile floor outside the governor's office and wished he were somewhere—anywhere—else. He and the captain had been kept waiting for nearly three hours, and Morgan sensed that even Sutter's monumental patience finally was wearing thin.

But suddenly the door opened and one of the governor's aides beckoned them forward with a slight bow and a perfunctory smile.

They were ushered into a very large office, dim but with enough light to see that the large French desk was occupied by the governor. The man was dressed in military uniform, festooned with even more gold braid and medals than Sutter wore.

"Governor Alvarado," Morgan said, removing his cap and bowing slightly, "you are most gracious to see us on such short notice. Allow me to introduce my good friend Captain John Augustus Sutter."

At the sound of his name Sutter marched right up to the governor's desk. When he came to a halt, his heels clicked smartly together and he gave a crisp salute, which he held until Alvarado, clearly taken by surprise, popped up from his desk and hastily returned it.

Sutter's right hand arched gracefully down to his creased trousers. "What a supreme pleasure, Your Excellency! You do me great honor by receiving me without an appointment. And sir, I must tell you that I have journeyed across half the world for this very moment."

Alvarado blinked. Morgan was sure that the Mexican was momentarily off balance, and that probably was a good sign.

"Captain Sutter, exactly what does bring you to me?"

"Fate?" Sutter smiled quizzically. "Dare I suggest even destiny?" He paused dramatically. "Who can say for certain? I am sure of only one thing—that this meeting one day will be recorded in the history books."

"Who *are* you?" Alvarado exclaimed with exasperation, his eyes darting to Morgan and then back to Sutter.

Morgan ground his teeth, searching for. . . for what? An explanation? An apology? Something to salvage the damage.

"I am," Sutter persisted with a bright, undaunted smile, "a friend of kings, nobles, and men of immense influence. May I present my letters of introduction? I believe they will attest to my character."

"Señor Beck, do you and your father represent this man as one of good character?"

"Yes, Your Excellency. He is to be trusted and has something important to say. His letters of introduction speak for themselves."

Alvarado's eyes locked with those of Sutter. "Then come, come, let me see them," he demanded, snapping his fingers with impatience.

Morgan thought his captain was going to salute, but instead Sutter swept off his hat with a flourish and placed it on a chair before opening the oilskin packet. He then removed the crucial letters of introduction. Morgan knew them to be from officials of the powerful Hudson's Bay Company as well as Russians from Sitka and the important British and American consuls Sutter had met in the Sandwich Islands. Even Eli had been impressed.

"Sit"—Alvarado's gaze touched the first letter of introduction, which Morgan recognized as one from the British consul—"down, Captain Sutter." His voice softened dramatically as he quickly thumbed through the other letters.

Morgan risked a glance at Sutter and the captain brazenly winked. The man's cool demeanor and unbridled confidence caused him to stand a little straighter.

When at last Alvarado had digested the letters to his satisfaction, he stacked them neatly on the outside corner of his desk.

"Brandy?" he asked with a warm smile.

"Yes, we will," Sutter said. "And thank you."

Morgan saw that somehow they had passed a test and he relaxed.

"So," Alvarado said as he poured the brandy, "you speak well, but you have yet to tell me anything. What brings you to Monterey?"

"I come to offer you my services," Sutter explained. "I want to conquer your inland wilderness. I want to civilize your Miwok Indians and reap for Mexico the wealth of the Sacramento river country."

Alvarado had been about to propose a toast but he paused and said, "I am sure you promise more than you can deliver—as did the earlier well-intentioned but naive padres."

"I am here as a businessman—not a missionary. I have—on the brig *Clementine* waiting in your harbor—cannon, supplies enough to outfit a post for one year, seed, and tools—enough to reap an abundant harvest."

Alvarado blinked and Sutter pushed on. "I also have determination and experience enough to win your confidence and trust."

"Then let us drink to trust," Alvarado said after studying Sutter very intently, "and to men of vision and destiny."

As they drank Morgan had the distinct impression that something very strong but indefinable passed between the two military officers, something he would never be able to share or even understand. He knew only that during the next few hours, he became just an observer.

At the end of that time Alvarado and Sutter were still poring over a map, speaking of Indians and arms, cannon and corn. Once Alvarado scooped up the captain's letters of introduction and said, "No one before has ever come with so many!"

Sutter merely laughed and then Alvarado laughed, too, and before their meeting was over, the pair were talking about dinner.

The governor looked up from the map of California spread out across his desk and seemed to notice Morgan for the first time since their introductions. "Ah, Señor Beck, what about you? Will you join us tonight?"

"No, thank you."

When the governor's eyebrows arched in question, Morgan quickly added, "My father asked me to give his regards to an old friend."

Alvarado did not bother to pretend disappointment. And neither did Sutter.

In The Tradition of *Wagons West* and *The Spanish Bit Saga* Comes:

RIVERS WEST

The author of **In the Season of the Sun** and **Scalpdancer** begins a multigenerational saga that will span the history of America, as seen through the lives of one family.

THE MEDAL
by Kerry Newcomb

From a nation born of strife and christened with patriots blood, there arose a dynasty of soldiers. They were the McQueens of America -- a clan hungry for adventure; a family whose fiery spirit would kindle the flame of a country's freedom. Keeping that flame from blazing into tyranny through the generations would take more than merely courage and determination. It would take a sacred secret: the proud legacy they called
THE MEDAL.

Look for the first two books in this series,

THE MEDAL BOOK ONE: GUNS OF LIBERTY
THE MEDAL BOOK TWO: SWORD OF VENGEANCE

on sale wherever Bantam Domain Books are sold.

AN239 -- 9/91

TERRY C. JOHNSTON

Winner of the prestigious Western Writer's award, Terry C. Johnston brings you his award-winning saga of mountain men Josiah Paddock and Titus Bass who strive together to meet the challenges of the western wilderness in the 1830's.

The final volume in the trilogy begun with *Carry the Wind* and *Borderlords*, ONE-EYED DREAM is a rich, textured tale of an 1830's trapper and his protegé, told at the height of the American fur trade.

Following a harrowing pursuit by vengeful Arapaho warriors, mountain man Titus "Scratch" Bass and his apprentice Josiah Paddock must travel south to old Taos. But their journey is cut short when they learn they must return to St. Louis...and old enemies.